The Infinite Cage

The Infinite Cage

Keith Laumer

A BERKLEY MEDALLION BOOK
published by
BERKLEY PUBLISHING CORPORATION

This book is dedicated to
Betty because of her
many faults

Library of Congress Catalog Card Number: 70-186648

SBN 425-02582-9

BERKLEY MEDALLION BOOKS are published by
Berkley Publishing Corporation
200 Madison Avenue
New York, N.Y. 10016

BERKLEY MEDALLION BOOKS ® TM 757, 375

Printed in the United States of America

Berkley Medallion Edition, July, 1974

[1]

Sergeant B. M. "Heavy" Dubell of the Jaspertown Police Department removed from his mouth the two-inch butt of a dead cigar, mashed it viciously in the chipped saucer he kept on his desk for the purpose, and shouted for Constable Kinch. There was no answer. He kicked his chair back, came around the desk, moving heavily, his broad, thick shoulders back, gut outthrust, cuffs jingling from the low-slung gun belt. A roll of acne-pitted fat overhung his curled collar; brown spots were scattered across his hairless head.

At the top of the stair leading down to the section of the jail known as the Annex he shouted again for Kinch. No answer. He thrust past the heavy steel-plate door and lumbered down the steps. At the bottom, the passage went straight ahead for a distance of fifteen feet, dead-ended at the cross-corridor. Sergeant Dubell rounded the corner and stopped dead. Twenty feet along the narrow corridor the heavy, iron-barred door of cell number 3 stood open. Dubell yanked his gun from its holster and went forward swiftly and silently.

Kinch lay with his cheek against the cell floor, snoring softly. Above his left eye a bruise which was turning from pink to purple ran up into the hairline. An overturned wooden stool lay beside him. Dubell swore and unlimbered his flashlight, shone it around the cell.

The prisoner lay on his side near the wall. He was naked, his body soiled, marked with small cuts, scratches, and bruises. His hair was long and tangled. He stared into the light with wide, unfocused eyes.

"What the hell," Dubell growled. He tried the wall switch; the bulb in the wire cage on the ceiling was burned out. Squatting beside Kinch, he checked the man's pulse; it was steady and strong. He must, Dubell surmised, have tripped over the stool. Clumsy damn fool. Now he'd have to carry him upstairs. Might even have to call Doc Fine. Cost the township money. Trouble. Have to do two men's work.

Dubell grunted, hauling the unconscious man to a sitting position, getting a shoulder under him. He didn't notice that the prisoner had moved until he saw him at the door. Dubell yelled and lunged to his feet, hampered by the weight across his back. The naked man skittered through the doorway and fell. Dubell dumped Kinch and jumped after him, to be met by the slamming of the steel door.

He hammered and shouted, but there was no response.

[2]

The prisoner lay on his back, staring at the light at the end of the passage. He was not aware that he had accidentally kicked the cell door shut; he paid no attention to the sounds coming from behind it. He had no memory of anything prior to now, but he did not wonder who he was, what he was, where he was, where he had been before he was here; nor was he aware of the absence of such memories. He was absorbed in the wealth of sensory impressions impinging on him, all of which had to be considered, classified, filed away. . . .

Gradually he became aware of a distinction between himself and his surroundings. He determined, by tentative movements, that the *me* comprised a hinged torso, to which were attached a *head,* with limited capacity for movement; jointed *legs,* rather more mobile; and *arms,* which were sharply limited in movement by a connection that held them in close juxtaposition at their terminal ends. The latter were elaborated into sets of smaller members, *fingers,* which, he found, moved quite freely. The names for these parts came into his mind effortlessly, unnoticed.

The arms bothered him. He sensed, somehow, that they should move more freely. The link between them, he deduced after careful introspection, was not a part of the *me.*

He tugged against the restraint, and suddenly a clear image came into his mind: he pictured himself rubbing the metal links against an abrasive surface; specifically, the concrete corner of the doorway beside him. He worked his way awkwardly into position and tentatively rubbed the handcuffs against the masonry, eliciting a metallic scraping sound. His arms, he quickly found, abraded more swiftly than the metal. . . . Metal was *hard*, he determined, savoring the concept. Body-stuff was *soft*. More carefully, he went on, rubbing the steel links back and forth, back and forth, attempting with partial success to keep his skin clear of contact. The pain increased for a time, then gradually lessened. A new sensation—*fatigue*—appeared, burning in his arms like slow fire; but he ignored it. He did not grow bored, or impatient. He was not aware of the passage of time; but time passed. Eventually the links parted.

He was delighted with the new freedom of movement, flexing his arms and hands as aimlessly as a baby playing with his toes. His eye was caught by the glossy crimson sheen of his wrists. Fluid, rich and red, was leaking from the whiteness of his wrists. There was pain there now, sharp, raw, attention-demanding. Involuntarily, he gave a low, complaining groan.

This was an interesting new phenomenon. He experimented with his mouth and tongue, searching for the combination that had produced such a novel and interesting effect. He managed smacking and clicking noises, but nothing so complex as the long, satisfying groan. Presently he tired of the game. The light drew him. He wanted to be closer to it. His arms and legs made aimless swimming motions for a few moments before an instinct pattern intervened. He came to hands and knees, swaying at first, but quickly gaining control, he crawled toward the light.

Encountering the stairs, he paused for a moment, then began to ascend, fumblingly at first, then more surely. His knees hurt, and his wrists, but it did not occur to him to stop, or to attempt to relieve the pain; he was not truly aware of it, any more than he was aware of the gravitational attraction of the earth, or the pressure of the atmosphere.

At the top, he paused, delighted by the change in scene. An inkling of the vastness of the world came to him. *Not-me* was so much greater than *me*.

He was fascinated by the new colors and shapes: the dun

7

and tan of the wall, the chipped green of the tile floor, the red splotch of the fire alarm. The light came from a point high above. He stopped under it and reached, and at once his chin struck the floor. He tasted blood in his mouth, and spent half a minute savoring this wholly new area of sensation.

The light hung far above him, beckoning, drawing him. He rose to his knees, then to his feet. Still his fingers failed to reach the glowing bulb. He willed himself to rise into the air, but nothing happened.

He moved on, passed through other rooms, came to a larger one. A pattern of bright points of glowing color at its far side attracted his attention. He went toward it.

His hands struck something invisible: the glass panel in the exterior door. He pushed against it, reaching for the tantalizing colors. It yielded, swung open. He took two steps, then fell headlong down the front steps, striking his head hard on the cracked pavement at the bottom.

[3]

Angelique Sobell had taken special pains with her *toilette* that evening, giving her hair a full fifty strokes before donning a black sateen blouse, a red oil-cloth skirt with a white plastic belt, white ankle socks, yellowish-white high-heeled shoes, somewhat scuffed. From a cigar box, she selected a pink coral ring, a Navahoesque bracelet with large dull-green stones, and a necklace of peeling pearls.

The reflection in the big, tarnished, bevel-edged mirror bolted to the back of the door posed provocatively, hand on hip to conceal the slight roll of flesh there, chest out and up, feet at right angles to emphasize the taper of thighs.

"Ke-rist," she muttered. "Baby's getting fat." She gave herself a final glance in the mirror, remembering to lift her chin to smooth out the throat line, and left the apartment, locking the door behind her. There were the usual odors of stale cookery, urine, and pot smoke in the stairwell; she descended slowly, one hand on the slightly gummy varnish of the handrail.

Outside, a light rain was falling. She passed stores that were closed and dark, a silent gas station, a parking lot. Light shone across the walk from a door ahead. There were dark shrubs at the foot of a short flight of steps. As she passed, she saw a man's foot projecting from the shadows at the edge of the walk.

Angelique halted, staring at the foot. It was bare, bone-white. There was a bare, dirty ankle, a scabbed shin. The other foot was doubled under the knee, which was a raw wound. The man was naked, lying on the grass. There was blood on his mouth, his hands, his knees.

"Good lord," Angelique whispered. She looked up at the chipped, black-edged gilt letters spelling out *Jasperton Police Department* above the lighted doorway.

"The lousy bums." She skirted the obstruction and hurried on.

In the next block she saw a tall, round-shouldered man emerging from an all-night liquor store.

"Henny," she called. He waited. "Them lousy cops," she gasped, coming up to him. "They gone too far this time. They thrown some poor devil out in the street buck naked. Beat up, maybe dead."

"Yeah?" The man had a deep, gruff voice. He looked along the street. It was a look that didn't want any trouble. He shifted the bottle-shaped paper bag under his arm as the woman grabbed at him.

"Right back there." Angelique hooked a thumb over her shoulder. "The guy is laying right on the pavement in front of the cop-house, right in the rain."

"It's none of my business—"

She pulled at his arm. "It won't hurt you to look, Henny!"

He came along, reluctantly. She towed him along the block, crossed the street against the light, approached the police station cautiously.

The man was still there, lying in the same position.

"Jeezus," Henny said.

Angelique went closer, looked down at the pale, whiskery face.

"He's breathing."

"He's got cuffs on him."

Angelique was studying the lighted door of the police station. The corridor behind it was empty, the windows beside it dark.

"Listen, Henny. Let's get him out of here."

9

"Nix, nix." Henny backed away.

"Get him up on your back; he ain't so big. We'll take him up to your place."

"Forget it." Henny started to turn away; Angelique took a deep breath as if to scream. Henny grabbed her arm.

"What the hell——!"

"Pick him up or I yell 'rape,' and baby, would they just love to stick it to you!"

For a moment, Henny hesitated. Then he swore, stooped, caught up the cold, limp, wet body. The arms dangled. The mouth lolled open.

"Ahhhgg," Henny snorted. "He stinks."

"Let's go."

Grunting, Henny set off at a half-trot, Angelique at his heels, looking back at the lighted door behind which there was still no sign of life.

[4]

His eyes opened; a strange face was looking down at him: pale, with garish lips, black smudges around the eyes.

"Hey——he's coming around," the face said, in a high-pitched voice.

He was in pain; pain that seemed to wash over him in waves, requiring some response. His throat tensed; his mouth and tongue moved as if by their own volition:

"My knees hurt," he said suddenly, unpremeditatedly; then he started to cry. He felt the big, hot tears running down his face. It felt good to cry; it seemed to relieve some sort of pressure inside him. He wailed, enjoying the relief.

"Hey, take it easy," the woman said. She stood; he could see her blurrily through the tears. He didn't want her to go; he wanted her to stay close and watch him cry. He reached impulsively for her and she ducked back.

"Hey, for Chrissakes," she said.

His eye fell on his wrist, the one he had reached out with. There was a shiny bracelet around it, pink and brown with blood. The skin was torn, adjacent to the metal; he could see the raw flesh, and the little tatters of skin. Blood had dried in a brown crust on his arms.

"It hurts," he said, and thought about crying some more.

He started to get up, but his legs felt very strange. He fell, grabbing at the bed as he went down, pulling the blanket with him.

"Oh-oh," he said. "I went to the toilet."

The woman swore. A man he hadn't seen before said, "Jeezus, Anj, for Chrissakes! The guy's a dummy."

"Well, don't stand around telling me he's a dummy! Take him in the john! The poor boob is sick, he can't help it."

"I ain't no night nurse!"

Grumbling, the man called Henny took his arm, lifted him. His legs still felt funny. He let them drag; he let his body go slack.

"Don't go cute on us, boy," the man said. "By God, I'd as soon throw ye back out in the street."

"Shut up, Henny. Come on, walk, feller. Work them legs." The woman's tone was much friendlier than the man's. He decided he liked her best. They walked him down a short hall, and the man took him through a door into a bathroom. It had brown walls and exposed pipes and a broken toilet seat, and there were scribblings on the walls.

"Don't read, do what you came for," the man said standing in the open door.

"I already did," he said. "I don't have to anymore."

In the hall, the woman laughed. The man swore. Together, they hauled him back to the room, dumped him in the bed. The bed was nice, he decided. He liked the bed. But he still hurt. He had forgotten about how much he hurt while they were busy with the exciting trip down the hall, but now the pain was clamoring for attention.

"Oh, boy," he said. "It really hurts," and started to cry, silently this time. It wasn't as much fun to cry silently, but it was a sincere crying now, an expression of great pain. The pain grew and grew, it was like a fire that caught in dry grass and spread, eating up the grass, growing swiftly bigger. He wailed.

"Please make it stop," he wailed. He kicked his feet, but that made it hurt worse. Lying still on the cot, he discovered, made the pain recede. He lay quietly, staring at the ceiling. There were patterns there: an overall pattern of little squiggly lines, and larger, darker blotches of

11

discoloration. He studied them, looking for the meaning in them. He had completely forgotten the man and the woman.

"Look at the sucker," the man said, reminding him. "Laying there now, happy as a pig in a ditch."

"Listen, feller," the woman said. "What's your name?"

"Lonzo," he said promptly. The name had popped into his mind as if it had been waiting there for that specific question. It meant nothing to him; it was an automatic response made by his mouth, not connected with the *me*.

"Lonzo what?"

He looked at her. She was wearing a black garment that was thin and wet, that clung to her body. He was intrigued by the bulging shapes outlined under the wet cloth, and put out a hand toward her. She jumped back. The man laughed.

"You keep your hands to yourself, Lonzo," she said sharply. "What's your last name? Where you from?"

"Sprackle," he said, hearing his own voice speak the strange word.

"That your name? Or your hometown?"

"I don't know."

"Lonzo Sprackle: that your name?"

"Fred. Freddy." He savored the new sound.

"Lonzo Fred Sprackle?"

"Horace. Seymore. Jim." There were many sounds available; his mouth seemed to know them all.

"Damn you, she ast you your name, boy!" Henny put in. "Don't get smartalecky now, or I'll throw you right back in the gutter you come from. Now what's your name?"

"Charles 'Chuck' Weinelt." He sensed other thought-forms moving behind the words, but Henny gave him no time to explore them.

"All right, Chuck; now where you from?"

"Lacoochee."

"Where's that at?"

"Florida."

"How'd you get all the way up here from Florida?"

"I . . . was walking."

"That's one hell of a long walk, boy. What the cops get you for?"

Lying on the cot, he looked at Henny. Henny kept asking questions, and he heard himself answering, but the answers didn't seem to come from inside him. It was interesting, waiting to hear what he'd say next.

"Vagrancy," his voice said. He wondered what *vagrancy* meant. But then the information was there, in his mind: *The condition or quality of being vagrant: one who strolls from place to place. From the old French* waucrant. . . .

"What'd they do to you?" Henny asked.

"They tried to finesse me." This was a new voice, he sensed. It felt different, hotter, tighter. . . . "They tried to ease me out of control. Damn traitors. Men I made. . . ."

"Huh?"

"They made me get in the car." Again the flickering sense of change.

"Then what?"

"She said there had to be some consideration. That's how she put it. Sweetly, of course. But some consideration. Damned trollop."

"Here, you, don't go talking foolish, now. I want to know what them cops done to you. They beat you up?"

Flicker. "Yeah. Pretty bad. But not too bad, you know? Just a warning, like. I got no grudge."

"Why they take your clothes?"

"*Cabrones. Hijos de la puta.*" He spat.

"Here, you, don't go spitting around here. And don't start talking Greaser. They taken your clothes and then they worked you over and then they thrown you out, right?"

"Hell, Henny," the woman spoke up. "You ain't finding out nothing. You're feeding him lines." She shouldered the man aside and sat on the edge of the cot.

"Now listen, sugar, you can talk to Angie. You tell Angie all about it. Them coppers picked you up, you was minding your own business, right?"

"Now who's feeding him lines?"

"How about it, sugar?"

Flicker, Flicker, Flicker. A sense of pressure, danger, urgency: "Hold it together," he heard himself saying. "I don't give a damn how you do it, but don't give the bastards anything."

"What bastards was them, honey?" Angelique inquired.

13

"Lousy IG types. Smooth-talking little devil. Any man in my outfit gives him anything, I'll see him shot."

"What outfit you with, sugar?"

"Link, Francis X. Major, AO 2355609. That's all you get."

"That's your name, Francis X. Link?"

"I said so, didn't I?"

"Where you from, Link?"

"Duluth. Why?"

"Hell, this guy's nutty as a pecan roll," Henny said. "He's having a big horse-laugh at the both of us." He stepped past the woman and grabbed the supine man by the shoulder, shook him.

"Smarten up, boy. I ask you one last time who you are and what they got on you. You rob a store? You kill somebody?"

Flicker. "Four of 'em," he mumbled. "Maybe five. Oh, God, I was scared. They came in through the door and it went off. I didn't mean to."

Henny swore and pushed the man back in disgust. "This joker's nuts," he said. "He's playing games."

Flicker. This time it was different. It was as if a door had opened, and the voice had pushed through it, taken over the stage.

"All right," Henny was saying. He broke off as the man on the bed pushed himself up suddenly on one elbow.

"I left orders I wasn't to be disturbed," he snapped. "Who are you?" His eyes flicked across the room. His expression changed, became suddenly wary. "What the devil's going on here? Where am I?"

Henny and the woman had recoiled at the snap in his voice.

"Why, ah, this here's my place," Henny blurted. "You was in bad shape, mister. We wanted to help you, was all—"

"You won't get far with this," the man on the cot said. He threw back the thin blanket, swung his skinny, pale legs to the floor. "Every police officer in the country will be after you—" he paused as his eyes fell on his own naked legs. He recoiled, as if to escape from his own body. He made a hoarse, distressed sound.

"Lookit here, Chuck," Henny said quickly, "you said

yourself they vagged you. They beat up on you and thrown you outside to die. Anj and me, we saved your bacon for you. You got no call——"

Flicker. "I want my mommy," the man on the cot said, and lay back on the pillow. His thumb went into his mouth. He rolled his eyes at the two people who stood over him.

"Hey," Angelique said weakly. "You're right, Hen. He's crazy as a bedbug."

Henny took two quick steps and caught her arm as she reached for the door.

"You're not running out and leaving the dummy here," he said.

"Wait a minute, Henny; listen," Angelique said. "Don't go off half-cocked. We got to think. We can't just dump him. He'll talk. He'll tell the cops about us."

Henny took a step back as if he'd been hit. "What you talking about, girl?"

"If we throw him out, we got to shut him up."

"You talking about killing?"

"Don't be a damn fool. We got to keep him here a while. They'll be looking for him. Later we can take him someplace—across the state line maybe."

They both turned to look at the subject of their discussion. He took his thumb from his mouth.

"I'm hungry," he said.

Henny swore. "Go get him a sandwich," he said to the woman.

"You got bread?"

"Use your own. You got me into this." Henny took out his handkerchief and wiped the back of his neck, his forehead, his chin, his upper lip. "I must of been nuts as the dummy, listening to you."

"I'll go get some sandwiches," the woman said. "You keep him quiet."

"Hurry it up," Henny said. "I don't like being alone with a nut case."

"Sure, you bet, Henny." She opened the door and glanced into the hall, then slipped through.

Henny pulled out a straight chair, sat in it, folded his arms, his eyes on the man on the bed.

"Just take it easy," he muttered. "Just don't get ideas."

2

[1]

It was two hours before Henny realized the woman wasn't coming back. He swore savagely, pacing up and down the room. He was sweating heavily; his stomach felt upset, as if he had eaten a batch of bad French fries. The man on the bed lay quietly, watching him, dozing occasionally. Henny stopped across the room and looked at him.

"I'll get some clothes on you," he said. "I'm getting you out of here." He went quickly to the curtain suspended from an angle of pipe in the corner to form an alcove, pulled out a blackish-green shirt and a pair of puckered, grease-stained khaki pants. He threw them at the man on the bed.

"Put them on!" he ordered.

The shirt had fallen across the face of the man on the bed. He plucked at it ineffectually. Henny swore and jerked it away from his face. The man laughed, pulled it back.

"Damn, you, I ain't playing pee-pie with you!" Henny said savagely. He caught the man by the still-damp brown hair, jerked him upright.

"Keep your hands off me, you, you big ape!" the man said, and kicked out; Henny jumped back, covering his groin with both hands.

"You rum-dummy, you could of ruined me!"

"I need a drink. What the hell is this place?"

"Just take it easy." Henny didn't like it when the crazy man seemed to speak rationally this way. He gave him the feeling that things were happening that were beyond his understanding; that something was being put over on him. It felt like a trap.

The man flopped back on the cot. "I hurt," he said. "I hurt all over. Get me a drink."

Henny took a flat bottle from the dresser drawer and handed it over. The man sat up, took a long pull, immediately retched, dropping the bottle, spewing liquor on the thin gray blanket. Henny swore luridly.

"I taken all I'm taking off you, you damn crum-bum. You're no better'n an animal. Get them clothes on."

The man lay on the cot with his eyes closed. "I'm sick," he whined.

"You'll be sicker 'fore I'm done with ye." Henny jerked the blanket off onto the floor. He checked at the sight of the other's emaciation. He had seen him before, but not laid out full length under the light.

"Can you stand up?" he muttered.

"No. Go away."

"Who the hell are you? No more crap, just who are you?"

"Sally Ann Seymour."

Henny made a sound that was half snort, half laugh. "You're the damnedest nut I ever seen. Get out of that bed, Sally Ann. We're going for a walk."

The man on the cot opened his eyes and looked directly at Henny. "I'm dying," he said. "I got cancer of the cervix. Spread all over hell. I got maybe a week. I ain't walking noplace."

"Cancer!" Henny was halted as if by a hex sign. "God damn," he said. Then: "Cancer of the cervix: that's some kind of female complaint!" Indignant at the trick, he grabbed the man by the arm, hauled him off onto the floor.

"Get them clothes on, boy. One more cute trick out of you and I'll work you over worse'n the cops ever thought about!"

The man wailed and scrabbled for the bed; then checked abruptly, staring down at himself. He gave a strangled squawk and fell back on the floor. His eyes had rolled up in his head. Henny dug at him with his foot, then kicked him lightly; but the man only snored, his mouth open, crescents of white eyeball showing under the lids.

Henny lifted him back onto the bed. He rubbed his hands on his thighs, mumbling to himself. Then he began pulling the oversized shirt on the slack arms.

It took him ten minutes to dress the unconscious man in the shirt and pants, pull a pair of worn sneakers onto his feet and lace them. By this time, the patient had begun to stir. His eyes opened. He looked around dully.

"Wha' happened?" he said.

"You flang a fit. Now get up."

The man rubbed a hand across his mouth. "Oh, boy," he said. "Oh boy. I don't remember a thing. What'd I do?"

"Let's go." Henny hauled at the man's arm and he stood, shakily.

"I'm not feeling too well," he said. "But I'll be OK. Just get me a cab."

"Yeah, a cab. Good idea. Sure. Come on, walk nice, now."

"I appreciate this, sir. You won't regret it. Was I much trouble?"

"Damn right, Sally Ann or whatever your name is." Henny was walking him toward the door.

"Chister. Wayne G. Chister. I'll make it right with you, Mr., er——?"

"Never mind that. Just be nice, now. You're going for a nice ride."

"Don't call my wife," Wayne G. Chister said. "Just worry her. I'll be fine, now."

"Sure, you'll be swell. Watch the steps."

Wayne G. Chister yelped as he took the first step. "My knee," he gasped. "Oh, my knee. And my hands hurt." He pulled back the overlong cuff of the shirt and stared at his bloody wrist, clamped in the steel wristlet with the dangling links of small chain.

"Oh, for the love of God, what's happened to me?"

"Nothing. A little joke. You're OK, Mr. Chister. Come on, you're going home, right? What was that address?"

"2705 Royal Palm Crescent, but what happened to me? Why am I wearing handcuffs?"

"Look, pal, the cops had you, see? Don't you remember?"

"No, no, I don't remember anything after——" he shut up abruptly.

At the street door, Henny peered cautiously out. No cars moved in the street. No pedestrians were in evidence. He looked at the man shivering against the wall.

"Look, Mr. Chinchy, you wait here, see? I'm going up to the hack stand; you just wait right here."

"I'm not feeling well, sir. Please hurry." His teeth chattered so that it interfered with his speech.

"Just don't go noplace." Henny ducked out into the drizzling rain and headed for the cab stand two blocks east.

[2]

He stood in the darkness of the hallway, listening to the voices in his head. Some of the voices were insistent, some faint. They seemed to be urging him to action; but the voices were confusing, conflicting. His legs and arms twitched in abortive response to the sense of urgency that the voices communicated to him.

A door banged loudly somewhere above, triggering something in his mind, opening a door. . . .

He flattened himself against the wall, slid away from the door into the greater darkness of the hall. Feet clacked on the steps. A fat woman came into view. She pushed out through the street door, paused to wrap her coat more closely about her, and was gone.

He leaned against the wall. His head hurt. He felt terrible.

This time I'm sick, a voice said in his head. *This time I'm really sick.* He put a hand against his forehead. His hand felt strange, too narrow—and hot. He had fever, all right, the voice told him. He hurt all over. His body felt strange. His arms and legs felt strange.

"I'm sick," he moaned, knowing that no one could hear him. "Please, somebody help me." It was not an actual appeal for help, merely the expression of his feelings: that he was a man who was in trouble, who needed help.

"But they don't care," he whispered. "Nobody cares." He wet his lips, and noticed the foul, sour taste in his mouth. He smelled the stale reek of the clothes he was wearing.

"What's happened to me?" he muttered. "I was never this bad before. . . ."

A flash of brilliant blue light lit the dark passage suddenly, winked out as swiftly, winked again. Through the glass panel in the door he saw the rotating flasher of a police car, just pulling to a stop at the curb. Terror was like a hand clamped on his heart.

"Oh, no, oh, God, no. . . ." He moved back farther, hearing car doors open, hearing feet clap on the sidewalk.

19

A beam of white light dazzled abruptly through the door, making stark shadows on the brown-yellow wallpaper. He shrank back into a wedge of blackness at the extreme rear of the hall. The door burst open. A large, uniformed policeman stood silhouetted there. Behind him, rain made slanting lines of twinkling brilliance in the light.

The cop turned and palmed another man into the hall ahead of him.

"OK, where is he?"

"He was right here. I swear I left him standing right here." The second man was big, round-shouldered, with a long, pale, soft face. Some part of his mind recognized him as a man called Henny.

"How come you went off and left him alone?"

"I told you, I was going for a hack—"

"Some service. Whyn't he get his own hack?"

"Like I said, he was drunk. I'm only tyrnna help. He says his name is Chisler—"

"Naw, that's you, Henny. You're mixed up."

"You got no call to badmouth me. I got rights like any citizen. I done nothing—"

"Let's take a look." The cop prodded Henny, who took a couple of aimless steps and called, "Mr. Chisley?"

"Let's go up and have a look-see at your flop," the cop said.

"There ain't nothing up there, I tell you he was right here—"

"Well, maybe he got tired waiting and went up. Let's go." The last two words with a whipcrack delivery. The two men went up the stairs.

The man hiding in the hallway stood trembling, sweating, feeling weak and hollow. There would be another cop in the car. He couldn't get out that way. He looked behind him, past the two large trash cans blocking the end of the hall. There was a metal-surfaced door behind them; it swung open silently.

Soft rain pattered down on him. Light shining past a torn windowshade to the right illuminated wet bricks, dented garbage cans, an overflowing wooden box, a rusty bicycle locked to a frame made of pipe. Across the way a narrow alley led out to a street beyond. He scuttled across the courtyard, keeping as near the wall as possible, skirting the obstructions. In the alley he paused to look back. No one was following him. His heart was beating painfully. His head hurt. His stomach hurt. His knees and hands and his face hurt. He sobbed once, and hurried toward the street.

It was a dark, narrow, shuttered street lined with old, high-built houses faced with dark green shingles and purple-gray stonework, with faded "Room for Rent" signs propped in the high arched windows. Lights shone behind a few of the windows. The rain fell steadily, making a whispering sound in the street. He shivered, feeling the cold, clammy cloth against him. In his head, voices whispered, but he paid no attention. He stood on the sidewalk, feeling the rain against his face, observing himself shivering.

Down the street, three men stepped from a doorway. They paused for a moment under the streetlight at the corner, looking in his direction now. They moved closer together. A match flared, and he saw lean, pale faces, dark eyes slanted toward him.

Flicker. There was a sudden churning sensation in his stomach. His heart began to thud heavily. His mouth felt dry. He turned and walked off quickly.

Feet whispered on the pavement behind him. He reached the corner, broke into a run. A dozen yards along the street a deep doorway cut back into the dark masonry. He skidded to a halt and ducked into the entry, and at once regretted it. It was a damn fool move, but too late now to change his mind. But what else could he have done? The way he felt, he couldn't outrun a one-legged panhandler. What was the matter with him? Couldn't even remember how he got here, down on Delaney Street, at like 2 a.m. for chrissakes.

. . .

Running feet approached, slowed. The three men passed the doorway, halted not ten feet away. Standing in the empty street, they looked both ways. One of them swore. Another spat. They were just boys, he saw; with long, oiled hair, soiled, bright-colored shirts and dark jeans.

"Where the hell he get to?"

"Can't be far."

21

One of the youths started to turn toward the doorway, and the man who was hiding there flattened himself into the corner where the shadow cast by the streetlight was densest. He heard steps come closer, turn away.

"An alley up ahead; you check right, Sal, I'll take left. Mick, you keep an eye out."

Feet retreated. He moved his head an inch, saw two of the lads moving off, fanning out. The third stood six feet away, his back to the doorway.

The hiding man knew he had to act fast. He wished that he didn't feel so sick. But it was now or never. He slid out silently; the boy's head was turned the other way. He clasped hands with himself and swung his arms as if he were swinging a baseball bat. The locked fists struck the boy on the side of the head, just above the ear; the boy's head bounced against the stone wall with an overripe sound; he went down on his face, slack. The man who had struck him caught his ankles, dragged him into the doorway. He knelt beside him, frisked him swiftly and efficiently, netting a five-inch switchblade, a package of cigarettes, and three crumpled dollar bills.

Without a backward glance he sprinted for the corner, rounded it, hurried along to the next cross street, a major avenue with lighted storefronts, an all-night movie. A cruising cab drifted toward him; he stepped into the street and flagged it down.

"Main and Third," he told the driver. He never rode cabs, but it was a good idea to get clear of the area fast. He hadn't liked the sound of the punk's head hitting that wall.

[4]

Leaning back in the soft seat, he watched the colored lights, the movement beyond the rain-streaked glass beside him. The *whick, whick, whick,* of the windshield wipers caught his attention. He watched the process of water striking the glass, being struck aside, and more water falling, to be struck aside in turn. . . .

The cab swerved to the curb and braked to a stop.

"Eighty-five," the driver said over his shoulder; but his passenger, watching the windshield wipers, did not notice;

he was engrossed in the complex patterns of colored light that changed each time the wipers swept past.

"Third and Main," the driver said. "That's what you ast for, right?"

The passenger turned his head and looked out the side window. He saw a garishly lit window covered with over-sized hand-painted posters advertising cut-rate patent medicines, in red letters on dirty-white newsprint. There was a narrow stand with magazines strung on a clothesline above the entrance. Behind the steamy window of a beanery, a fat man scraped burnt grease from a hot-plate.

"How about it, Mac?" the driver said. "This where you wanted to go?"

Flicker. "No," a voice said. "Lord, no. Not here. Can you take me home?"

"Where's that at?"

"Brycewood. Tulane Street. The Tulane Apartments. Number 907."

"You ribbing me or what, Mac? There ain't no such street. Not in Jasperton, there ain't."

"Jasperton?" He heard the voice say. He waited to hear what it would say next.

"Hey, you all right, mister?" The driver was looking at him in the mirror. He threw an arm over the back of the seat and stared back at his fare.

"I'm afraid I don't feel too well," the voice said. "To tell you the truth, I don't know just where I am."

"Maybe I better get a cop."

"Yes. That's a good idea, driver. Find a policeman."

The driver grunted. "Where you from?"

"Caney. Caney, Kansas."

"What you doing in Jasperton?"

"I can't really say. I wonder . . . if this could be what they call amnesia?"

"You forgot your name?"

"I'm Claude P. Mullins. No, I haven't forgotten my name. I just . . . don't know . . ." the voice trailed off.

"You get hit on the head?" The driver was looking at him. He felt his head; it was tender in several places. His wrists hurt abominably. His knees hurt. *Flicker.*

"The sons of bitches. They worked me over good."

"Who?" the driver asked.

"The damn cops. I done nothing. They don't give a man a chance."

"Maybe you better get out here, mister."

"Give me a break, pal. Run me out to the edge of town, OK?"

"That'll be two bucks."

He felt in his pockets, found some crumpled bills.

"Sure," he said. "I got dough. Get me out of this town. I seen enough of this town."

"Caney, Kansas, huh?" the driver said as he pulled away from the curb.

"What's that mean?" the man in the passenger's seat said suspiciously.

"That's where you said you was from."

"I never been west in my life."

"Suits me, Mr. Mullins."

"Why you call me that?"

"Ain't that your name?"

"Hell, no. I'm Stick Marazky. Why?"

"I thought you said it was Mullins."

"I'm no damn Mick."

The driver wagged his head and drove in silence for a few blocks. He turned left at a Shell station, went past dark houses, billboards, a cafe. Dark trees closed in on the road. Weeds grew rank on the shoulder, shining green in the beam of the headlights.

"This where you want out?"

The man looked out into the wet night. *Flicker.*

"Why are you stopping here?"

"You said take you out of town. OK. This is the city limits."

"You can't leave me here."

The driver put his elbow over the seat back and studied his passenger.

"What are you, nuts, or what? Or maybe you got a funny sense of humor. Two bucks, Mister."

He felt over his pockets, found three wadded bills. He gave two to the driver.

"Please," he said. "I'm sorry to be troublesome, young man, but I seem to be having an attack of some kind. I live at the Sunshine Motel, at Indian Beach. If you'll take me there, my wife will pay your fare. I seem to have only one more dollar with me——"

"There ain't no such beach around here, mister. Look, I better run you over to the hospital. You're in no shape to be running around loose."

"Yes, yes, I'd appreciate that, young man."

The cab did a U-turn and gunned back into Jasperton.

[5]

He leaned back in the seat, listening to the voices. Some of them seemed far away and dim, others were close, right inside his head. But then they were all inside his head. Or his head was outside all of them. The concept became fuzzy. It made his head hurt to think about it. It was easier just to listen to the voices:

"... creep puts his hands on me again ..."

"Varför skulle de bry sig om det?"

"... Temos tempo de fazer planos. Mas agora fale-me de si ..."

"... just wait till next time, that's all ..."

"Endlist bist du wach. Du schläfst, das ist gut ..."

"... I promise, I won't do it again, I swear ..."

"Get out. Go on, get out, get out now!"

"... curioso, vero? Quei teschi non sembrano più grossi di biglie ..."

"... lay me down to sleep, to sleep, for God's sake. That's a laugh. I lay me down to sleep...."

"... à propos de fête, il serait temps que je rebrousse chemin ..."

"... tomorrow, first thing tomorrow, for sure ..."

"Cual es la dificultad? Tenemos que sacudirnos el polvo de aquí ..."

The car swerved suddenly, shot up a curving drive, and braked to a stop under a wide overhang. Light shone through a rank of glass doors fronting a lighted lobby with a green tile floor. A woman in white sat behind the desk. The driver climbed out, opened the rear door.

"You just sit tight, mister. I'll be right back. What was that name again?"

Flicker. "Harkinson," a voice said promptly. "J. W.

Harkinson. Look here, who are you? What is this place?"

"Do me a favor, mister. Don't change your name so much, OK? Harkinson. That's a nice name. Stick with it, OK?" The driver turned and walked toward the doors. The man in the car watched him, a squat bandy-legged figure in a mackinaw and a flat leather cap. *"Don't change your name so much,"* he had said; *"Harkinson . . . nice name . . . stick with it . . ."*

He sat watching the rain run down the glass. A large man in a blue slicker appeared, strolling along the walk in front of the building. He wore a uniform cap and a pistol at his hip.

Flicker. The man in the car ducked down out of sight. His heart was pounding painfully. He had to get away, fast. He didn't ask himself why; he simply knew that he had to make his escape now, at once.

Raising his head cautiously, he saw the policeman standing by the hospital door. The light shone on the wet slicker. The cop yawned. The man in the car slid quickly over into the front seat, got behind the wheel. The policeman was looking away, along the drive. He started the engine, pulled gently away. The headlights shone along the cedars lining the drive. In the street, he gunned it, squeaking the tires, cursed, slowed. He didn't want to attract any attention now. He drove swiftly through the night street, heading for the edge of town. Once past the city limits sign, he opened it up, putting distance between himself and the town.

[1]

The cab ran out of gas fourteen miles west of Jasperton. When the engine sputtered and stopped the driver, who had been gripping the wheel, staring ahead into the rain—which was falling harder now—started as though awakened from a deep sleep.

Flicker. He clung to the wheel, not steering, merely hanging on. The vehicle, which had been traveling at forty miles per hour, coasted down a gentle grade, gradually trending left across the centerline. As the road curved off to the right, it left the pavement, bumped along the shoulder, losing speed, angling down into the drainage ditch. At a speed of five miles per hour, it struck a highway route marker, snapping it off short, and came to rest, nose down, in a weed-choked gully.

The driver let out a shuddering sigh and unclenched his hands from the wheel.

"Oh, golly," he said. "Oh, golly oh, golly . . ." He found the door handle and climbed out into ice-cold ankle-deep water. The car was sitting at a steep angle. It looked as if it might roll over at any moment. Water was gurgling in the ditch, sluicing around the front wheels, which were crimped at an angle against a twenty-four inch concrete drainage tile.

"I didn't mean it," he said. "I'm sorry." He backed away from the car and scrambled up the bank. It was a very dark night; he could faintly see the yellow centerline of the road running off for a few yards in each direction. Trees beside the road made masses of deep black against the slightly lesser blackness of the sky. In the ditch the headlights of the car were still burning, shining on wet weeds; enough light reflected from them to enable him to pick his way along for a hundred yards or so before the darkness closed in again.

He came up over a low rise and saw a light off to the right, perhaps half a mile ahead.

"Please, ma'am," he mumbled half aloud. "My scout troop got lost, and I . . ."

Wasn't berry season. "Ma'am, my ma is sick in the next town, and I set out to visit her, and . . ."

He didn't know the name of the next town.

Flicker. "Harkinson," he said suddenly. "Name's Harkinson." He went on, heading toward the light now, muttering the name to himself.

A wire fence barred his way. He yanked at the strands, succeeded in gouging his hand painfully on a barb. Backing away, he followed the fence line to a gate which stood open.

A hand-painted sign attached to a post showed a palm with the finger spread, under the legend "Sister Louella, Spiritual Counselor."

He went up along the drive, paying no attention when a dog began to bark hoarsely from somewhere off behind the house. There were lights in two windows, shining cheerfully through colorful curtains. A big, shaggy collielike dog came racing up to him, halted ten feet away, barking frantically. The man snapped his finger, advancing toward the dog.

"Here, boy," he said. "Nice old feller." He walked steadily toward the dog, which ran excitedly to and fro, wagging its tail, barking, but less stridently now. The man reached out and fondled the dog's head carelessly, scratched behind its ears. The animal sniffed at him, made a whining sound, fell in beside him, and escorted him to the porch.

A light went on—a bare light bulb against the narrow paneling of the porch ceiling. The screen door opened and a man stepped out.

"Who's that?" he called, shading his eyes under the light.

"Harkinson's the name," the visitor said promptly.

"We don't know any Harkinson," the man said; the dog bounded up onto the porch, tried to jump up on the man, who thrust him away.

"What is it?" the man on the porch said. He was staring

28

down uncertainly, frowning. He backed away as the newcomer started up the steps, ducked inside the screen door, latching it hastily. The stranger tried to open the door.

"What do you want?" the man said through the door. "I've got a gun in here."

"I want to come inside. I'm cold and wet." The visitor hugged himself and shivered.

"Where'd you come from?"

Flicker-flicker. "Back there." He waved a hand.

"Car broke down?"

"It wasn't my fault," the visitor said quickly. His voice sounded different now, less sure of itself. "I'm a Boy Scout," he added. "Please, mister, I have to telephone my ma." He snuffed and wiped his nose with his forefinger.

"What is it, Les?" a new voice said; a woman's voice, high-pitched, slightly wheezy.

"Heard Shep barking and come out to see and here was this feller. Says he's a Scoutmaster. Car broke down."

"What's the matter with him?"

"You better move on, mister," the man behind the door said.

"Now, Les." The woman opened the door and stepped out. She was bulky, with a vague, muddy face, tight-twisted gray hair, a small, garish mouth. She flapped a hand at the dog as it muzzled her knee.

"Why, he's crying," she said. "What's the matter, mister?"

The man sobbed, knuckling his eye.

"Shep likes him," the woman said. "How'd he get past Shep?"

"Damn fool dog. Better come back inside, Lou."

"Who are you, mister?" the woman asked.

Flicker-flicker-flicker. A confusion of voices. . . .

"H-harkinson," he said tearfully. "J. W. Harkinson."

"You sick or something?" the woman gasped and started as the sleeve fell away from his wrist, exposing the bloody area.

"Saints preserve us," she gasped. "Les, looky here."

Les came out cautiously. He stood beside the woman, staring at the thin man in the sodden shirt and pants. His face was pale and hollow-cheeked. His mouth was cut and

29

bruised; his dark hair was plastered against his forehead. He had stopped crying. His expression was calm now, almost unconcerned.

"Let's see that hand," the woman said. She reached, gingerly took his fingers, automatically turned the hand palm up, brushed the other hand across it.

"That's a handcuff on him," Les said sharply. "This feller's broke from the police."

"I can see that," the woman said. "What did they have you for, Mr. Harkinson?"

Flicker. "I'm terribly sorry. I seem to have suffered a breakdown. I'm not feeling at all well." He tottered, and the woman caught his arm.

"Les, get his other arm. Can't you see he's sick?"

"Wait a minute, Lou—what do we know about this fellow? For all we know—"

"He's hurt and sick. Get him inside."

They assisted him into the house, across a pseudo-Oriental rug that was worn thin, along a mustard-colored hall, into a small bedroom. Les switched on an exposed 40-watt bulb suspended from the ceiling by two strands of twisted green-covered wire. There was a single bed with a chenille spread, a rocker, a white-painted dresser, a hooked rug. A framed brown rotogravure of a painting of Christ hung against the yellowish wallpaper.

They lowered him to the bed. The mattress was hard, stiff at the edges, sagging in the center. He lay back; the pillow crackled as if stuffed with straw. He closed his eyes and sighed, relaxing.

"Les, get that iron-saw and cut these manacles off this man."

"Lou, we got no call to go mixing in police business. I'll drive up to Olsen's and telephone the sheriff—"

"You'll do nothing of the kind. What have police ever done for you and me but give us trouble?"

"They'll give us more when they find out we helped a fugitive from justice."

"You just get that saw, Les."

The man grunted and left the room. The woman went out, came back with a towel. Carefully, she dried the patient's face and shoulders and chest. She took great care with his arms, clucking as she dabbed bloody water away

30

from his hands. He watched her without curiosity.

"It's not too bad," she said. "Just the skin torn. Not deep."

"It hurts," he said.

"I know—"

"My legs hurt." He tried to sit up and she pressed him back.

"You just rest easy, now, Mr. Harkinson."

He frowned at her. He licked his lips, looking worried now.

"How did I get here?"

"Your car broke down you said; you walked to the house."

"Was I in an accident?"

"Not's I know of."

"I'm suffering a good deal of pain." He lifted his hands, stared at the bloody wrists encircled by the bright-steel cuffs with the dangling chain.

"What's the meaning of this?" he cried.

"Don't you remember?" the woman spoke sharply.

He let his hands down gingerly. The woman covered his chest with the towel.

"No. Nothing. I'm sixty-seven years of age and I've never been sick or in trouble a day in my life."

Les came back in with the hacksaw. The woman rose and met him.

"He's talking pretty strange," she said. "But there's no harm in him."

"What'd he say?"

"Said he didn't remember about the trouble with the police. Told me he was sixty-seven years old."

"Why, he's not over thirty," Les said.

"Let's get those things off his wrists," the woman said.

It hurt when Les began sawing. The woman held the steel band steady, making soothing sounds. It took Les half an hour to saw through the tough metal, another half hour for the other. The woman bathed his wrists in warm water, applied a salve, bandaged them.

"Let's get his britches off and get him in bed," she said when she finished. Les helped her. He exclaimed when he saw the man wore nothing under the trousers.

"Don't take on, Les, I was a practical nurse for years,"

she said; but she hissed at sight of his knees.

"They're scraped raw as hamburger," Les said. "Looks like he was dragged. Maybe come off a motorsickle on a gravel road."

The woman cleaned and bandaged his knees. They dressed him in a pair of Les' pajamas. The woman removed the damp bedspread and together they got him under the blanket. Throughout the process, he lay as passive as a doll, complying with instructions but otherwise paying no attention to the proceedings.

"You hungry?" the woman asked.

"No," one of his voices said.

"You go to sleep," she said. "You'll feel a lot better in the morning."

[2]

He lay in the dark, waiting for what came next. The voices in his head muttered, but he didn't want to hear them now; he wanted to think of all the new experiences, the new sounds and sights and smells and sensations. He *thrust* at the voices, and they were gone. He thought nothing of this, was not even aware of having done it. Now he could give his full attention to the savoring of sensory impressions.

There was no light here; but there were other things: the feel of the sheet under him, the lumpy mattress beneath that; the pressure of the bandages; the dull ache of his knees and the sharper, more insistent pain in his wrists. There were odors: a stale smell of cooking, a mothball odor from the blanket. And sounds: the moaning of the wind, the rattling of the sash in its frame, the soft, insistent drum of the rain. He knew what all these things were, drawing the knowledge effortlessly from behind the voices that clustered so thickly about him.

Blue-white light stuttered beyond the windows, followed almost at once by a terrific crash of sound.

Flicker. Panic surged through him. He sprang from the bed, ran for the door, seized the knob and twisted; but it failed to yield. Lightning dazzled again; this time the thunder was almost simultaneous. He howled and pounded frantically on the door. Feet thudded; the latch rattled and the door was flung inward, knocking him sprawling.

A gigantic figure clad in a billowing white garment stood silhouetted in the doorway, its head a mass of bulging coils. He yelled in terror and squeezed his eyes shut.

"What in tarnation's got into you, Mr. Harkinson?" Sister Louella demanded. "You having a fit, or what?"

The man on the floor moaned and covered his eyes with his hands.

"What is it?" Les called, hurrying up behind the woman.

"He's afraid of the storm," the woman said. "That's all. Nearly scared me out of my skin, the way he set to yelling and carrying on. Now you get up, Mr. Harkinson."

He opened his eyes, rolled them around the room like a horse smelling smoke.

"Ah didn't mean it, Lawd!" he cried. "I ain't nigh ready, Lawd!"

"Ready for what?" the woman inquired, amazed.

"Ready fo' glory, Lawd!"

"Mr. Harkinson, you get up off that floor and stop this foolishness in the middle of the night!"

"You got de wrong pahty, Lawd. This po' sinner's name is Fedral Relief Thompson!"

"He's talking crazy," Les said. "He's out of his head."

"Just a minute," the woman said sharply. "He's possessed, that's what he is. You—Mr. Thompson. . . ?"

"Yas'm." The man spoke more calmly now; but he was still trembling.

"Where do you live, Mr. Thompson?"

"Up past Robeson's, down nigh to de crick."

"What town?"

"Neahest town Dothan." His voice shook as he spoke; his eyes roved the room. "What place dis?" he blurted. He scrambled to his feet, looked down at himself.

"Sweet Jesus, what I doin' here?" He backed away from the man and woman. "I swear, I ain't never messed with no white lady. No, suh. Not never, no suh—"

"Now, you just calm down, Mr. Thompson," Sister Louella said firmly. "You're among friends. Nobody's going to hurt you. I just want to talk to you. Sit down, there on the bed."

He stared from the man to the woman and back.

"Y'all must be Yankee white folks," he whispered.

"Just sit down, Mr. Thompson."

He backed uncertainly to the bed, sank down on it, huddled there, looking up worriedly. Sister Louella pulled the chair over to face him and sat in it.

"Now, you came here for a reason, didn't you, Mr. Thompson? You have a message for someone, don't you?" Her voice was pitched higher now, and trembled with excitement.

"No'm I ain't got no message."

"You may speak to me, Mr. Thompson. Just tell me what it is that's brought you here. What's troubling you?"

"Ma'am, I don't know how I come to be in this place. I swear to Jesus I don't know." His voice shook so that it was barely comprehensible.

"Now, don't you be frightened of a thing," Sister Louella said. "Of course it's confusing for you at first. But you just be calm, and think, now. There's something unfinished on this side of the veil that's bothering you. You can tell Sister Louella. Speak now."

"Just let me go," he said. "Just turn me loose, now."

"Now, you buck up, Mr. Thompson. You've come here to tell me something. Speak, now!"

"Oh, Lawd," he said. "Oh, sweet Jesus."

"Speak freely, Mr. Thompson. Let's start with yourself. How long since you passed over?"

"I ain't never goin' drink another drop o' gin," he said. "I promise, Jesus, not another drop. Not ever."

"When did you die, Mr. Thompson?" Sister Louella demanded, sharply.

Flicker. The man sitting, trembling, on the edge of the bed gave a hoarse cry and recoiled against the wall, gibbering.

"Mr. Thompson! Mr. Thompson!" Sister Louella was on her feet, bending over him.

"He's having a fit," Les cried. "He's crazy as a bedbug, Lou!"

"Mr. Thompson, speak to me!"

"Lemme be," he muttered. "Damn you, Trish, lemme be!"

"Speak, spirit!" Sister Louella whispered. "Who are you?"

"Get the hell away from me, Trish."

34

"As soon as you tell me who you are."

"I'm Dubie, damn you! You know that!"

"Good Lord," Sister Louella breathed. "Another spirit's took possession." Then, louder: "Speak, Dubie! What did you come here to tell me?"

"I'll kill you; I swear . . ." his voice died away in a mumble.

"You have no power over me, Dubie. Speak, now. Who do you want to contact? What's your message for this side?"

"Awrrr."

"He's addled, I tell you, Lou," Les declared. "He's a crazy man. Next thing he'll take a butcher knife to us!"

"Shut up, Les. Don't you see what this is? This is a natural medium. Probably don't even know it." She shook the slack figure slumped back on the bed.

"Speak, Dubie! You can deliver your message now!"

"I'll give ye a message: get away from me and leave me be or I'll cut your heart out!"

"I'm calling the sheriff!" Les cried.

"You'll call nothing, Lester Choate! Don't be a bigger fool than God made you. Dubie! Speak up, now! What's the tidings you've come to pass across to this side?"

"Lou, just a minute now," Les said. "I've been with you a long time, but if you start talking like you're starting to *believe* in this spook stuff—"

"Get out of this room, Lester Choate! Get out of my house. I've got my hands on the biggest thing ever come my way, and I won't have your black thoughts driving it away! Dubie! You still there?"

Flicker. "*Kurrrattt!*" the man on the bed grated, rolling the *R* ferociously.

"Come on now; come through, restless spirit. Speak!"

The man on the bed stirred. His eyelids fluttered. He stared up at Sister Louella.

"Who are you?" she whispered.

Flicker. "Ferd Malone. That's my handle. Wh . . . where am I at?" He twisted his head to look around the room.

"Speak, Ferd Malone!"

"I need a drink."

"After, Ferd Malone. After you speak with me. What's it like on the other side?"

35

"Oh, boy," the man on the bed said. "Oh, boy, oh, boy."

"Look here, Ferd Malone. You've passed over, you understand? You're across the river now. What's it like over there?"

"Hey," the man said weakly.

"Tell me about death, Ferd. How did it come to you? How did it seem to you when you crossed over?"

"Dead? I'm not dead. My God, I'm as alive as anyone. I—"

"Face up to it, Ferd. You've died, but death is just a door, just a passage to a higher state. Now, tell me what it's like; what you've seen—"

"Call my lawyer. He'll tell you."

"What year did you die, Ferd?"

"You're crazy." The man tried to sit up, was forced back by the woman's powerful hand. "What are you trying to do to me?"

"You've got to accept it, Ferd. You've died and went to your reward. Now you're back, speaking through Mr. Harkinson here—"

Flicker. "Harkinson," he said in a different tone. "My name's Harkinson. J. W. Harkinson."

"Drat. We've lost Ferd." Sister Louella sat up straight. "But I see it now: Mr. Harkinson's a spirit voice, too!"

"Listen, Lou—"

"If you can't keep quiet, get out of this room, Les," Sister Louella snapped. "Now, Mr. Harkinson, you just relax. You relax and let the contacts come through—"

"I don't feel well. I don't feel well at all," he said.

"You're fine. You're just fine. You just relax."

"I have a bladder condition. I need medication."

"Sure, I'll see to that—just as soon as we get that message through here to the loved one on earth. Who wants to speak now? Just speak, you there on the other side. It's all right."

"I'll pay. I'll see you're well paid for your trouble. Just telephone my wife, Mrs. J. W. Harkinson, at 345-2349. Call collect. Reverse the charges."

"All right, Mr. Harkinson; I'll see your wife gets the message. You go ahead now."

"Tell her—tell her I've had a seizure. I . . . don't remember a thing. I woke up—and here I am. Tell her bring my pills. Tell her to get Doc Ferguson. Tell her hurry."

"Now, who's your wife, Mr. Harkinson? Where can I find her?"

"Right here in St. Louie. Parkside Terrace. You phone her at 345-2349. Tell her hurry."

"All right, Mr. Harkinson. Now what else did you wish to say to her? Any messages from other loved ones on the other side?"

"That's all. Just tell her to hurry with my medicine. I've been taken bad."

"Les—you got the number. Go call Mrs. Harkinson. Tell her we got a Class A Number One contact with her departed."

"Aw, just a second here, Lou—"

"You do's I told you!"

"She'll think I'm crazy."

Sister Louella turned a triumphant look on her partner. "Not if they's a Mrs. Harkinson at that number, she won't. Don't you understand, Les? We're onto something big—so big it takes my breath away!"

"I'll make the call," Les said. "But it'll be a wrong number, you'll see."

[3]

Sister Louella sat by the bed, crooning softly to the man who lay there, eyes shut, breathing through his mouth.

"Just rest easy," she murmured. "Everything's fine. . . ."

He opened his eyes; for a moment he looked vaguely about the room; then his expression sharpened; his eyes became alert.

"Amazing," he said.

"What is it, Mr. Harkinson?"

"Why do you call me by that name?"

"Les is gone to make your call, Mr. Harkinson. You just linger on here awhile."

The man raised himself on one elbow.

"You take it easy, Mr. H. You just lie quiet."

"Who are you?" the man asked sharply.

"Me? Why, I'm Sister Louella. I taken you in and made

37

you comfortable here. You were in bad shape—"

"Louella who?"

"Why, Louella Knefter." She laughed an embarrassed laugh. "Been so long since I used it I near forgot."

"Where do you live? What town? What state?"

"Just outside Springfield. Look here, Mr. Harkin—"

"My name's not Harkinson. Poldak. Arthur Poldak." He sat up, swung his legs over the side of the bed. He looked down at his lean thighs; he touched his knees and winced.

"Absolute verisimilitude," he said. "Amazing."

"What's amazing?"

"Sitting here having a conversation with a hypnogogic illusion," the man muttered. "Tactile, auditory, visual—everything. It's perfectly real—as real as any other experience."

"Mr. Poldak—when did you pass over?" Sister Louella asked abruptly.

He looked at her critically. "Are you asking me when I *died?*"

"That's right. When? What year?"

"I'm as alive as you are, Mrs. Knefter." He smiled, a crooked, not altogether happy smile. "You think I'm a ghost?"

"I'm a medium, Mr. Poldak. You've passed over—I know it may be hard for you to grasp that—they say sometimes a spirit has a terrible time understanding what's happened. But it's nothing to be upset about. You've passed to the other side, but I'm here to receive your message. You must have something you wanted to say to a dear one left behind."

The man on the bed laughed again, a short bark. "I'm dreaming you, and you think I'm a ghost. Remarkable."

"You can speak freely to me, Mr. Poldak. Tell me about passing over—"

"What's the date?"

"Why, August 10—"

"Well, as of midnight August 9 I was still alive and kicking. I'm in my bedroom at home in Scarsdale, Mrs. Knefter. I'm asleep—or half asleep. And I'm dreaming all this. I'm a psychologist. This is my field, you know, dream research. Guggenheim grant, Columbia. I've been trying for an experience like this, but I had no idea—" He broke off, shaking his head.

"You must have died in the night. You're a spirit, Mr. Poldak. You're speaking through my, uh, assistant. He's a very sensitive medium. I've already spoke to half a dozen spirits on the other side tonight."

"I wonder . . ." the man looked at his hands, prodded the bandages on his wrist. "I wonder if we've been missing something?" he said, talking to himself. "Is there any possibility that there's something in the idea of the Ka? The wandering spirit that leaves the body during sleep?"

"You bet your sweet life," Sister Louella said. "I'll guarantee you, Mr. Poldak, you're not here in the flesh, no siree."

"I'm inclined to agree with you." He pinched the skin of his forearm. "But it's real flesh. Or the illusion of real flesh. How can one be sure?"

"All my life I've wanted to know what it's like—passing over, I mean," Sister Louella said in a low, urgent voice. "Tell me that much; just tell me what it's like. Does it hurt? Were you afraid?"

The man looked at her. "I suppose in your own way you're as much an earnest seeker after truth as myself. All right—as a fellow researcher, I'll tell you all I know."

"Yes?"

"I went to bed normally. Had a little trouble dropping off. Usually do, since I ordinarily test various sleep-inducing routines. A matter of preparing the mind to dream, you understand. I remember feeling the onset of stage two drowsiness—my own term. Then—I was dreaming this. That's all."

"Just like that. No pain, no suffering."

"But I'm not dead, Mrs. Knefter. Somehow, I seem to be occupying a body not my own—or dreaming that I am—"

The outer door slammed; Les's voice swore. His feet tramped heavily along the hall.

"Hope you're satisfied," Les said. He stood in the doorway, slapping his wool cap against his leg. His jacket was soaked; water dripped from the end of his nose.

"What happened?"

"I put the call through, lady answered. Said she was Mis' Harkinson—and that her husband was sound asleep in bed. I asked her to go check, and she said if he was a corpse he was snoring pretty good. Thought I was some drunk. Hung up on me."

"Well—I declare." Sister Louella turned back to the man sitting on the bed. He stared back vacantly. Saliva ran from the corner of his slack mouth.

"Mr. Poldak?" she said uncertainly. The man made a bubbling noise and sank back on the pillow. Sister Louella stood up; her eyes were bright and intent.

"Les," she said. "We got us a medium here, all right. But not the ordinary kind. It's not the dead speaking through him. It's the living!"

"Aw, come on, Lou—you're raving."

"We'll see who's raving when we get rich on this." She lifted her charge's legs onto the bed, covered him with her blanket.

"Go on to bed, Les. Adam is what we'll call him. Adam Nova. In the morning we start parlaying this poor drownded rooster into a million dollars cash."

4

[1]

In the days that followed, Adam's wounds healed. He was allowed to get out of bed, to wander about the house and grounds. In the alternation of *dark* and *light,* in the rhythm of his own sensations of hunger and sleepiness he had perceived patterns. Now the search for other patterns occupied his attention. He became aware of *time* as the matrix against which events occurred. At length, the distinction between an *event* and an *act* dawned on him. This was a most delightful discovery. He experimented, moving his body, touching things, making sounds. As a result of Les' cursing and blows he learned to control the bodily functions of elimination, following the prescribed rituals. And always the voices spoke, sometimes faintly, at other times so loudly that the *me* retreated into dimness. He disliked these times; he fought back, at first feebly, then more surely. He learned to push the voices away at will, holding the *me* in control.

The *Les* and the *Sister Louella,* also known as the *Lou,* were near him most of the time. Once, he remembered vaguely, they had not been near; now they were near. It was an observed datum, like other data. He was not curious about this, or any other abstraction. His mind was fully occupied in exploring the spectrum of sensation, of immediate physical experience.

The Les and the Sister Louella spoke to him frequently. He made no effort to comply with their instruction and requests. The idea of linking actions to words had not occurred to him. He spent most of his time lost in thought, poking and prodding at himself, feeling the textures of wood and cloth and glass, making noises with his mouth.

One day he said "hungry." He had felt pangs in his stomach and had ignored them, as usual. But suddenly his mouth had formed the word.

Sister Louella stared at him.

"You got a possession, Adam?" she demanded. In a vague way he understood that the word "Adam" was connected with the *me*. He gave no answer. He was busy trying his tongue in different positions.

"Food," he said.

"Who are you? Who's speaking?"

His mouth twitched. He felt a stir of irritation arising from frustration.

"Adam," he said.

"Why—why, yes, Adam. You're hungry?"

"Ham and eggs," he said distinctly. "Toast, butter, jam, coffee, orange juice." He paused, delighted by the sound of the words. Always before the voices had made such words. Now it was different: the *me* was making its own words.

"Veal birds. Macaroni and cheese. Spareribs. Cream of wheat. Alberjawskrty." He paused, feeling that there was something wrong with the last sound.

"De viande," he said. "Frommage; poissons, l'escargots, de la bière, des fruites."

"Les," Sister called. "Come here!"

"Matt. Kött. Ost, fisk, knäckebröd. Hamelfleisch, bröt,

schnapps, schnitzel. Carne, garbanzos, cerveza. . . ."

"Les, he's talking. Some gibberish, but some of it's just as plain! He said he's hungry. Wants ham and eggs!"

"Well, what's so wonderful about that? I could use some ham and eggs myself."

"Listen, Adam," Sister Louella said earnestly. "You want to eat, you have to ask for it. You understand?"

"Eat," he said.

"Now, you tell Sister Louella; say, 'I want my breakfast.' "

"Jam. Sausage."

"Say, 'Please, Sister Louella, may I have some nice breakfast?' "

"Eat. Hungry."

"Aw, hell, Lou, you can't teach no grown man to talk," Les said. "Give the poor dummy his breakfast."

"Give me my breakfast," the man said. "Eat. Hot. Salt. Hungry."

Sister Louella beamed and patted his hand and bustled away. Les stayed behind, staring shrewdly at him.

"You wouldn't be pulling somebody's laig, would you, Adam?" he said softly.

"Shut up, Les," the man said calmly. Les jerked as if he had been struck.

"Don't you go giving me your jaw," he blurted. "I'm onto you, you slick little devil."

The man called Adam wasn't listening. He was busy discovering how far back he could bend his fingers before the bad-feeling became unendurable.

[2]

"We been feeding and coddling this feller for nigh two months now," Les said. He was sitting across the kitchen table from Sister Louella, over the scraped dinner plates. "You been letting your regular work go to hell—"

"You know I don't allow that kind of language in my house, Lester Choate," the woman said sharply.

"But you let this tricky little rascal come here and upset everything, make a fool of you—"

"That's enough of that, Les. I'm tired—"

"It ain't near enough. I've been with you a long time,

42

Lou. I can't set by and watch some dirty little confidence man trick you out of house and home. I can see which way it's going—"

"You listen to me, Les. This is my home. I run it to suit me. If you don't like it, you're free to leave, just anytime."

"Don't think I don't know what's going on," Les said sullenly.

"What's that mean?"

"I can hear. I got ears—and eyes."

Sister Louella stared at the man.

"You been drinking."

"Where would I get licker?" Les muttered.

"You been drinking, after you swore on the Book you'd never touch another drop; and you sit here and insult me, and lie to me!"

"Wait a minute, Lou; I swear I never—"

"Don't go perjuring your soul to hell. Lean over here; let me smell your breath."

"Damn if I will," Les blustered. "I taken about all I aim to take off you, Lou."

"Dirty old bitch," a voice said from the door. "You're fat, and you stink, and if it wasn't for the meals and the bed I'd of been long gone."

The man and the woman at the table turned to stare.

"Good Christ," Adam said. His eyes looked vague. "The dummy's reading my mind!"

"Don't believe a word of it, Lou," Les said, his words an echo superimposed on the other's.

"Adam!" Sister Louella gasped.

"Leave the dirty louse to me," Adam and Les shouted. "He can't talk about you like that!"

Sister Louella came up out of her chair, caught Les' arm, threw him half across the room. She stood gaping at Adam.

"Adam," she gasped. "Was that you saying them things?"

"Sure it was him," Adam said, echoing Les. "You seen it with your own eyes, heard it—" both voices cut off abruptly. Louella turned to stare at Les.

"He's reading your mind," she whispered. "Speaking your thoughts out loud."

"No. He's tricking you, Lou," Les and Adam said.

"Shut up, Les! Not another word!" Sister Louella whirled on Adam.

"What's he thinking? Tell me, Adam. Speak it out!"

"I'll kill him," Adam mumbled. "Filthy hobo. Dirty, rotten, sneaky . . . coming in here, ruining everything . . . the old bitch believes him. My God. He's really doing it. Everything I think . . ."

Les covered his ears and jumped to his feet. "He's a liar, a trickster!" he and Adam shouted together. Les put his head down and charged past Adam, out into the hall. They heard his feet, taking the stairs three at a time.

Sister Louella sank into a chair.

"Adam," she gasped. "You really did it. You read his dirty little mind." She broke off. "Can you . . . can you read mine, Adam?"

He put his hands to his head, frowned.

"Sister Louella, can I have a cookie and some licker?"

"Read my mind, Adam. You can do it. Come on, honey, try for Sister Louella."

Adam looked at her, thinking of the cookie. He *reached*.
. . .

"Sweet lord, if this works I'll make a million," Adam said.

Sister Louella uttered an exclamation. "Praise God, he's really doing it," Adam cried in synchronization with the woman. "He's really reading me. But—what if—Adam! That's enough! Don't read any more, you hear?" they said together. Sister Louella stepped forward and seized him by the shoulders, shook him.

"Adam, stop that now!" they chanted in unison. "Stop it! You got no right looking in a lady's thoughts that way!"

Flicker. Adam fell silent, staring at her vaguely.

"A real, honest-to-lord mind reader," Sister Louella murmured. "Why, I can't hardly see the end to what we can do together, Adam. Brother Adam, I better call you now. A man with a gift like yours. . . ."

[3]

It was three weeks later. Adam sat on a straight chair, alone in the semidarkened room. He was dressed in an elderly tuxedo, formerly the property of the late Mr. Knefter,

44

a handsome costume with brocaded lapels and vest and a wing collar. Sister Louella had cut it down to fit Adam's slight body, which had filled out a little on a diet of macaroni, potatoes, chicken-and-dumplings, and *apfel strudel*. He got on the straight chair, his hair neatly combed, his body in a position that was somehow not quite symmetrical, his hands lying on his knees, one palm up, the other down, like a pair of objects that had been dropped carelessly. He sat quietly, studying the design of the wallpaper. His scrutiny was not purposeful, not even conscious. His mind automatically scanned data, asking *what*, but never *how*, or *why*. He noted the discontinuity where adjoining strips had been imperfectly matched. If asked, he could have given the number of rows of amorphous shapes that made up the design, horizontally and vertically; he could have drawn the outlines of the shapes themselves. In his thoughts there was no distinction between the important and the trivial.

Having exhausted the possibilities of the wallpaper, his attention wandered to the *voices* coming from the next room. He had learned to sense the direction and distance of a *voice*-source, not deliberately, but in the same way that he had learned to trace audible sounds, instinctively. There were twelve *voice*-sources. He did not think of them as people. It would not have surprised him if the *voices* had issued from stones or trees. He did not, in fact, think of the sources as entities separate from the *voices*. He merely listened, observing, filing, recording. . . .

". . . sakes, nice turnout, didn't expect old Mrs. Kleek . . ."

". . . like stale cabbage, no housekeeper . . ."

". . . doing here, damned old charlatan, Lydia's idea, keep peace in the family, can't she see . . ."

Adam's attention wandered again. He was listening to the sequence and texture of the sounds given off by the house as it accommodated to the gusty wind that pressed against it, as if testing it for weakness. A mental image of the dynamics of the house formed in his mind. He saw where the stresses were, where the first failures would occur. . . .

". . . where are you? Answer me!" a more distant voice penetrated his concentration. This *voice* was different from the others; more urgent, more purposeful. The words "urgent" and "purposeful" did not come into his mind, but the concepts were there. He was not alarmed, merely interested.

"I'm Arthur Poldak! Answer me! Where are you?" The *voice* rang with a hard purpose; it intrigued Adam. He listened closely for more, but there was nothing, only the vague muttering subcurrent that underlay the *voices*.

Adam's interest flagged. He played a game with the nearby *voices,* separating one from another, teasing a *voice* closer until he felt his throat tense, his tongue about to begin mouthing the words; then pushing it back, holding it at a distance, hearing it without letting it push the *me* aside. . . .

He tired of the game and devised another: tracing the lines of memory, reevoking the past with the vivid clarity of total recall: back past the days with Sister Louella, his wanderings in the city, the concrete-floored cell. . . .

There, all memory ended. It was as though a light had gone out, leaving his mind in darkness.

But not quite total darkness, he saw, peering past the barrier. It was like a corridor leading into darkness. He took a hesitant step, felt the parameters of his awareness close in almost to nothing. But a faint thread of dim consciousness remained. He followed it. Back. Back to a beginning.

Pain, and the impingement of sensations in a chaotic flood. Light, sound, pressure, heat, cold. Now, standing outside himself, he was able to put words to the phenomena that had accompanied the birth trauma. He had been small, then, he sensed now. He saw himself as the days and weeks and years passed, growing physically, at last able to stand, to walk.

But not to talk. Not to feed himself. Mentally, he remained an infant.

Idiot, the word came into his mind. *I was born an idiot.*

Vaguely, through the dim, unfocused perceptions of his early unformed mind, he saw the rooms where he had lived; the cot on which he had slept, the oversized highchair where the gruel had been spooned into his unheeding mouth. He lived again the empty hours of the endless days.

. . . He saw himself wandering through a door accidentally left unlocked, finding a place where things with sharp smells were stored: the asylum kitchen. He ate: sugar, lard, paper—which he spat out—cold stew, chocolate. A smooth, hard thing jumped from his grip and made a loud sound, and after that there were sharp pains in his bare feet, and red fluid had stained the floor. He sat down in the puddled liquor, cutting himself again on broken glass. He made unhappy, bubbling sounds—he had been taught not to make loud noises, at the cost of hundreds of hours of patient switch-wielding by a succession of sweating attendants. He licked his hands. The taste of blood and rum nauseated him. He vomited.

. . . His clothing—a loose coverall—was sticky and clammy wet. He pulled at it; cloth ripped. He tore away the garment. . . .

. . . He was outside. A dim recollection of running and jumping with the others took form. He ran down across a ragged stretch of uncut weeds, into sparse woods. Soon he tired; he sat on the ground and made bubbling sounds, but no one came. He rose and wandered on. Sharp things jabbed and scratched him. He ate aimlessly: leaves, bits of rotted wood, a small, feathered object with a foul smell that came apart in his hands. He vomited again.

. . . It was dark. He lay, shivering, making small, mewing sounds. He fouled himself, and made gobbling noises. He slept. . . .

. . . Daylight came. The trees thinned. Instinctively, he angled his aimless course to follow the line of least resistance. At times he halted and lay down, curling around the pain in his stomach. Then, without purpose, without awareness, he would rise and wander on.

. . . Night again. Cold. Pain. Then spots of bright light, coming toward him. The lights stopped. He emerged from the brush and into the dazzle, fascinated. Sounds. Men coming forward, making sounds.

"What the hell you doing out here stark naked, boy?"

"It's one of them damned preverts. Out cruising."

"Somebitch is tore up. What happened to you, boy? Somebody roll you, take your clothes?"

He made bubbling sounds and reached for the shiny thing at the man's hip.

A swift movement, a blinding light and a flash of pain.
. . .

. . . He was lying on a warm floor. There was movement around him, light that glared down from above. He opened his eyes and stared at it.

"Somebitch's coming around. Hey, you." Something dug into his side. "What's your name?"

"Leave me work on him, Sar'nt Dubell. I'll make the sucker talk plenty."

"You get out there and clean up the mess he made in the car, Kenny, like I told you!"

The sounds the men were making with their mouths had carried no significance to him; the conception that sounds might have meaning had never occurred to him. From time to time the man kicked him, lightly at first, then harder. He mewed and tried to move away from the pain, but it followed him. He gobbled and got to his feet, and a blow sent him back to the floor.

"Take him downstairs, Kenny. Somebitch's a dummy. Must of escaped from someplace, maybe that home up to Belleton."

"Hell, you think he could of walked fifteen mile through wild country barefoot?"

"He's faking it, Sar'nt. Leave me work him over."

"Lock him up, Kenny. Then clean up where he puked over by the door."

. . . The man Kenny hustling him along a passage, down steps, pausing at the door. Clank of metal. Door opening, a hand thrusting him inside.

A blow on the head knocked him down.

"I ain't soft like Dubell. I don't buy the act. And I don't like queers. You're going to talk to me, boy."

The beating went on and on. After a time, he was no longer aware of it. . . .

The door opened; Sister Louella came in, massive in dark blue satin. Her doughy face was slightly flushed. Her eyes had an unusual shine.

"Come along, Brother Adam, our guests are waiting for you."

[4]

"Just remember what I told you, Adam," she whispered, walking him from the room, along the hall. "Do just like we practiced. . . ." She held the new purple velveteen hanging aside. Faces turned to stare. Adam gazed back, noticing the variety of shapes and sizes and textures and colors; of hair growth and of baldness, the evidences of decay, illness, the effects of time and gravity. . . . They were all different, but all alike. There was a subtle and powerful pattern here which he could perceive, but could not grasp in its entirety. . . .

"Ladies and gentlemen, meet Brother Adam," Sister Louella was saying. "Brother Adam, you set here." She guided him to the big chair with the carved mahogany arms, seated him ceremoniously. He settled into a random position, his eyes fixed on the wart on the cheek of the elderly Mrs. Dunch.

"Brother Adam's tired, he's spent the day meditating and composing his thoughts for this evening's session," Sister Louella said. "He's promised to do his best for you folks this evening; I've told him how much you were counting on him, how great the need was for his gifts."

Several people shifted in their chairs. Sister Louella bustled across to pull the drapes closed across the front windows.

"Brother Adam works better in a subdued light," she explained. She had noticed how dowdy the tuxedo looked in the level rays of the late sun striking across the room.

"Now, Brother Adam's gift is not like my own," Sister Louella stated. "My work with the readings you all know; you know how much we can learn of our fates from the study of the character and destiny lines. But Brother Adam works more direct. He senses his truths by direct ether transference. Now, just to start off—Adam—I'd like you to tell me the names of these lovely people. Just start anywhere and go round."

Adam blinked; he raised a hand to his eyes, caught sight of his fingers, turned them over, peering closely at them. Someone shuffled his feet; someone cleared a throat.

"Now, don't go into a meditation, Brother Adam," Sister Louella said sharply. "Give me the names, start with Mrs. Kleek. . . ."

He looked around the room; the name meshed with a

49

pattern centered on the elderly woman seated nearest the door.

"Mrs. Emma Kleek," he said. He looked at the man beside her. "Mr. Horace Levy. Mrs. Doris Dunch . . ." He proceeded, calling off the names of all the people in the room; he hesitated, then continued:

"Lester Choate; Gus Pendleton . . ." As he paused, Sister Louella spoke up:

"That's enough, Brother Adam, you've named all present. Now—"

"Hummph," Mr. Levy said. "What's that prove? Anybody could have told him our names."

"Well!" Sister Louella gave him a bittersweet smile. "I don't suppose you meant nothing by that, Horace." She used a thumb to hitch up a slipping strap. "Brother Adam, s'pose you give Mr. Levy a further reading." She gave him a look which an observer would have called significant. He caught her *voice* clearly:

"Tell his full name, address, wife's name, children. Give his birthday—not the year. Got to respect his privacy. . . ."

"Hyman Nicoliavitch. Levenowski," Adam said. "248 Shadyside Drive. Sheila MacKenzie Levy. No children. October 21."

Horace Levy sat up and uttered a grunt expressive of astonishment which he quickly covered with a cough.

"Very clever," he said. "Except he got my name wrong," he added. "And he says I got no children. What about Seymour?"

"What's got into you, Adam?" Sister Louella said, mock-playfully. The smile was a grimace now. "Now, you straighten up and stop funning with Mr. Levy."

"You change your name, Horace?" Mr. Grant asked, giving the older man a shrewd glance.

"What, me? Why should I . . ." Mr. Levy's voice faded off.

"Why should I lie?" Adam said. "It's something dishonorable I should change my name? For convenience, that's all. It's not like I took a name like O'Reilly. . . ."

"Hey," Mr. Levy said weakly, gaping at Adam with his mouth open.

"Adam—you stick to what I told you!" Sister Louella's silent voice came across with a snap.

"What the heck, the boy's right," Mr. Levy said in a strained voice. "I was, uh, just testing him. I was born Levenowski, it's true. What I'm wondering, how did he know? How—"

"What about Seymour?" Mr. Grant cut in.

Mr. Levy took out a large, not-too-clean handkerchief from the side of his pants and mopped at his face.

"Should I tell them the boy is adopted?" Adam said. "Shelly's boy, from before—"

"Now that's enough out of you, you low-life!" Mr. Levy roared, leaping to his feet, pointing a plump, quivering finger at Adam. "You shut your mouth, you hear me?"

Adam shut his mind to the cacophony of voices, audible and inaudible. He closed his eyes, sorting out the odors in the air: human body-odor, leather, perfume, tobacco, dust, the stew Sister Louella had cooked up last night. . . .

"Adam—sit up, smile!" Sister Louella's thought slashed at him. He opened his eyes. Mr. Levy was on his feet, his face red, his hair rumpled.

". . . and the rest of you, you should be ashamed to sit here!" he was saying. "You'll see, it's you he'll be insulting next!"

"Horace, now don't take on that way," Sister Louella said quietly. "Brother Adam didn't mean a thing. He was just mixed up, was all. You set down and let me give you a nice cup of tea and we'll go on with the reading. Adam, you speak to Mrs. Dunch now. Doris, you just set and Adam will—"

"Not me, no thanks," Doris spoke up shrilly, holding up a brown-spotted hand sparkling with rings, heavy with bracelets. "Just leave me be. I'll just sit here and listen."

"I'll be next," Mr. Grant said into the silence. He looked at Adam through narrowed eyes. "Go ahead, Mr. Adam. Tell me the same kind of things you were telling Horace."

"Adam—you remember what I said! Name, birthday—safe things!"

Adam looked at Mr. Grant. He was a small, peppery man of about fifty, with reddish hair, gray at the sides, a leathery, freckled skin, pale blue eyes under bushy brows.

"Aneas M. Grant, Box 456, RFD Route 1. December 2. . . ." Adam's voice trailed off, his attention caught by another, deeper voice; a buried *voice,* faint and faraway.

"Idealia," he whispered. "Dead and gone these twenty-one years, but alive in my brain and heart every day and every night. . . ."

"Adam—what's that nonsense!" Sister Louella spoke up quickly.

"Be quiet!" Mr. Grant said in a choked voice. "Go on, boy."

"That September," Adam said. "So long ago; but only yesterday. More than I deserved, more than I ever dreamed of. I told her I loved her, and she said . . . I love you, too, Aneas. . . .'"

"Now, Adam—" Sister Louella subsided at Grant's curt gesture.

"Did wrong; did so many things wrong. I was a fool, lost the thing I wanted more than anything on earth. But I was young. I didn't know better. Now it's too late, and I'll regret it the rest of my life. . . ."

"Mr. Adam," Grant said in a strained voice. "Do you—are you in contact with her—in the hereafter? Is that . . . can you . . . can she—" He broke off.

"Damn fool," Adam said. "Taken in by this damned fool woman and her partner. Ought to have my head examined." As he spoke, Adam's face twitched into a variety of meaningless expressions; his eyes were fixed on the rosette of brilliant purple light exploding from the belly of the decanter filled with colored water that occupied the center of the doily on the table.

"Brother Adam! Now, you get aholt of yourself!" Sister Louella said shrilly.

"He's—reading my thoughts," Mr. Grant said. He came to his feet, his hands pressed to his head. "By the living God, he's actually reading my thoughts!"

". . . reading my thoughts," Adam echoed.

"You go on to Miz Abrams now—" Sister Louella said.

"Not me!" Mrs. Abrams rose, holding out a hand like a traffic policeman forbidding entry to a one-way street. "Count me out, Louella. Palm reading, yes, OK. It's expected. But feeling around inside my head—never!"

Others were rising. Mr. Grant sat staring across at Adam. Everyone was talking. Sister Louella's voice rose above the hubbub:

"I was jest going to serve my special cake," she cried.

"Brother Adam has to rest now; let's just set down, everybody, and . . ."

"I'm going," Mr. Levy stated firmly; he picked his hat from the end table and placed it squarely on his head with an air of finality.

"Coming, Mr. Grant?"

Grant's face looked gray. He got to his feet, left the room without a backward glance. The rest followed, the talk dying. Sister Louella fluttered around the departing guests like a mother bird whose nest is threatened.

A spotlight sprang up from a point just beyond the gate, illuminating the throng on the porch. Car doors clacked open. A large figure in khaki jodhpurs and a blue blouse with a sheriff's department patch appeared, stalking ominously forward.

"Why, Officer Pendleton," Sister Louella said, her voice pitched abnormally high.

The deputy halted at the foot of the porch steps, looking up rather uncertainly at the group gathered above him.

"Miz Louella, I, uh, got a complaint here. Uh, I, uh, hear they's fortune-telling going on here."

"Why, the idear," Sister Louella said weakly.

"I got a paper," Deputy Pendleton went on. "Swore to and signed." He patted his pockets.

"Signed by who?"

"Lester Choate."

"Ha! That little worm!"

Mr. Levy started down the steps with the air of a man with important business elsewhere. Deputy Pendleton stepped into his path.

"Hold on, here, Mr. Levy. I ain't through—"

"What, you're arresting me?" Mr. Levy demanded. He looked around at the others crowding down the steps. "He's arresting me? What's the charge?" He looked from Sister Louella to Mr. Grant to Mrs. Dunch.

"Wait a minute, Mr. Levy. I never said I was arresting you—"

"In that case, I'm going." He started past Pendleton, who backed to keep pace with him.

"You're a witness, Mr. Levy. I got to have your statement—"

"Statement? What statement? I'm visiting my acquaint-

53

ance, what more is there? You got a law against this?"

"Mr. Levy, was there fortune-telling going on in there?"

"Fortune-telling? Me? Fortune-telling? I'm a business-man, Mr. Pendleton. You think I go for fortune-telling? A social call, no more." He rounded the deputy and strode away. The others were spreading out, edging past on both sides.

"Mr. Grant—what about you? Was Sister Louella offering to tell fortunes for money?"

"Horace told you: social occasion," Grant muttered, and kept going.

"Who you got out in the car?" Sister Louella asked as the rest of the party dispersed, with Deputy Pendleton standing uncertainly in the middle of the walk as they streamed past.

"Got Les."

"You tell that dirty little sneak to stay away from me."

"He signed the complaint," Pendleton said sullenly. "I got my duty to perform."

"What'd you expect to find here?" Sister Louella demanded. "Crystal balls? Gypsy cards?"

"Les says you got some kind of loony here, Louella. Man with a police record."

Sister Louella gasped. Pendleton eyed her sharply.

"So I guess maybe I better see this fellow. He inside?"

Sister Louella backed away. "You can't. He ain't well. I haven't had time to redd up, place's a mess. You come by tomorrow—"

"Now don't give me trouble, Lou. I got my job to do. Let's go inside." He put a hand on the butt of the pistal at his hip. Sister Louella emitted a faint squeak, went up the steps sideways. At the door she turned.

"You got a search warrant?" she asked breathlessly.

Pendleton pulled a paper from his pocket and slapped it on his knuckles. "Right here, Lou."

"Well—you might's well come in, then."

5

[1]

Adam watched them come into the room. He caught fragments of panicky thought: *"Adam—just set quiet, don't do nothing, don't say nothing out of the way, just answer his questions . . ."*

The man halted in the archway from the hall and looked at him. He was a big, rangy man, well past youth. Adam sensed in him the stir of an animal urge to violent action inhibited by uncertainty, now that he was inside the house:

"Paltry-looking fellow. Sick. Fool woman taken him in like a stray cat. Wasting my time. That Les made a fool of me, big arrest, nothing here. . . ."

"Who's this?" Pendleton asked.

"That's Brother Adam. He's staying here with me now. To help around the place. I needed somebody once Les left."

Pendleton looked heavily at Sister Louella. "Les said this fellow come here a month before he pulled out."

"Well, maybe that's right. But he stayed on to help, me being all alone, and all." She attempted a simper, which caused Deputy Pendleton's jaw to drop. He cleared his throat.

"Where you from, Mr. Adam?"

Adam caught Louella's hasty thought: *Out west.*

"Out west," he said.

"Where out west?"

"Brother Adam come here from Phoenix, ain't that right, Brother Adam," Sister Louella said quickly, and shot Adam a grim flicker of a smile.

"Let him answer," Pendleton said sharply. "You a minister of the gospel, Mr. Adam?"

Adam gazed incuriously at him.

"Well, Lordy, with all this excitement Brother Adam looks to be coming on to one of his spells."

Pendleton raised a hand to scratch at his scalp, straightened his cap instead. He turned to Sister Louella.

"This fellow not quite right?" he enquired in a carrying *sotto voce*.

"It comes over him sometimes," Sister Louella said quickly. "He just kind of tunes out, like. But not violent nor nothing like that. Why, Brother Adam's that sweet-natured—"

"How'd he come to be here?"

"He was overtook by night and needed a place to rest his head, and—"

"A tramp? Hoboeing, was he?" Pendleton looked speculatively at Adam, as if estimating his weight.

"His car broke down on him."

"Where's it at now?"

"Why—" Sister Louella's mouth opened and closed. "I don't rightly know."

"Didn't he have it towed in?"

"Why—I never thought about it."

"How you know he had a car?"

"Then I'd like to know how he got here," Sister Louella said with a note of indignation. "Fourteen miles from town, he never walked no fourteen miles. Not in his condition . . ." her voice trailed off.

"What condition was that?"

"Why—why, he had a cold. Sneezing and coughing something terrible. Why, he could hardly walk across the room, not to say nothing about no fourteen miles—"

"Hey," Deputy Pendleton said, and his hand went again to the pistol butt. "A couple months back—less'n a mile from right here—a stolen car, city cab, we found it off the road in the ditch. There was a tab out on a man—" He swiveled to give Adam a swift up-down look. He jerked the pistol from its holster, levered back the hammer, aimed it from the hip in Adam's general direction.

"Five eleven, one-twenty, brown hair and eyes," he said. "You'll do, mister. Get up on your feet."

Sister Louella yelped and lunged for the policeman's arm. He half turned and the gun went off as she crashed into him; the slug smacked into the plaster wall six feet from the chair where Adam had been sitting.

But Adam, rising swiftly as Louella moved, had launched himself in a perfectly coordinated tackle. He struck the deputy at knee level; Pendleton went down and back, his skull smacking the baseboard with a dull impact. Adam rolled free, scrambled to his feet.

"Crazy goddamn gun-happy cops," he snarled. Pendleton uttered a groan and rolled over on his back. Sister Louella, knocked aside by the tackle, made gobbling noises and pressed both hands to her bosom.

"Brother Adam," she wailed.

"You got a car?" Adam demanded. "Yeah, you got a car . . ." His voice faltered. "Must get the car—go away," he muttered.

"Adam, what's got into you?" Sister Louella keened. "Oh, lord, what's going to happen to me now, you striking the deputy and all—"

"Sister Louella," Adam said. His voice sounded half strangled, as if he were speaking under a severe strain. "Get the car keys. Quick."

She backed away from him. "Adam—you stay away from me, now. I always been good to you, Adam, you know that—"

"Won't hurt you," Adam enunciated awkwardly.

"Do as he says."

"W-who?"

"Walt. Walter M. Kumelli. Have to . . . *use* him. His voice knows. Now do what I told you, damn you!" The last words came in a snarl.

Louella fled.

[2]

Adam/Walter stood in the center of the room. Adam was most interested in what was taking place. Some of the urgency of the Walter voice had communicated itself to him, along with the strong distress emanations from the woman. When the stranger had drawn his gun, he had felt Walter push the *me* aside, had watched as Walt had attacked the policeman, had dimly felt the impact, noted the agility with which Walt had bounced to his feet.

57

Tie him up, Walt dictated. Adam heard and understood; but he recognized that Walt referred to skills and concepts he did not possess. Voluntarily, he stepped aside, let Walt take over, while he, Adam, remained present, aware, not interfering. . . .

[3]

"Where we going, Adam?" Sister Louella asked in a voice that quivered with anxiety. Hunched over the wheel, squinting along the dusk-lit road through the dusty windshield of the nine-year-old Dodge, Adam gave no answer. The trick of balancing the *Walt/Me* equation, using Walt's skill and knowledge while he, Adam, retained overall control, required all his attention. The twilight was fading fast. The car wandering off the road, bumping on the shoulder. Louella screeched and grabbed for the wheel. Adam cuffed her back.

"Lemme alone, dammit. Want to wreck the car?" A pause. "Sorry, Sister Louella. Please . . . let me . . ." His voice trailed off.

"Oh, Adam, I don't know what's come over you. You was never like this. That *is* you, ain't it, Adam? Not. . . ?"

"It's me, Adam. Walt is helping me . . . got to concentrate." His voice hardened. "Something funny . . . feels damn wrong. Can't get any more speed out of this tub. . . ."

"Adam, what will we do? The police will be after us, they'll send me off to jail, I couldn't stand that, Adam, why don't we just go in and tell 'em——"

"Get across the state line," Adam cut in, ignoring her proposal. He wiped a hand across his face. "Got to get a map. Need money. Make it to Atlanta . . ."

"Right here, Adam, I got a map." Louella rummaged in the dusty glove compartment, spilling out a broken plastic windshield scraper, a beer-can opener, gnawed pencils, a tattered Shell Oil Company road map, folded out to show the northern section of the state.

"Where are we?" Adam snapped, glancing aside as she held it out.

"Right here, about twenty miles west of Springfield."

"What's the next main road we cross?"

"That's State 42; just past Oakdale."

"We'll head south there. About fifty miles to the line. You got money?"

"Money? No, Adam, just some silver, is all, I never had time—"

"Got to have money." Adam stared fiercely out at dark weed-grown fields, scrub woods, billboards, power poles. Ahead, a shabby service station squatted by the road; faded pennants strung from the dim-lit pumps fluttered half-heartedly. With a squeal of rubber, Adam cut across the highway, swerved to a halt before the pumps. He picked up Deputy Pendleton's revolver from the seat beside him, thrust it inside his coat and got out of the car.

"Adam—what you going to do!" Sister Louella called after him in a frantic whisper.

"Shut up, damn you!" he snarled. Then he added, "I'm sorry, Sister Louella," and turned toward the station. Inside, a lean, round-shouldered man in a rumpled dark-green workshirt and pants was sitting on a folding chair reading a newspaper. He laid it aside reluctantly and came out.

"Fill her up?" he muttered, not looking at Adam as he went past him, headed for the pump.

"Right," Adam grunted. He walked toward the station.

"Hey," the attendant called after him. Adam looked back from the door.

"Nobody allowed in the office," the man said, and gazed up at the moving numbers on the pump. Adam stepped inside. The cash register was on a scarred, black-stained oak desk against one wall, under a calender showing a smiling girl wearing high-heeled red shoes.

"Hey, you!" Adam ignored the man's shout. There was a pay telephone against the wall, surrounded by a halo of penciled numbers and black finger marks. Dusty oil cans were stacked on a counter. There was cracked green linoleum on the floor. The room smelled of tobacco juice and sweat.

The man was in the door, jerking his thumb over his shoulder.

"Out!" he snapped. "Who do you think you are, mister—"

"Where's the toilet?" Adam asked in a flat tone.

"Round the side. Ask for the key, I'll give it to you—"

"Get over by the telephone," Adam said. The man's mouth opened; his expression was a complicated one reflecting the pleasure of righteous outrage mingled with incipient fear.

"Boy, you get the hell out right now. Three sixty for the gas, and—"

Adam jerked the pistol from his coat.

"Do what I told you, farmer," he said in a low, deadly voice. The man made a gargly sound and his legs began to tremble violently. His face looked suddenly gray.

"My God, mister—" He broke off and lurched past Adam to the telephone, turned to face Adam, his hands raised from his sides.

"Pull the wires out," Adam commanded.

The man turned, holding his eyes on Adam as long as possible, groped the receiver from the hook, gave it a feeble pull. The armored cable held firm.

"You can do better," Adam said. The man gave a hearty heave, and the phone flew from his fingers, banged against the wall.

"Get some cutters," Adam commanded. The man sidled past, his eyes flicking from Adam's eyes to the gun in his hand. He fumbled a drawer open, eased a hand in, came out with a pair of diagonal pliers. He went back to the telephone and cut the wire.

"Open that register," Adam said.

The man groped, got the drawer open, stepped back.

"Get it out, damn you; stack it on the desk."

The man did as ordered. Adam reached across and scooped up the rumpled bills, not looking at the money, watching the attendant.

"Let's go around back," Adam said. The man's knees began to shake again.

"Oh, sweet mother of Christ," he wailed in a bubbly voice. "Don't kill me—"

"Get out there!" Adam snarled. The man tottered past him, out the door, Adam behind him.

"You got the money," the man said in a broken voice, "killing me won't help—"

"Shut up!" Adam handed him the key he had lifted from the hook as he left the station, a heavy brass key wired to a section of broom handle worn smooth and black by handling.

"Open the toilet."

The man had trouble getting the key in; he fumbled and clattered, got the door open. Adam caught his mumbled voice:

"... oh, God ... dead on the floor ... blood on them white tiles. Dirty, fall in the urinal ..."

"Don't be afraid," Adam said. "He won't hurt you."

"Wha?" The man stared at him, his face loose.

"Get inside."

The man took a step, hesitated.

"You ain't going to kill me, mister?"

"Just go inside," Adam mumbled. The images from the man's mind were fascinating; he studied them, overriding Walt.

"You can't get away with this," the man said. Adam didn't answer. His eyes were fixed on a point on the wall three feet to the left of the attendant's right elbow. The attendant was looking at the gun, watching the muzzle sink lower. He shifted, swallowed.

"Boy ... you put that gun down, now," the man said, his voice breaking on the words. Adam showed no sign of having heard. The man leaned forward, his hand coming up—

"Get in there 'fore I blow a hole in your guts!" Adam barked, and jerked the gun up. "Got to be careful," he went on as the tall man stumbled back, half fell into the room. "Can't let Walt ... but don't know. ... Close the door, damn it! Lock it!" He jerked the door shut, turned the key in the lock, withdrew it and tossed it into the weeds growing up through the bumper of a derelict car. He turned and walked quickly back to the Dodge. Sister Louella peered out at him.

"Adam? What—did you do to that man. . . ?"

He didn't answer. He got in the car, started up, switched on the headlights, pulled out on the highway, and gunned away to the west.

[4]

They crossed the state line into Kentucky at half past eleven. It was almost 2 a.m. when Adam pulled into the driveway of a run-down motel with a broken neon sign reading

BIDE-A-WILE TOURIST COTTAGES
acancy

"What's this place?" Sister Louella inquired anxiously, awakening from an uneasy doze. "Why you stopping, Adam?"

"It's . . . a sleeping place, Sister Louella. There are rooms. Each has a bed, a chair, a window—"

"I know what a motel is, Adam. Not what I meant. What you mean, bringing me here?"

"We have to sleep," Adam said. He was fingering the steering wheel, studying the pattern of the cracks in the perished plastic.

"Well, the idear! You just drive us right on to . . . to . . ." Sister Louella faded out, staring out the window at the sagging black screen enclosing the porch beside the building bearing the sign "Office." A light went on inside. An elderly woman in a chenille robe appeared at the door, shading her eyes against the glare of the headlights.

Adam switched off the engine.

"Yes?" the old woman called. She came out on the porch, descended the steps painfully.

"Folks needing a room?" she quavered. "I have a lovely double, let you have it for twelve dollars, late as it is . . ."

Adam gazed up at her as she came up.

"How many would there be? Just the two? Well, I'll tell you what, why don't I just let you have it for eleven. Ten, that is. I meant to say ten, see, after midnight we cut the rates a dollar. Or two."

"I'm tired," Adam said. He seemed to be addressing the horn button.

"How far you folks come today? My, I'll just bet you're beat, on the road all day and all. I have genuine Simmons mattresses in each and every room. We don't believe in the air-conditioning, gives a body sinus, but we have a lovely breeze this time of year. Nine dollars to you. Number one, my finest room. Handmade slip covers. Make coffee right in the room. Don't have television, noisy, you know. Private bath. Commode and shower. I'll tell you what, I'll let it go for eight dollars. . . ."

"Well," Sister Louella said.

"Lovely double bed," the old woman said.

"This . . . this is my cousin," Sister Louella blurted. "Second cousin. We'd want two rooms."

"Just pull right in there to number one, sir," the old woman said quickly. "I believe I can help you just fine. I just happen to have another room open. Right next door."

Adam obediently moved the car, parked it crookedly before a slightly asymmetrical frame cottage with chalky-white siding and a warped porch with two doors. The old woman unlocked them, snapped on lights.

Adam followed Louella inside. There was a dowdy rug, a square iron bedstead with a threadbare coverlet, an upholstered rocker, a massive dresser with a mirror and a Gideon Bible, an easy chair with crocheted antimacassar.

"This is just a lovely room," the old woman said. "I've had more compliments on my rooms."

"How much will it run for the two?" Sister Louella asked sharply.

"That's eight dollars each," the old woman said, but hurried on as she saw Louella's lips tighten. "But I'll let the two rooms go for twelve—"

"Ten," Louella said. "Adam, give the lady ten dollars."

"Well," the old woman said. She took the proffered money, led Adam to his room, wished him a quavery good-night, and left.

Adam stood in the center of the rag rug listening to the faint background susurrus of *voices*. He was learning to tune them down, shut them out at will. But they kept him company. There were so many of them, and they spoke of so many things.

The door in the side wall opened a crack. Louella peeped through, quickly withdrew, and closed the door. Adam went to it, pulled it open.

"Adam, what . . ." Louella said, staring at him uncertainly.

"Walt is gone," Adam said. "I don't like Walt."

Sister Louella gave him an uncertain look. "Brother Adam . . . sometimes I don't rightly understand. I know you hear the voices and all. But how is it when you hear 'em?"

Adam thought about it.

"I just hear them," he said.

"No, really," Sister Louella said. "Set down here, Adam. Tell me how it is. Do they just speak up? Is it like someone talking out loud to you?"

Adam sank into the rocker. "The voices are always there," he said; his eyes were vague, his mind focused inward. "Millions and millions of them. If I try . . . I can . . . tune them in. Like a radio. Or I can . . . shut them out."

"Can you pick and choose, Adam? Can you hear anybody you like?"

Adam thought it over. "I can hear you, Sister Louella—but you told me not to listen in to you. And I can hear Mrs. Moody. Then, if I . . . reach out . . ."

"Can you listen in on—say—the President? Famous people?"

"I don't know what that is," Adam said.

"Lord, Adam—what a gift you got, and don't know how to use it. Listen: before—in the car, on the way here—when you was talking so rough and all. You talked about a Walt. Like he was you. Is that how it is, Adam? When you speak in tongues do you turn into the other person?"

"Walt tried to push *me* away," Adam said slowly. "I didn't like that. But Walt . . . knew what to do. That's why I let him in," he finished with a note of discovery in his voice.

"But you can keep him out if you want?"

"Oh, yes," Adam nodded.

"And call him when you want him?"

"Yes," Adam said hesitantly. "He's there; I can feel him. But I don't want to . . . I don't like . . ."

"That's all right, Adam, I don't want you to call up Walt. Walt's a mean man, Adam, you understand me? I think he'd do bad things. You want to stay away from people like that Walt."

"Yes," Adam agreed.

"But there's others," Sister Louella went on, "who're good. Nice people, important people. You can speak with them, too, Adam—can't you?"

He looked at her in his slightly unfocused way, as if he was not quite listening.

"Adam, suppose you was to go out looking for a body;

some movie star, say. Some singer everybody knows—everybody except you, I mean, seeing's you don't know much. I mean you got a whole lot to learn about the world, Adam. Could you find them?"

"I don't know, Sister Louella."

"Try, Adam. Take . . . take Mr. Billy Graham, now. He's a wonderful preacher. Reverend Graham. Can you summon him?"

Adam thought about it. The name meant nothing to him. His thoughts wandered. . . .

". . . listening to me, Adam!" Sister Louella was saying sharply. "I taken you in, stood up for you. You realize I given up my home, just on account of you? Not that I begrudge it. But you owe it to me to try, Adam."

"Yes, Sister Louella." Adam said. But his attention was divided between the woman who was present and the other woman some fifty feet distant, who was laboriously dialing the telephone. He listened to the hum of her mind as she peered near-sightedly at the numbers:

". . . *gun. Right on the seat of the car. Bank robbers. Seemed ordinary, but you never know . . . drat!*" Adam sensed that she had made a mistake and was starting over.

"Adam! You listen, hear? What I'm saying's important!" Louella broke in.

"Yes, Sister Louella. I was just listening to Mrs. Moody."

"Who's Mrs. Moody?"

"The old woman. The one I gave the money to."

"Land sakes. What's she doing? Not that we got any right to pry. . . ."

"Operator," Adam said. "Give me the police."

"Adam, don't say things like that. It's enough to scare a body. . . ."

"Just any police," Adam said. "I don't care what police. I live alone, you see. I manage the Bide-a-Wile Motel, out on 42, north of town. . . . Bide-a-Wile. . . ."

"Adam," Sister Louella gasped. "What—you mean—is that what—?"

"Now, see here young lady, it doesn't matter whether you can spell the name of my motel," Adam said. "Point is, I want to talk to the police . . . about a murderer."

"Murder!" Louella was on her feet. "Adam, she—the

lady runs the place—is she. . . ?"

Adam smiled placidly up at her, not quite looking at her.

Sister Louella rushed to the door, slammed out onto the porch. Adam followed, watching with incurious attention as she waddled across to the office, jerked the door open, disappeared inside.

"*. . . of course I'm sure,*" Mrs. Moody was saying. "*You think I'm in the habit—what's that? No, I haven't found a dead body,*" Mrs. Moody's train of thought swirled suddenly into a chaos of excited thought fragments:

"*. . . kill me—help—too late—run—*"

He withdrew, feeling distressed. He had caught the fringe of Sister Louella's thoughts; they were not like her usual bland voice. There were fear and anger there, and other, even more elemental impulses. Adam closed his mind to them, let his thoughts wander to an analysis of the pattern of a spider web in the corner of the ceiling.

Louella burst into the room. Her hair was awry, her face a strange blotchy color, her eyes wild.

"Adam, we got to go—right now!" She caught his arm, dragging him from behind the chair, out across the porch, down the steps. He got behind the wheel.

"Get started, Adam," Sister Louella gasped. "Get away from here, quick, police'll be on the way already, hurry, Adam!"

He fingered the steering wheel, smiling at the instrument faces. Louella switched on the key, making a grating sound; the car lurched.

"Adam—you ain't forgot how to drive?"

"I want to sleep, Sister Louella," he said.

"You want to hang?" Sister Louella almost screamed. "I pushed her, and she fell! If she dies, they'll say I killed her! Start this car! Get Walt to help you!"

Some of her urgency penetrated to Adam. He realized that she wished to travel in the car now. There was something about Mrs. Moody that was unclear, but he hardly noticed that. Holding control, not allowing them to swamp him, he *felt* through the hubbub of available voices, found one that seemed somehow right, let it slip into his brain.

His hands went to the starter and the gearshift; his feet tramped pedals. The engine sprang to life; he felt himself backing, braking, accelerating forward, cutting the wheel.

His left hand switched on the headlights; his right shifted to high. His arms manipulated the wheel, swinging the car out into the highway. Resting quietly in one corner of his brain, Adam watched with interest as his body drove the car off into the night.

6

[1]

They slept in the car, parked in the shelter of a dense grove of live oak trees, somewhere south of Paducah. It was hot in the car, and the mosquitoes were bothersome. Sister Louella huddled in the back seat, while Adam stretched out under the wheel and slept soundly.

It was barely dawn when the woman woke. She sat up, pushed at her hair, rubbed her eyes, straightened her clothes.

"Adam," she said. "Wake up."

He sat up, gave her his aimless smile.

"We need to find a rest room," she said. "A Howard Johnson, maybe. Someplace nice. Lordy, I feel like I slept in a haystack."

Adam started up, pulled back into the road. This time he was hardly conscious of the mechanics of driving. They passed through a small town, at Louella's command stopped at an Uncle Rube's Flapjack House. Inside, Sister Louella disappeared into the ladies' room, leaving Adam to pick a table.

"Get a nice one by the winder," she commanded him. "Just look at the menu till I get back."

Louella returned, her eyes puffy and her face blotchy with insect bites; but she had washed her face and combed her hair. She seated herself and looked at Adam critically.

"Go wash up," she said. "I'll order."

Adam spent almost a quarter of an hour in the men's

room, the better part of it playing in the water. The patterns the soap scum made as the water drained from the bowl were fascinating. At length he wandered back out. Louella hissed at him as he sat:

"You give me a turn! I thought you'd went off someplace and left me stranded. How much money do you . . . do we have?"

He took it out and showed it to her; she took it, counted it, tucked it away in her purse.

"Seventy-one dollars," she said. "Not much, but maybe we can manage for a while. But Adam—we have to figger out what we're going to *do*."

The waitress brought plates of flapjacks, butter, syrup. For a few minutes they ate. Over coffee Sister Louella reopened the subject.

"Adam, you got a great gift. Question is, how do we use it? Straight mind reading's no good—not unless you got plenty of money behind you. In fact, I'm thinking we need to stop thinking about any kind of show business." She stared at him with an expression of concentration.

"You don't follow the pattern," Adam said.

"What?"

"The speech pattern. When you feel excitement, you adopt an alternate pattern."

"I don't know what you're talking about, Adam. We got more important things to think about—"

"Before," Adam said, "you used the locution 'we have.' Now you say 'we got' . . ." He seemed to lose interest, gazing at the scattered grains of sugar on the table. "Randomness," he muttered. "Distribution patterns . . ."

Sister Louella pursed her lips. "I can speak excellent grammar when I take the time. Mr. Knefter insisted on it. But sometimes . . . but you're right. I need to pay attention to the little things. They're going to be important. But, lordy, Adam, where do you get all those big words?"

"I get the words from the voices," Adam said. "Sometimes I have a thought, and I don't know the word. But I . . . reach out and find the . . . the concept in a *voice*, and I see the word connected to it."

"Adam, there's money in this," Louella said reverently. "Big money. And of course, service. That's the important thing."

Adam belched. Sister Louella jerked and gave him a look of outrage.

"Well! You got . . . you have no more manners'n a hog, Adam! You have to learn how to behave."

He scratched the end of his nose, went on to explore the nostril.

"Adam, stop that! You're a disgrace! No telling what you'll do next!"

Adam paused, considering. He nodded. "I see . . . there are so many patterns. Patterns of behavior and patterns of exception to the patterns."

"Never mind that, Adam," Sister Louella said fiercely. "I'm not going to be partners with any man that picks his nose in no . . . in a public place!"

"Partners?"

"Certainly. I'm cutting you in for a full share. You don't think I'd try to take advantage of you, do you Brother Adam?"

He smiled vaguely at her.

"Only thing is," she added, "we have to figure out just how to go about it. But don't worry, Adam. I'll think of the best way. Just you let me think it over awhile. Now finish your coffee. I don't like setting here with everybody staring at us."

[2]

Sister Louella bought a pack of playing cards at the J. C. Penney store at Pineville, Tennessee. An hour later, in a motel room south of town, she dealt out a hand of poker. She looked at her cards.

"What am I holding, Adam?"

"Five pieces of paper," he said.

"Adam, sometimes I forget just how dumb you are; how uneducated, I mean. What's on the cards? What numbers and such? What suits?"

"King of hearts," Adam said, "four of spades . . ." he named all five cards. "My God," he went on dreamily, "he can do it. He can really do it—no!"

"Adam, you stay out of there! You just look at what cards I'm thinking of, that's all!"

"I'm sorry, Sister Louella."

"You have to practice," the woman said. "I can see this ain't—this won't be easy. You've got a lot to learn. Now . . ." she dealt new cards. "Try again."

Adam named the cards.

The next time, he made two errors. Louella looked at him indignantly.

"You were thinking those words," Adam said mildly.

"All right, I had the ace-king-queen and maybe I *was* thinking of the jack and ten, but you have to be able to tell the difference. You can't make that kind of mistake, Adam."

They practiced, Louella intentionally thinking of other cards than those she held. Little by little, Adam learned to distinguish the difference between thoughts of what was *real* and what was *imaginary*. He found the latter concept so absorbing that he spent most of the next few days— when not working with Louella—in sorting through the *voices*, examining imaginary concepts. In many voices, he realized, the real and the unreal were blended, sometimes inextricably.

[3]

"Adam, you got a million-dollar talent," Sister Louella was telling him. "I mean you *have* a million-dollar talent. There's no end to the wonderful works you can perform. But before we can bring your gifts to the world, we have to have operating capital, you understand? It's not the money, lord knows—but a body has to have cash on hand in this world before she can accomplish anything."

"Yes, Sister Louella," Adam said. It was merely a sound he had learned to make which had the effect of soothing the woman.

"So that's why first you have to raise us some funds," Sister Louella said. "Not that I hold with gambling; in fact it will serve 'em right. They want to throw money away, why, who better than us to profit? In a good cause. Turn left here."

Adam obediently turned left. They were in a street of neon lights, windows with displays of liquor, small dine-and-drink establishments with photos of topless females decorated with feathers and sequins, bright-lit "book" stores placarded with announcements of adult material available inside.

"Park anywhere here." In the next block Adam found a spot. He parked the car deftly, with a casual skill that still surprised Sister Louella.

"That's the place," she said, indicating a bar across the street with a window bright with glowing beer ads and cardboard cutouts of women holding glasses.

Inside, they took a table. Louella ordered beer. When the waiter brought it, she gave him an arch look, and said, "Go on, Adam. Ask the man."

The waiter looked at him.

"I understand a fellow can play some cards hereabouts," he said, with the rehearsed intonation of an amateur actor.

"Who told you that, Jack?" the waiter growled.

"Mr. Johanssen, at our hotel," Louella spoke up. "Mr. Nova—that's my, ah, my husband here, well, he likes his cards—"

"You got a bum steer, lady."

"Looky here, you, I paid five dollars for—"

"You got swindled. No action here, lady. Maybe you better blow; you and this sport you're with."

"Well, the idear!"

"Out." The waiter jerked a thumb. "Whilst I'm still being nice about it."

[4]

On the sidewalk, Louella soothed her feelings by talking loudly of the complicated vengeance she would exact, through legal channels, just as soon as certain parties unspecified heard of the incident.

"That's not real, Sister Louella," Adam said. "Why do you say things that aren't real?" He looked at her with interest.

"Well, I never! You got your nerve, Adam, after all I done . . . did—for you."

"It's pleasant for you, satisfying," Adam said. "Yes, I see that. When you speak as if a thing were real, it becomes real. In this way you can neutralize most of the aggression, and—"

"More big words! You got too many of 'em, Adam!

Sometimes I get almighty sick of you and your fancy talk, calling me a liar—"

Adam was nodding. "Yes, by directing your anger at me, you relieve the necessity for verbal retaliation—"

"You shut up, Adam! One more word and I leave you right here on this sidewalk! You can beg all you want, but I'm through—"

". . . and by uttering empty threats, you achieve a temporary sense of power; a sense of having vast forces of reward and punishment at your disposition, without of course, being called on to exercise any such powers."

"Get out," Sister Louella cried, clapping her hands over her ears. "It's not you talking; it's some professor someplace. You're just like a walking grave-robber, you dip in anyplace you like and look at what a body's thinking, nothing's private from you, you pry and sneak and . . . and . . ." she broke off with a sob.

"Oh, lordy, Adam, what are we going to do?"

"I'm hungry," Adam said.

"That's just it—we haven't got any more money, Adam! Except for your stake, we're flat broke! I was counting on you winning something for us; I gave that Mr. Johanssen my last five-dollar bill—and now . . ." She snuffled, probing in her handbag for a handkerchief.

"They're playing cards," Adam said. "Hit me. Eighter from Decatur. Again . . . Little Joe. . . . Once more, lightly but politely—goddam, bust!"

"Where?" Sister Louella gasped, clutching at his arm. "Can you tell where?"

The waiter emerged from the bar. "Go on, get moving," he snarled. "Tough luck, coppers. That getup wouldn't fool a kid o' six," he spat past Louella, and went back inside.

"He must be crazy," she said. "Come on, Adam. Find that game. Blackjack, they're playing, sounds like. You remember blackjack. It's the easy one. We'll find it and you just do like I taught you, and our troubles is over. Are over."

[5]

Adam led the way across the street at a long diagonal, being saved from being struck by a cab by Sister Louella's

72

grab at his arm. He went fifty feet along the sidewalk, past a bright-lit grocery store featuring strings of onions, olive oil, heaped fruit, and wine in straw baskets, hesitated before the mouth of an alley.

"I don't like the look of this neighborhood, Adam," Sister Louella said. "Are you sure—"

Adam started into the alley; Louella plucked at his sleeve, then followed. A light bulb burned over a door twenty feet from the street. They went toward it.

"Adam," Sister Louella hissed as he halted before the door, "this time you take a peek at what he's got on his mind; see what's the right thing to say, hear?"

Adam cocked his head. "You wait back there, Sister Louella," he said. "They don't like women."

"Don't like women? What do I care what they like? Without me—"

"They wouldn't let me in with you. No women at all." Adam was looking dreamily at the pattern of cracks in the brown paint on the door.

"Why, the nerve!"

Adam knocked on the door: two, three, two. He turned to the woman. "You'd better go now."

"But—you can't—you don't know how—Adam! You still got your ten dollars? Will you be all right, alone? And where'll I meet you?"

The door latch rattled; Louella fled. The door opened and a small, sandy-haired man in rolled shirt sleeves frowned at Adam.

"Yeah?" He took a cigarette from behind him and fitted it between his lips.

"Pittsburgh Ace said to say hello to Harv and the boys," Adam said.

"Yeah?"

"I'm in town a day or two. Just thought I'd drop by."

"Come on in." Adam followed the man inside. There was a hallway, dark brown with a light brown stripe. A light burned in the ceiling ten feet along. Light shone from an open door.

"Where do you know the Ace from?"

"The Coast; around. You know."

The man grunted, went along to the lighted door. Steps led down. The air had a cool, damp feel as Adam reached

73

the lower corridor. Voices came from a room at the end. The sandy-haired man motioned Adam ahead. Five men looked up from a table as he entered the room. There were cards and money and glasses on the table, stark under a brilliant light with a metal shade.

"Who the hell's this?" a large man with bluish jowls barked.

"Charlie Webb," Adam said. "From Denver and San Antone. The Ace said look you up."

"Yeah?" The man lifted a cigar from an ashtray, drew on it, blew smoke out, looking Adam over.

"You just sprung, hah?"

"Yeah," Adam said.

"Yeah, you look kind of green. How's the Ace?"

"Not good," Adam said.

"Oh?"

"He's dead."

The big man nodded, seemed to relax. "You in on that one?"

"No. I just heard."

"What was that name again? Webb?"

"Ducktail, they used to call me, up Detroit way."

The big man seemed to lose interest. He picked up the deck. "Let him in, Brownie," he said to the man on his left. Chairs were shifted. Adam sat down.

"Blackjack," the big man said. "Five ante."

Adam slid his ten-dollar bill onto the table. "Deal me two hands," he said.

The big man dealt. Adam looked at his cards. A king-ten and a nine-three, the small cards up. The dealer had a four showing. He didn't look at his down-cards.

"How about it?" he said, squinting through cigar smoke.

Adam smiled vaguely. . . .

"*. . . ten coming up, bust him wide open,*" he caught the dealer's thought.

"I'll stay," he said. The big man frowned, went on to the next man. The ten broke him. The next two men stood on their cards. The last player took two cards. The dealer looked at Adam, peeled off a card for himself. A jack. He turned over his hole-card: another jack. He grunted and paid.

Adam won the next five hands, including his deal, unavoidably lost two in a row when the dealer drew twenty-one, won four more straight.

"You're hot tonight, Webb," a paunchy, bald man said. "Anybody care if I deal a hand of five-card?"

"Go ahead."

He dealt. Adam looked at his cards. He had a 2-3-5-9 of mixed suits, a 9 in the hole. He opened for five.

There were a possible straight and two low pairs showing. The pot reached forty-five dollars. He raised, was raised back by the pair of eights. Three players stayed in. He raised again and all three folded.

The pair of eights smiled lazily at him. "Pretty proud of that pair of nines, aren't you, Rube? Up five."

Adam saw the five and raised ten.

"Ten more," the eights said promptly. Adam saw the bet and raised another ten—the last of his funds.

"You nuts?" the pair of eights said angrily. He stared at Adam, then cursed and folded his hand.

"Looks like your bluff didn't run worth a damn, Sol," the sandy-haired man said.

"You're too damn lucky," the bald man said. "Who is this guy, Harv?"

"Brownie dealt it," Harv said. But he was looking thoughtfully at Adam.

"How much this mug bring into the game?" the bald man asked. "He's showed one ten-spot. He's got over two hundred of the game's dough in twenty minutes flat."

"Let's see what you got on you, Webb," Harv said.

Adam didn't move. The man on his left stood, kicked back his chair, grabbed Adam's upper arms and hauled him to his feet.

"Check him out," he grated. The man called Brownie frisked him efficiently.

"The sucker's clean. Not a thin dime on him. The ten was it."

"That ain't nice, Webb," Harv said. "We don't like hustlers around here." He stood, balled his fist, and drove a short, straight right to Adam's stomach; he promptly doubled over and vomited his dinner on Harv's shoes.

There were several more blows after that, and much

swearing. His feet were bumping up steps; a door was being opened and cool night air blew in.

"Don't come around lots, palsy," someone invited, and then a brick wall struck him in the face.

[6]

Sister Louella used the ten-dollar bill which had been neatly folded and tucked in Adam's shirt pocket to buy iodine, Band-Aids, two Cokes, and two hamburgers, and one night's use of a hot, ill-ventilated room above a Chinese laundry.

"We ought to have the law on 'em," she said for the tenth time as she applied a bandage to the cut on Adam's jaw. "Over two hundred dollars you had, won fair and square—"

"I cheated," Adam said.

"They had no call to whip you! They could have hurt you bad, throwing you out on the pavement. I don't see why you didn't see it coming, and—"

"I did. But there was nothing I could do. They were much stronger than I."

"I declare, Adam—you act like you didn't care a thing about being robbed and beat—"

"Beaten."

"How can you think about grammar when you're bleeding in half a dozen places!"

"I don't think about it, Sister Louella. It's just that . . . I've listened to so many voices . . . and I've absorbed the underlying usage patterns—"

"You and your dern patterns!"

"Correct grammar is merely the commonly accepted form of the language. I've noticed—"

"Adam, I don't care a thing in the world about all that," Louella cut him off sharply. "I care about how we're going to stay alive until I figure out how we're to make the most of your gift! So far all we've done is run and hide, like scared mice. Why, it's ridiculous. You could be the most powerful man in the world—with me to guide you, o' course."

"I could get a job," Adam said.

"Job! You? What can you do? That's useful, I mean. I

76

mean that somebody would pay you for? You're helpless as a baby, Adam. And you're frail. Nobody'd hire you—"

"Man-Ball Chong would," Adam said.

"What's that supposed to mean? I bet you're not even listening—"

"He's the man who lives downstairs."

"You mean that old Chinaman? Hire *you?* What on earth for?"

"To operate the steam press. Sweep up. Go for food to the restaurant on Apex Street. Talk to the customers. Write bills—"

"What's all this, Adam? When'd you talk to him?"

"I was . . . listening. Just now."

Louella gasped. "Land sakes, I keep forgetting. In a way it's like you was some kind of magic, Adam. You can really hear what that old Chinaman's thinking?"

"Hwài ér dz. bù tiñg hwà de syí fu. bù gei chyán de kè ren taì dwo. O rè. Kêshr wo men de wâu li hái you fan. You fang dz."

"Lordy," Sister Louella said. "What's that mean?"

"Nothing. Just . . . aimless thoughts. But he needs a *ching saû gung rém.*"

"I don't know what you mean. What's that, some heathen Chinese you were talking?"

"A man to sweep," Adam said. "Yes, he needs me."

"And you'd take orders from a Chinaman? What's he willing to pay? But you're not strong, Adam—"

"Two dollars an hour. One fifty if I eat in."

"Take the two," Sister Louella said quickly. "Now, just sit still until I get you patched up, Adam. We don't want that Chinaman thinking you're some kind of roughneck."

7

[1]

Life in the Chinese laundry was placid, serene, unvarying, and exhausting. Man-Ball Chong, after his first surprise on receiving a job application from a Caucasian, albeit a sickly-looking one, had been even more astonished to discover that the applicant spoke perfect, fluent Cantonese—of the dialect moreover of his home village, from which he had departed over forty years before. He had accepted Adam's offer—even conceding a salary of two dollars an hour, since the strange little man seemed to be adamant on the point—and put him to work sweeping, operating the steam iron, writing bills, and dealing with the Caucasian customers—and, after a few days, the Chinese patrons as well. They seemed pleased to meet an American who spoke Cantonese like a native of China.

Oddly enough, for all his willingness to work, Adam had declined to empty slops, act as servant to Madame Man-Ball or to young Tina Ching, his son's impertinent wife, or to swab the toilet. These chores remained in the province of the half-witted lad, Wing Lu.

The new employee had been remarkably quick to master the intricacies of the operation of the ancient, creaking steam-press, Man-Ball noted. When the apparatus acted up, as it did frequently, he had only to glance at it, it seemed, and Adam would at once take the appropriate corrective action, just as he himself would have. A clever worker, Adam—for an American. Man-Ball, after a few days, found himself feeling quite kindly toward his new employee.

On Wednesday of Adam's second week at the laundry, a trio of sleek-haired, olive-skinned, black-eyed youths entered the shop. Busy at the steam press, Adam hardly noticed their entry. Absently, he monitored their *voices:*

"Cuidado . . . chino viejo, gringo enfermizo . . . caja . . ."

"Oscuro aquí—nadie puede vernos de la calle . . ."

"Me gustaría saber cuánto dinero—ganancias de todo el día . . ."

"Mr. Man-Ball," Adam said. The old man glanced at him impatiently. Adam did not look up.

"They're going to rob the store," he said in Chinese.

"What's that? They're what?"

"The biggest one has a gun. The one behind him has a knife. So does the other . . ."

Mr. Man-Ball stiffened for a moment, then smiled, bowed to the youth who had swaggered forward.

"Excuse please," he said, and reached under the counter, brought out a gigantic nickel-plated .44 caliber revolver of French manufacture, aimed it at the putative customer.

"You will stand quite still," he said. "Adam—call the police."

The three youths halted in mid-swagger. All six eyes stared at the gun. It continued to point steadily at the third pearl button on the maroon shirt of the leader.

"No disparará," one of the lads said.

"Gritaré," the others said. *"Luego atácalo, Chico."*

"No lo hagan, muchachos," Adam said. He had come over to stand beside Mr. Man-Ball. *"Disparará, seguro."*

"Who're you?" the leader of the trio said. "You work for this Chink?"

"Mario—you don't want to get Chico killed, do you?" Adam said to the third youth, who was edging off-side. Mario stopped.

"How do you know my name?"

"Mr. Man-Ball, if they leave and promise not to try it again will you let them go?"

"Jeĭ syè rén de hwà bù jr chyán," the old man said.

"Will you promise never to try to rob Mr. Man-Ball again if he lets you go?" Adam asked Chico.

"Sure." *Not until tonight, when the old devil's asleep. We'll wreck the joint . . .*

"No, you won't," Adam said. "I won't let you, you see. I'll be listening."

79

"I didn't say nothing," Chico mumbled. "I said OK, sure, that's all."

"Give me your promise, Chico. Your real promise."

"I already—" *Damn you—I'll get you—*

"This is your last chance, Chico. If you won't give up the idea, I'll have to go ahead and call the police."

"All right, I said so, didn't I?" *What is this creep, the evil eye, second sight* . . . Inobtrusively, under the cover of scratching his nose, chest, and other places, Chico crossed himself.

"You others—you promise too?"

"They do what I say," Chico snarled.

"They won't come back, Mr. Man-Ball," Adam said. "You can put the gun away."

"Get out," Mr. Man-Ball said, and waved the gun. The three boys fled.

Mr. Man-Ball smiled at Adam and weighted the big revolver on his palm. "Someday I must purchase some ammunition for it," he said.

[2]

Later that week, Adam discovered mathematics. In teaching him to play cards, Louella had pointed out to him the distinction between *none* and *one*, between *one* and *two* and *many*. But he had thought of each number as an entity in itself. Four was not two two's, any more than water was hydrogen plus oxygen. Like the Chinese ideographs he had learned to identify on the laundry slips, each number was unique. Then, late one afternoon, while folding the towels for the Iranian restaurant in the next block, he made the discovery that two ones were two; and two two's four, and two fours eight. . . .

Completely absorbed in this astonishing revelation he had stood unmoving, staring at the patch of sunshine that slanted down through the grimy window above the moving garment rack, exploring its ramifications. He jumped almost at once to the concept of multiplication, from that to squares and cubes, then on to arithmetic and geometric progressions. The concept of algebra appeared dimly, tantalizingly—

"Adam," Mr. Man-Ball spoke suddenly. "Are you well?"

"Yes, fine, thank you, Mr. Man-Ball." Adam felt a little dazed, as if he had been spun in a centrifuge at high speed.

"You're a strange man, Adam. Sometimes I wonder . . . tell me, what did you do before you came here?"

"Nothing," Adam said. "I traveled with Sister Louella . . ."

"I see. Where did you learn to speak Chinese?"

Adam had been warned by Sister Louella against disclosing his ability to hear voices unheard by others. "Oh, around," he said, and smiled, slightly out of focus.

"And Spanish. You must speak it well, else the youths who came here to steal money would not have been so tractable."

"They weren't really bad," Adam said. "They wanted money to buy things . . . shiny, bright-colored things. . . ."

"A man best heeds advice in his own dialect," Man-Ball quoted. "And one day I heard you speak to the India man, Mr. Balani, in yet another tongue. I wonder, Adam—why do you, a scholar, toil here as a laundryman's helper?"

"I like it here," Adam said. "It's peaceful. And you pay me money, and I buy food for me and Sister Louella."

"You must have traveled widely, to have mastered so many languages. You are a man of many abilities, Adam, though in some ways you seem curiously innocent. Your talents are wasted sweeping floors. Have you no desire to better your station in life?"

"Yes. Or Sister Louella does. She wants me to make a great deal of money, so she can carry on her Work."

"You are indeed devoted to your sister, Adam. An admirable characteristic. But what of you, yourself? Have you no ambition?"

"I want to know more about numbers," Adam said; his attention was wandering back to the magically complex structures of which he had caught the merest glimpse.

"Ah, numbers. So you are a mathematician as well. Hmmm. I have a nephew who owns an import business. He is in need of a bookkeeper, one who knows both English and the old tongue. He is an exacting man, but perhaps . . ."

"Yes, bookkeeping," Adam said; he caught a glimpse of Mr. Man-Ball's confused concept of arithmetic, involving an abacus and his fingers. "I'd like that, Mr. Man-Ball."

"I'll speak to him. Though it will doubtless lose me the services of my handyman. But one owes it to talent to see to its flowering."

Three days later, Mr. Man-Ball notified Adam that he had made an appointment with his nephew, Mr. Lin, for an interview. He looked at Adam critically.

"I don't wish to give offense, Adam," he said, "but your present costume might give LinPiau an erroneous impression. If my memory serves me rightly, you've worn that same shirt and trousers each day since you entered my employ."

"Sister Louella washes them—"

"Indeed. But there is a certain lack of dash in your selection of garments, Adam. You have a week's wages due you; why not come along with me—we have time before the meeting with LinPiau—and select a more flattering outfit?"

"Sister Louella doesn't like me to waste any money."

"One must spend in order to earn," Mr. Man-Ball stated firmly. "Come."

He took Adam along to a Hong Kong import shop operated by a tiny wafer of a man with almost-black skin, straight, blue-black hair, piercing eyes, and an ingratiating manner. His name was Mr. K. Krishna, and he was both surprised and delighted at Adam's fluent Urdu.

"Certainly, Mr. Man-Ball, I will be so happy to assist you to select an appropriate suit of clothes for Mr. Adam. And underclothes, and shirt and tie as well, everything, I have it all in stock, a fine selection, the best materials, and our tailors—"

"I know about your tailors," Mr. Man-Ball said in his utility English. "Chinese workers, sit cross-legged on tables in Indian factory, cut, stitch by hand, for five Hong Kong dollars per day."

The proprietor fluttered his hands. "As to that, Mr. Man-Ball—"

"No matter, Mr. Krishna. Show Mr. Adam plenty fine clothes, for man who will take important job."

Half an hour later, clad in a handsome suit of dark-blue

worsted, a light-blue shirt, and a maroon tie, Adam looked at his reflection in a mirror. An impression stirred in his mind, triggered by the sight of himself thus clad.

"Haircut," he said. "Shoes."

"Ah—a good thought," Mr. Man-Ball agreed. He paid Mr. Krishna, led Adam first to a Thom McAn, where he purchased a pair of imitation-leather, imitation-Italian shoes, then to a barber for a trim.

"A transformation," Mr. Man-Ball said afterward. "Mr. Adam, you now present the appearance of a man of substance. My nephew will be impressed. Please do not disabuse him."

[3]

Mr. Lin was a short, stout, neatly tailored man of thirty-five, with a round face, a receding hairline, thick glasses, and a brisk manner that bordered on the impatient.

"Well, Uncle Chong, come in, have a chair, you too, Mr. Adam, sit down, sit down." He gave Adam a sharp look. "I understand you speak Chinese?" he said in that language.

Adam smiled. "Yes."

"How many dialects?"

"Oh . . ." Adam tuned in on Mr. Lin's *voice*. . . . "Mandarin, Shanghai, the coastal barbarisms . . ."

"Ah! Remarkable! The very ones I encounter in my business. I understand also that you're an experienced bookkeeper."

"Not experienced, perhaps, nephew," Mr. Man-Ball spoke up, "but skilled. Test him. Ask him questions."

"You know double-entry bookkeeping?"

Adam reached out, found the information he needed —in the mind of a man named Clyde P. Springer, in Cincinnati, as it happened—and delivered a short, concise lecture on double-entry bookkeeping.

"I guess you know your stuff, all right," Mr. Lin said admiringly. "Well, maybe I could try you in the position." *Brother—if I can hire this clown . . . start him at thirty-five a week, work him up to say forty . . . paid that last joker sixty-five. . . .*

"What kind of salary did you have in mind, Mr. Adam?"

"Start me at sixty-five," Adam said. "I'm worth it."

"Forty," Mr. Lin said flatly. *A bargain even at forty—if he can do the work . . .*

"I'll start at forty-five," Adam said. "At the end of a month, you'll raise me to sixty-five—if I prove I can do the work."

"Out of the question."

"You paid more to the miscreant who absconded last week, nephew," Mr. Man-Ball said mildly. "Why not accede to Mr. Adam's request?"

"Well . . . for your sake, Uncle," Mr. Lin said grumpily, feeling pleased.

"When can you start, Mr. Adam?"

"I have some work to finish at the laundry—"

"He'll be free to report in the morning," Mr. Man-Ball said quickly. "Come, Mr. Adam. We'll take a cup of tea together before dinner."

[4]

Sister Louella yelped when Adam entered the room. "You give me a turn," she exclaimed. "Where'd you get the suit, Adam? Coming in like that. Why, it looks real nice. You didn't . . . how much did it cost, Adam? You know I told you—"

Adam explained about the suit and the job. Sister Louella uttered a little cry of pleasure when he came to the part about the forty dollars a week.

"Lord knows we can use it," she said. "Why, I don't know how we been keeping body and soul together on the thirty you been bringing in."

"I'm glad you're pleased," Adam said, his mind on the figures he would be working with tomorrow.

"Just don't go wasting any more cash on fancy clothes. Lordy, I could use a new dress and some things myself— what I had in the suitcase is just pitiful. But I can wait until you get your raise."

"That's nice," Adam murmured, lost in the intricacies of a mathematical analysis of the linoleum pattern.

Louella went on with her running commentary on the shortcomings of her present life by contrast with the rich, full existence she had given up in order to accompany Adam on his travels, as she got out paper plates (used for several previous meals but still servicable) and napkins, assembled sardine sandwiches, poured out a soft drink for Adam, a beer for herself. Adam ate abstractedly, replying to Louella's conversation absently; he had developed the ability to scan the surface of her thoughts sufficiently to reply with a word at appropriate points, while occupying his mind with other matters. By the end of the meal, he had thought his way through analytical geometry and was nibbling at the conception of calculus.

[5]

His first day at Mr. Lin's establishment was a hectic one. The office where he was to work was on the second floor of what had been constructed as a warehouse some sixty-five years before. Mr. Lin had walled off, painted, carpeted, and air-conditioned the front fifty feet of the upstairs loft. The ceiling was acoustical, the lighting indirect. An exceedingly pretty Chinese girl, whom Mr. Lin introduced as Lucy Yang, his third cousin, hammered a typewriter in the corner of the office. People came and went, telephones rang, while sounds of labor came from below, and shouts, horns, and engine-rumblings rose from the street. A Muzak system played innocuous tunes, which were audible in the interstices of the din.

Mr. Lin assigned Adam a desk behind a three-sided, head-high glass partition, indicated a stack of ledgers and a filing cabinet, and took himself off, after suggesting that Lucy might explain anything that was unclear.

Adam sat for a while, gazing at the wall and musing over the periodicity of the calendar hanging there. This led him to consider the structure of the week, month, and year—purely as abstract patterns, not as subjective entities.

"Something bothering you?" a melodious voice asked. Lucy Yang was looking across at him, smiling slightly. She wore a tight-fitted armless dress with a small stand-up collar, in shiny blue brocade. The slit in the side showed a pleasing length of smooth thigh.

"Why do three hundred and sixty-five days make a year?" he asked, hardly aware that he was speaking aloud. It was merely the verbalization of the question puzzling him at the moment. "Three hundred and sixty days would be simpler."

"Are you kidding?"

"No."

"Well, because that's how long a year *is,*" Lucy said reasonably. "What's that got to do with the price of rice?"

Adam searched for a connection, failed to find one. "Tell me," he said.

"Tell you what?" Lucy rose and ambled over, leaned in the entry to the cubicle. "What's this about a year?"

"It seems arbitrary. If we used three hundred and sixty days instead—"

"How can we, when everyone else uses three sixty-five? And in leap year it's three sixty-six."

"Why?"

"I don't know. Something to do with making Christmas fall on the winter solstice."

"What is that?"

"The shortest day of the year."

"Aren't all days the same. . . ?" But even as he asked the question, Adam realized they were not. He had never consciously noticed, but it was true that darkness fell at an earlier time now than it had in the beginning.

"You don't seem to be very well informed," Lucy said. "For a bookkeeper." She had had two years of college, and intended to get two more, as soon as she had saved the necessary money.

"There are many things I want to know about."

"Like why there's three hundred and sixty-five days in a year." Lucy gave a charming little lift of the shoulders. "Let's look it up in the dictionary."

Adam followed her to the large volume laid out open on top of a bookcase stuffed with advertising material, catalogs, price lists, and brochures.

"Here it is . . . 'the time of one apparent revolution of the sun around the ecliptic.' "

"What is the ecliptic?"

"Look, Mr., ah, Adam," Lucy said, and flipped the book shut, "this isn't an astronomy class. Mr. Lin hired you to keep the books."

Adam caught from her a sense of the meaning of the

word *astronomy* . . . and stood transfixed by the concepts it implied.

". . . you OK, Mr. Adam?" Her voice was alarmed. "You looked like you were going to faint. Here, sit down." She helped him back to his chair.

"You sure you feel like working? You look awfully pale. Are you eating properly?"

"The world," he said. "The sun . . . patterns . . ."

"You just sit here, Mr. Adam. I'll get somebody—"

"No, I'm all right. It was such a marvelous thing . . . the ecliptic . . ."

Poor guy's sick . . . crazy, maybe. Harmless, but . . . I'd better . . .

"Please excuse me," Adam said, making an effort to conform to the behavior pattern he sensed was expected in this situation. "I haven't been eating too well. I was just thinking about . . . things . . ."

"You sure you're OK?"

"I'm fine."

"Look, you can read the dictionary on lunch break; right now I think you'd better dig into the books. I'm afraid the last fellow left them in a mess. . . ." She lifted down a large ledger, opened it on the table in front of him.

"This is the current transactions. The last date is two weeks ago. Here are the invoices . . . receipted bills . . . check books . . ." She rattled on, indicating the scope of the task ahead.

"You'd better start with these accounts receivable," she finished. "Match them up with the deposits, here . . ."

Adam looked blankly at the stack of papers. He picked one up, turned it over, and looked at the back.

"Have you been listening, Mr. Adam?" Lucy asked with some asperity.

"Yes."

"You understand what I said?"

"Yes."

"Well—why not get started?"

Adam smiled his vague smile.

"Look, Mr. Adam—look at the name on the bill, and see if it's paid. Here's the listing. . . . Oh, here, I'll help you to get started. What's that first one?"

Adam turned the paper around and gazed at it, inverted. Lucy stared at him.

"Mr. Adam—can't you *read?*"

"Ah . . ."

The girl pointed a manicured nail at the words printed across the top: "Far East Imports, Inc."

"Far East Imports," Adam took the words from her mind.

"For a minute there," Lucy said, "I wondered about you." *Good night, if Harry hired an illiterate bookkeeper.
. . .*

Adam had noted the realtionship between written symbols and spoken words before, but he had never been called upon to make use of the system. Now, as Lucy read aloud, pointing out the text as she went along, Adam swiftly analyzed the system, noting the multiplicity of symbols, the system of organization. He took their meanings from Lucy's mind, went on to apply the pattern to the next example.

"Well, you get the idea, Mr. Adam. Now read them off to me the way I was doing, and I'll find the check record here. . . ."

Adam obediently read aloud the document in his hand. Lucy started to nod, then glanced over at the paper. She gave Adam a look half exasperated, half amused.

"Pretending you couldn't read—and now you're reading Chinese!" She laughed. "I think I'm beginning to get the idea, Mr. Adam. You've been kidding me—and I fell for it." She stood, still smiling. "I asked for it, sticking my nose in. I guess I sounded pretty snooty, asking you if you knew your job. I'm sorry."

"Thank you, Lucy. You've been a great help."

"Any time, Mr. Adam," she said gaily, and went back to her desk.

8

[1]

Adam had not been surprised by his ability to master the reading of both English and Chinese in a quarter of an hour. Nothing truly surprised him, since surprise implies expectation and preconception, and Adam had no preconceptions. He accepted the existence of everything he encountered as naturally as a child accepts the miracles of daylight and rain and the lights in the sky.

Neither did he find anything extraordinary in his ability to remember perfectly any datum which came his way. He had had no experience of the usual painful learning methods: the requirement for repetition of verbal symbolisms or physical acts necessary to impress the information on the subconscious filing system known as memory. His memory was exposed, naked, to the raw data. He received them as newsprint receives inked type, in toto, in precise detail.

While sensitive to all new information, endlessly fascinated by all that impinged on him, he was devoid of curiosity in its ordinary sense. He absorbed facts, followed lines of inquiry, stored data; but lacking all sense of amazement, he was never caught up in wonderment, beset by a driving urge to seek out answers, or attracted to a particular line of inquiry as potentially fruitful of astonishing new discoveries. Thus, having mastered reading, he read what fell into his line of sight; he never went browsing in search of new intellectual stimuli. He read colorful brochures detailing the advantages of postage meters and Kwik-Freeze Noodles; Chinese newspaper accounts of the observance of obscure festivals; aging correspondence from the files: whatever passed his desk, or fell under his eye in the course of bringing order to the chaos of the accounts of the Dragon Import Company.

He was a remarkably effective accountant, after the first few days of exploration of patterns. His particular habits of mind were ideally adapted to running down and searching out discrepancies, unhindered by any sense of boredom with the routine. He quickly discovered that the relationship between the figures in the ledgers and the actual transactions of the company during the six years of its existence was so tenuous as to be negligible. Mr. Lin, a highly perceptive buyer, a shrewd bargainer, a persuasive salesman, had no grasp of economics whatever. So long as there were sufficient funds in the business account to pay the salaries and bills, he questioned nothing. If, in spite of a steadily increasing volume of trade, that account seemed never to increase markedly, he attributed this to inflation and the rising cost of living.

As the placid weeks passed, Adam delved deeper, turning up leads, following lines of inquiry through dusty heaps of records, through cartons of retired files—Mr. Lin never threw any business paper away, possibly through some faint cultural heritage of respect for the written word. Adam assembled figures. He added and subtracted. He made comparisons. He compiled data. . . .

At the end of the fourth week, Mr. Man-Ball called on his nephew to inquire after Adam's progress. Having seen Adam almost daily in his capacity as landlord, he was aware that his protégé was apparently doing well. But knowing both Adam and Mr. Lin, he felt it politic to appear at this time to remind both parties diplomatically of the projected raise in pay.

"He's doing all right, I suppose, Uncle," Mr. Lin said offhandedly. "Stirs up enough dust, dragging all the old records out of the storage closet. Seems to love to root around back there, perfectly happy digging for figures, writing 'em down, adding 'em up. Strange fellow."

"And he has found all in order?"

"I suppose so. He hasn't said otherwise."

"Surprising—in view of the somewhat informal methods you've employed in the past as regards your balance sheets, not to mention the dubious circumstances under which your previous bookkeeper departed from the firm."

"As long as I have money to pay my bills—"

"I know. You're content. But what if the check to which

your former employee was apprehended in the act of forging your name was not his only peccadillo?"

Mr. Lin waved a hand. "Nonsense. It was just a sudden impulse, and he got caught—"

"An accident. Foolish of him to make the attempt here in the neighborhood, where you're known by sight. Perhaps he'd been made careless by long success."

Mr. Lin frowned. "Well—I can call Adam in and ask him." He pushed a button, asked Lucy to tell Adam he wanted to see him. Adam arrived half a minute later, his hands dusty, cobwebs in his hair. He smiled his unfocused smile.

"Well, Mr. Adam," Mr. Lin said heartily, "you've been with us for almost a month now. Books all in good shape, are they?"

"No, Mr. Lin," Adam said.

Mr. Lin frowned. "What's the matter with them?"

"All the figures were incorrect. I've been correcting them. I'm almost finished."

"Incorrect in what way?"

The question confused Adam. Automatically, he reached out to draw on the knowledge of Mr. Clyde P. Springer, his usual source of clarification when confronted by a perplexity in his work.

"Funds have been systematically drained from the company since its third week of operation," he said crisply. "The method used was a combination of false billings and figure juggling. At first an effort was made to make the transpositions appear accidental, but for the last few years false entries have been made quite openly; I presume because no one ever checked the books."

Mr. Lin, impressed by the sudden briskness of Adam's tone, checked the automatic contradiction he had been ready to utter. He got to his feet.

"Show me," he said.

Adam showed him. For an hour he delivered a nonstop lecture on the inadequacies and inaccuracies of the company's records.

"The stock will be short by at least these amounts," Adam said, handing over a lengthy list. "I haven't checked the inventory lists yet, but there may be pilferage losses, too," he concluded.

"How much?" Mr. Lin demanded, tight-lipped.

"The shortage? I don't have the final figures, but something in excess of seventy-two thousand dollars in cash over the last six years, plus stock shortages."

Mr. Lin made a choking noise. "But—how could one man. . . ?"

"There were several customers in collusion with him," Adam said. "They're listed here." He handed over another neatly typed sheet. "And he was also assisted by the stock clerk, at least two of the drivers, and a warehouseman."

"How . . . how do you know all this?"

"It was an inevitable deduction from the pattern here in the records."

"Can you name the people involved?"

"Oh, yes." He did so.

Mr. Lin stood amazed at the revelation. "Tung Loo? He's been with me for years—and so has Sally Wu—and Chin . . . and they're back there right now, robbing me blind! Look here, Adam—how long have you known this?"

"Since my third day here."

"Why didn't you tell me at once? They've probably carted off another thousand dollars' worth since then!"

Adam was suddenly uncertain. "I . . . I didn't . . ."

"He undoubtedly wanted to give you a complete picture—to be quite certain," Mr. Man-Ball put in. "Knowing your loyalty to your old employees, he wouldn't have wanted to speak up prematurely."

"Old employees," Mr. Lin muttered. "We'll get to the bottom of this right now!" He started from the room.

"A suggestion, Nephew," Mr. Man-Ball said softly. "Would it not be wise, perhaps, to telephone your legal adviser? It would be desirable to take them all in one swoop, would it not, rather than to alarm them by precipitate action, perhaps allowing some of the birds to escape the net?"

"I suppose so," Mr. Lin said. He dialed a number, spoke briefly, and left the room. Lucy, who had been listening with total absorption to Adam's revelation let out her breath in a sigh of astonishment.

"Well! You certainly play them close to your chest, Mr. Adam!"

He smiled past her and returned to the task of entering the last week's figures in the ledger.

Sister Louella was delighted with the hundred-dollar bonus and the raise to sixty-five dollars per week when Adam reported it to her that evening. The subject came up quite by accident when she made a comment on the trials she had endured in recent weeks, her usual dinner table conversation.

"How come you didn't tell me right away?" she demanded when Adam produced the hundred dollars and handed it over. "And you got your raise! Well, it's about time. If that Chinaman knew what kind of rare God-given talent he's got setting down there scratching numbers on a sheet of paper . . ." Then she fell to musing aloud on the improvements in circumstances the new affluence would provide.

For the first few days of their residence in the Man-Ball household, they had occupied a single room, Louella sleeping, fully clothed, on the bed, while Adam made himself comfortable on the floor with a blanket and a sofa cushion. On the day that Adam had entered Mr. Lin's employ, Louella had arranged for an additional room—a tiny box-room three doors from her own, formerly a storeroom—in which a cot was placed for Adam. The chamber's single window looked out on a vista of brick wall three feet distant—a view Adam had studied with intense concentration for most of one evening, analyzing the stress patterns in the structure from the design of cracks in the masonry.

"We can fix the room up, now," Sister Louella said. "Get us some nice curtains, and maybe a television. It wouldn't be a luxury—Lord knows I need something to occupy me while I'm waiting." She gave Adam the reproachful look which he had long ceased to notice.

"Course, I'll save the most of it," she added, tucking the bills away in her bosom. She had gained weight in the last month, on a diet of canned spaghetti, bread, sweet rolls, beer, and Chinese food which Adam procured at the restaurant three doors away and brought up in paper cartons. "And out of the sixty-five, I guess I could put away twenty. Now, with the eighty I already saved, in three months . . ." She sipped her beer, contentedly projecting her financial plans.

"When we have enough," she said aloud, "we can bring your gift to the world, Adam. And we'll do it right, this time. A lovely dress for me, you in your suit, hire a nice hall, print up tickets. . . ."

Adam had been sitting idly, his head cocked at a slight angle not indicative of attention, merely a random placement. He had not been listening to Sister Louella's comments, having grown accustomed to the general tenor of her store of conversation, which contained nothing to engage his interest. For her part, she no longer expected answers from him. She was quite content to talk to herself, uninterrupted.

As usual when not otherwise occupied, Adam was listening absently to the voices that always murmured in the background. He had grown quite adept at sorting out one from another, amplifying one, tuning another out at will. He had gathered a great deal of data in this way—data that were of no more practical use to him than the fund of information in an encyclopedia is useful to the volume itself, and for the same basic reason: the impulse to make useful connections and act on the basis thereof was lacking.

Now and then, Adam would recognize a familiar voice, as in a crowded city one occasionally sees the face of a stranger one has seen before. He had encountered a Mr. Wayne C. Chister, sensed in his thoughts a lingering fear of insanity dating back to a curious hallucination of a few months earlier. He had lightly brushed the thoughts of a Mr. Harkinson, and had hesitated for a moment, confused as to whether *his* name was Harkinson. . . .

There you are—don't go away! I'm Poldak. Where are you?

Adam listened interestedly to the excited voices. He found it curious that the voice seemed to be addressing him directly, but the idea of replying to it did not occur to him.

I have to get in touch with you. Call me—collect. Area code 920, 496-9009. You must! I've been trying to contact you—looking for the woman—Louella Knefter . . .

"I don't think you should do that," Adam said aloud.

"What?" Louella said. "Do what? Plan for the future? Lord knows if I don't, who will?"

"I didn't mean that . . ." Adam's thoughts drifted on. . . . .
. . . *like it, can't forget it, hit over the head and my gun
took, by that damn little shrimp. . . .*
"Adam! You listening to me?"
"No."
Sister Louella snorted. "Don't know why I waste my
time, Adam. I think sometimes you don't appreciate a
thing I've done for you, running off like I did, living here
in such conditions. . . ."

[3]

There was tension in the air at the Dragon Import Company. Mr. Lin had fired five men and a woman; two of the
men were now in the hands of the police department,
lodged in jail. Mr. Lin had taken to patrolling the
warehouse, the packing rooms, the shipping dock, staring
suspiciously at his employees. His manner with his
customers had also suffered; two firms whose proprietors
he had long been in the habit of entertaining at long
luncheons at Kwan Luck had been among those
apparently—but not quite probably—implicated in the
embezzlement. He had refused to see these former asso-
ciates when they called, and had given instructions that no
further orders were to be accepted from them. Even Lucy
Yang seemed subdued in her manner. Adam noticed none
of this; or, more accurately, he noted the change, but attached no more significance to it than a schoolboy might
to a change in the style of women's hats.

At the end of the workday, a week after retribution had
descended on the thieves—who were doubly indignant at
being caught out by a total stranger, and an American at
that, after so many years of routine success—Lucy spoke
to Adam:

"It's not your fault—you just uncovered it. And I guess
we all knew there was a little hanky-panky going on, but of
course we didn't know it was so big—I mean, I guess we
just had the idea Mr. Lin could afford a little here and
there—but what I mean is—everything's so different now.
And they blame you, Mr. Adam."

"Yes," he said.

"Is that all? Don't you care?"

Adam thought about it. "No."

"You're a strange one, Adam, even for an American. You're sort of tuned out of things, aren't you? All you care about is your ledgers, adding up your numbers."

"It's very interesting. Mike told me . . ." He broke off, realizing he had been about to launch into a discussion of prime numbers gleaned from a student at MIT. Louella had told him never to mention the voices.

"Sometimes," Lucy said, "I think you're kidding me—like you did that first day. I think that dumb act you put on is just—an act. But why?"

He shook his head vaguely.

Maybe he really is crackers. He never looks right at me . . . or rather, he's as likely to talk to my chin or my ear as my eyes.

"I'll look at your eyes if you want me to," Adam said.

Lucy felt a prickling at the back of her neck.

"Why . . . did you say that?"

"Because . . . they're very pretty eyes," he said. The remark was not an effort at a sophisticated change of subject; he had merely been struck, quite suddenly, by the beauty of the girl's bright, jet-black eyes, the long lashes, the delicately arched brows.

Lucy gave an exasperated but ladylike snort, not displeased, and returned to the last-minute chores of covering her typewriter, locking the desk, putting on her light coat.

"Come on, Mr. Adam," she urged him as he hovered by his desk. *As if he's forgotten he's supposed to go home now . . .*

They left the room together. It was quiet in the old building; their feet seemed to rattle with unaccustomed loudness on the stairs. As they reached the ground floor and started toward the side exit, three men stepped out of concealment to bar their way. They were masked, dressed in shapeless coveralls, and carried short, stout clubs.

Lucy gave a sharp cry and jumped back, then stood rigid as one of the men menaced her with his club.

"Stay out of the way and you won't get hurt," he said to her in Chinese. He took a step toward Adam and, without warning swung a vicious blow at his head. Adam leaned aside almost casually, kicked out, struck the man square in the groin. The attacker shrieked and fell, clutching himself. The second man snarled and moved in, aimed a blow at Adam's neck. Adam bent his knees to duck under the swing, caught the arm as it went past, put his right forearm behind the elbow, and jerked the wrist down. The joint went, with a complicated sound of bone and gristle. Its owner helped and fell on his face in a dead faint. The third man backed, threw down his club, and fled.

"Adam," Lucy whimpered. "They . . . would have killed us."

"Sons of bitches," Adam snarled, and aimed a kick at the head of the man who was groaning at his feet: he subsided into snoring unconsciousness. Adam turned and gave Lucy a fierce look which faded, to be replaced by his usual rather vacuous grin.

"I . . . I never saw anything like that," the girl said. "Only in the movies. You—you just *annihilated* them."

"They wanted to hurt us," Adam said apologetically.

"You were wonderful." Lucy stepped to him, put a hand on his shoulder, kissed him swiftly on the corner of the mouth. "You really are full of surprises, Adam." She laughed shakily. "It's as if you were half a dozen different men. . . ."

Adam touched his mouth where she had kissed him. "That felt very pleasant," he said. "Do it again, Lucy."

"Adam—with this man lying here in agony—and the other one . . ." she looked at the arm lying at an abnormal angle and shuddered. "We have to call the police."

He came close to her and reached out a hand. She ducked back.

"Adam! Stop that."

"Why?" He looked genuinely interested.

"Because—I don't want you to. I gave you a kiss because I . . . because you deserved it. But . . ."

"I have a curious feeling, Lucy. I want to be close to you. It's very strange. I've never felt this sensation before . . ." He seemed to be talking to himself.

"Well, it's normal enough—but don't let it get out of hand," Lucy said, with a return of her usual self-confident manner. She looked at Adam. "What do you mean, you never felt this way before? Am I the first girl who ever kissed you?" She smiled sardonically.

97

"Yes."

Lucy was surprised by the candor of the answer. "Well, you *have* led a sheltered life——"

"I want to touch you," Adam said in the tone of one deciding what to have for dinner. "I want to press against you; I want to lie in a bed with you and put my hands on your bare skin——"

"Adam! That's enough! You really handled these thugs, and I admire a man who can take care of himself. But——"

"You don't feel the same desire?" Adam said. "Somehow it seems—it should be a mutual impulse. . . ."

"No, I don't! Now let's go." She turned away, went rather warily around him toward the warehouse office.

"It's quite a pleasant feeling," Adam said. "But it's like the need for food; it requires a satisfaction." He was still speaking analytically, like a medically trained cancer victim describing his own terminal symptoms.

"I know all about the feeling," Lucy said sharply. "But you're not my type, Adam, I'm sorry."

"I don't understand." The idea of reaching out to sense Lucy's thoughts didn't occur to Adam. Louella's frequent stern admonitions to him to never look into her mind had left a powerful inhibition against tuning in on the *voice* of any female present.

Lucy looked back at him, frowning. "I don't know whether this is another of your put-ons, or what, Adam. Sometimes you seem so wise—and other times you're like a little kid. Look, I like you, OK? I work with you, and I enjoy talking to you; I think you're a nice guy. But that's all. You don't turn me on. I don't want you groping me, or trying to kiss me. Clear?"

"Clear—but you said you understood the feeling I have——"

"Look, I'm a healthy girl. Some men turn me on, some don't. No offense, but you don't."

"Why?"

She looked at him angrily. "Well—you asked for it. You're not attractive. Not that way. You're too . . . skinny. You comb your hair funny. You stand funny, kind of as if your bones were broken, or made of rubber, or something. You get these dopey looks on your face. And your clothes—you've worn the same suit every day since you came to work here. You've got no style, no . . . personality." She nibbled her lower lip, looking thoughtful. "I guess that's really it, Adam. You've got no personality at all. It's as if—you weren't anybody in particular. As if you aren't really here, somehow."

"The desire to be close to a person and touch them is dependent on all these factors?"

"God, you make it sound like something in a laboratory. I don't know, Adam. It's the great mystery of life. Why do you go for one person and not another? Do you go for every girl you see?"

"No, only you."

"Try looking at another woman. Maybe you'll get the same result. And I must be nuts, talking to you as if this was really the first time. . . ." She paused, studying his face. "But, gee, maybe it really is for you, Adam."

"I've looked at many women," Adam said in the same mild, analytical tone. "Sister Louella . . . I've never had a wish to press my body against hers."

"Your sister, for God's sake?"

"Sister Louella is her name; she's not a relative. I have no relatives. I—"

"Adam—you're living in sin with a woman, and you come on all innocent with me?" Lucy said teasingly. She had seen Louella once, from a distance.

"What is sin?"

"Oh, brother, the questions you ask. Let's skip it, OK?"

Lucy went in to the telephone, made her call, came back out.

"Mr. Lin said to wait here. He's calling the police. Do you think we ought to . . . tie them up or something?"

Adam reached out, sensed a level of thought in the two men that was associated with deep sleep.

"No. They won't wake soon. I still have the feeling, Lucy. It's not pleasant, now. I sense that it's only pleasant when the impulses it gives rise to are satisfied."

"Try not to think about it," Lucy said shortly.

"Ummm. That's very difficult. It would be much easier if you allowed me to put my arms around you, and touch you. I want to feel your body, to—"

"Adam—you said you don't feel this way about Sister Louella?"

He thought it over. "No."

"So you see how it is. You don't want her—and I don't want you. I don't mean to sound cruel, but . . . there it is."

"Oh, I see; it would be very unpleasant for you to take off your clothes and press yourself against me. Yes. Terrible." He felt a shudder shake his body.

"It's not that bad, Adam," Lucy said contritely. "There must be plenty of women you'd like. . . ."

"But I like you, Lucy," Adam said, sounding surprised. "I don't need to look for another woman."

"You do if I don't return the feeling, Adam."

"Perhaps you'll feel differently later," he suggested.

"I doubt it," she said gently.

"Sister Louella is physically repellent to me because her shape and the texture of her hair and skin aren't pleasing," Adam said thoughtfully. "Possibly I displease you for similar reasons. You mentioned the way I comb my hair—"

Lucy laughed, a trifle desperately. "For God's sake, Adam—it's . . . *you*. You're a skinny, sick-looking, creepy-acting fellow with a physique like an invalid and no more sex appeal than a dry mop. Go out and take up weight-lifting, and find out something about men's fashions, and learn to Watusi, and how to light a girl's cigarette, and order wine, and drive a sports car, and maybe grow some sideburns or a mustache, and get a line of conversation, and learn to look at a gal as if she excited you. Even when you're telling me you want me to strip and rub up against you, you sound like you're telling symptoms to a doctor!"

Adam listened intently. He nodded slowly. "Thank you for the suggestions, Lucy. I'll start at once."

She stared at him, threw back her head and laughed.

"Adam, you really had me going. I'll say one thing, it's the weirdest pass a girl ever had thrown at her. You're a character, Adam. Come on, that's Mr. Lin now."

9

[1]

Adam climbed the two flights of steps to the room, no more aware than usual of the mingled odors of the laundry and of Chinese cookery, of age and dirt and stale cigarette smoke. His attention was focused on the sequence of muscular contractions involved in climbing the steps, the resultant increase in his pulse rate and the depth of his breathing. In the way that had become automatic with him, he reached out, fingered through the vast mindfield of voices, tapped it for additional information on the point under consideration. He had developed the ability, quite unconsciously, to abstract only that level of thought that interested him; no longer did he tune in a mass of unrelated ego data—name, age, address, personality traits—along with the facts.

In this instance, it was an Air Force medical officer whose education he absorbed—a man who had been, for fifteen years, conducting a study of physical fitness and the effects of diet and exercise thereon. It was not necessary for Adam to verbalize or rationalize the data he scanned. It was merely absorbed, stored, ready for use, quite as if he himself had devoted a decade and a half to its acquisition. He diagnosed his own physical condition, noting the discrepancies from the ideal in his lung capacity, muscle tone, the flexibility of joints, the resiliency of his vascular system; the atrophy of organs, the damage and underdevelopment due to injury, poor diet, lack of exercise, inadequate sleep.

There was no major disease, he deduced; none of the symptoms that would have caused the major to mark a prospective subject as unfit to participate in one of his programs. He was, in fact, an ideal subject. It would be interesting to subject the organism to rigorous training and to observe its reactions.

"Well, you're late, Adam," Sister Louella said. She was in the big second-hand rocker by the window. Her bulk almost filled it. She lifted a plump hand and let it fall back. "Your dinner's cold."

"Yes," Adam said. "Sister Louella, we've been subsisting on an improper diet. It's necessary that we begin nourishing ourselves correctly."

"Well, I never had any complaints of my cooking from Mr. Knefter," Louella said. "Is that the thanks I get, fixing you a nice dinner—"

"Poor nutrition causes ill health, Sister Louella. Good health is essential to physical beauty, as well as maximum efficiency of the organism."

Louella wagged her head. "Lordy, what's got into you, Adam? I admit you're no Clark Gable, but you've filled out some since we came here, and—"

"You've become fatter, Sister Louella," Adam pursued his line of thought. "Much fatter."

"Well, I never!" Louella stared, then burst into tears. Adam watched her with a mildly puzzled expression.

"The condition can be corrected, Sister Louella," he said. "It's only necessary to eat less, and of the proper foods. We've been subsisting almost entirely on starches and sweets—"

"You've got some nerve, Adam Nova! Calling me fat to my face! I've always been well filled-out; and there's plenty men admire a well-fleshed woman!"

"Really?" Adam said, interested. "Personally, I find obesity repellent."

Louella uttered a wail, heaved herself from her chair, and rushed into the adjoining room, slamming the door. Adam gazed abstractedly after her for a few moments, then went to the shelf where their small store of food was kept. He looked over the macaroni and noodles, the crackers and peanut butter and doughnuts.

"Organically grown vegetables," he murmured. "Wheat germ, whole grain bread, yoghurt. . . ."

He checked the box where Louella kept the money. It was empty. He went to the door through which she had

102

disappeared and tried the knob. It was locked.

"Sister Louella," he called, "I need money to buy the new foods."

"Go away," she bleated.

Adam considered this. "Very well," he said. "Good-bye, Sister Louella."

He was almost at the hall door when the inner one burst open. Sister Louella stared at him, red-faced, blear-eyed.

"Adam! Where are you going?"

"I have no specific destination in mind. My intention was only to go away so as not to cause you further distress."

"You can't do that! You can't just run off and leave me here among these heathen!"

"I believe I can," Adam said quite soberly. "I know of no obstacle—"

"Looky, Adam, I'll fix what you want. You just set down and rest now and I'll get just the kind of things you say. I was just . . . being silly. I . . . I knew you were just teasing me about my weight and all."

"Oh, no, I was quite in earnest. The new foods will help, you'll see."

"All right, Adam, just don't do anything foolish. I know what to get. I almost went into the health food end once myself, after Mr. Knefter passed on. Soy beans and the like. Goat's milk. You just wait here and I'll be back directly."

"I think it will be better for me to begin my aerobics program at once."

"Sure, Adam, whatever you like." Louella bustled to the sewing basket she had improvised from a cardboard box, rummaged, came up with a small cache of folded bills. She departed, still uttering reassurances. Adam stayed behind just long enough to remove his coat and tie, then went down to the street. He stood by the entrance to the laundry and drew a dozen deep breaths, letting them out slowly. Then he set off at a jog trot along the crowded sidewalk, concentrating on breath control: inhaling for four paces, exhaling for four.

He was in the second block when a police car squealed to a halt at the curb and two uniformed men jumped out.

Adam paid no attention to their shouts; it didn't occur to him that their appearance had any connection with himself until he felt the impact of the flying tackle that brought him down.

[2]

Adam woke slowly. His head hurt. Also his face. He touched it; his upper lip was badly swollen and his nose was sore, scraped raw. He was lying on a cot in a room with walls that had been painted green a very long time ago. An overweight policeman in shirtsleeves was standing over him. Beside him was Mr. Lin, his round face pink-cheeked and smiling.

". . . full responsibility, Sergeant," Mr. Lin was saying. "I'm sure there's some simple explanation."

"Well, you don't never know," the policeman said darkly. "The guy don't stop when we yell; and he tore right by the bus stop and the bus was just pulling in, so he wasn't running for no bus."

Adam sat up. His head throbbed.

"Aerobics," he said.

"What's the matter, don't this guy talk American?" the officer demanded.

"Of course," Mr. Lin spoke up. "Adam, Sergeant Tully is curious as to why you were running."

"I've embarked on a program of physical fitness," Adam said. "Initially, I intend to tone up my heart and lungs by jogging."

The cop frowned. "I heard of guys out in the suburbs doing roadwork down the back lanes, but nobody don't go for no run through Chinatown, fer Chrissakes."

"Adam does," Mr. Lin said crisply. "Adam is something of a, ah, character, Sergeant." He winked at Adam. "But quite harmless, I assure you."

"Yah—he don't look like no tough guy, I'll give you that," Tully looked at Mr. Lin appraisingly. "Kind of a lot of action with you this afternoon, Mr. Lin. Them two bums your boys brought in, and before you leave the station house, this bird. I don't guess there's no connection?"

"You're not suggesting Mr. Adam was involved in the apprehension of the thieves, Sergeant?" Mr. Lin smiled at the joke. The sergeant grinned wryly back.

"Go on, get him out of here, Mr. Lin. And tell him next time he gets in a hurry call a cab."

[3]

At Mr. Lin's bemused suggestion, Adam sought out a gymnasium and health spa in the run-down commercial section half a dozen blocks from the laundry. He listened interestedly to the inspirational pitch given by a rather youngish man with abundant hair, carefully styled, and a slight bulge above the belt. The main impact of his message seemed to be that if Adam brought in six new members his own membership would be free.

"I'm quite willing to pay the usual fee," Adam assured the man. "My interest is in improving my physique, not recruitment. May I ask what method of training you employ personally?"

The man admitted that his personal interest in athletics extended only as far as observing the World Series on TV. "But we've got highly qualified trainers, Mr. Adam," he reassured his prospective customer. "The boys'll take you in hand and design a program tailored to your individual needs, like."

Adam signed up, paid his initial fee of thirty-eight dollars, and purchased the appropriate costume of T-shirt and sweat pants. His personal trainer was a bulky youth with an undershot jaw and sleepy eyes, and a habit of glancing sideways and rotating his shoulder forward each time he passed a mirror. He led Adam to a wheelless bicycle frame, positioned him atop it, and told him to peddle.

Half an hour later Adam went in search of his personal counselor, found him asleep on a bench outside the steam room. He was on the point of remonstrating when it occurred to him that the major might be of help. He tuned his thoughts. . . .

"Bench presses . . . about seventy pounds, three sets of six reps. Triceps curls, ten pounds, three sets of six; military press, fifty pounds, three sets of six; incline curls.
. . ."

Dutifully, Adam sought out the required apparatus, which he recognized easily with the major's help. It was a

105

well-appointed gym, red carpeted, bright-lit, with chrome-plated metal fittings and red-plastic upholstered benches. There were many fellow customers present, mostly plump, post-middle-age businessman types; but they appeared to be mainly occupied in steam-bathing, chatting, gently peddling exercisers, and sipping fruit drinks at the Vitabar. As a result, Adam found the equipment virtually unused and at his disposal. Following the running instructions of his invisible coach, he adjusted the bench press apparatus for the proper weight, dutifully attempted the prescribed exercises.

Pressing seventy pounds, he discovered, made him weak and dizzy. After a few repetitions his arms burned as if fires had been lit inside them. This circumstance in no way discouraged him. He made no actual conscious connection between the exercise and the pain in his arms and the dizziness. He proceeded as instructed, watching the bright-shot darkness gather. . . .

". . . damned fool, working out without his trainer, busts a gut and then he sues and they'll say it's all *my* fault, damn it!"

"He's OK. He's coming around."

Adam sat up. "Sorry," he said, taking his cue from the major. "I've had a long layoff. I'm out of shape. Shouldn't have tried my old routine. I'm OK."

Mollified, the manager sent him to the showers and admonished him to take it easier next time. And to bring a friend along for a free sample workout.

Adam was back the following day, Mr. Lin having granted him an extended lunch hour for the purpose. This time, carefully following the major's advice, he reduced the weight on the bar bell to sixty pounds for his bench presses, did a cautious six reps, rested a full five minutes, did six more. The major took him step-by-step through nine more exercises, thrice reducing the weight after observing Adam's reactions, once adding five pounds when he proved more capable at the lateral raise than anticipated.

At the end of an hour and a half, Adam was trembling, sweating, and nauseated. The trainer looked at him dubiously as he tottered toward the showers.

"You look kind of green, Mr. Adam. You OK?"

"Fine," Adam said. He enjoyed the infrared room, the

camphor-inhalation room, the dry-heat room, and the sauna, as well as the cold plunge and the mineral baths. Afterward he consumed a two-thirds-of-a-quart-size Hi-proteen drink made of milk, honey, pecans, and wheat germ.

As he drifted off to exhausted sleep that night, a dim, faraway voice called: *". . . where are you? Poldak here, damn it, I know you're out there, somewhere . . . but where? Answer me! Poldak here. . . ."*

Adam ignored the voice and let sleep wash over him like a rising tide of warm soapsuds. . . .

The next day he woke moaning. Sister Louella was bending over him, frightening in curlers and cold cream.

"Brother Adam, you having a seizure? Are you took bad?"

"I'm fine," he groaned, and moved experimentally. Every muscle in his body, it seemed, ached in its own way.

"Fine business," the major's voice assured him. *"Nothing to worry about. Just shows you the areas that need development. You'll feel better when you warm up a little."*

With difficulty, assisted by Sister Louella, Adam got out of bed. He took a hot bath, then hobbled about the room until he had loosened up sufficiently to dress and go down to the office. His muscles continued to hurt, but not cripplingly. Lucy asked him if he had had an accident, which he denied, without explaining.

The following day he started for the gym, only to be halted by the major's voice.

"Rest today. A workout tears tissue down; that's why you're sore. You need forty-eight hours to build it back up again. On your off-days you can walk and practice your eight-count breathing."

He complied dutifully. Monday, Wednesday, and Friday were his workout days. He appeared at the gym religiously at 11 a.m., did his hour and a half, which gradually shortened to an hour and a quarter. By the second week he was no longer nauseated at the end of the session. The pain in his muscles had faded. In the third week, he increased his repetitions to eight, the following week to ten. After a month, he added five pounds to his lighter weights, ten to the heavier ones, and went back to six reps. His trainer came by occasionally to observe, cautioning him to suck air in audible gasps through pursed lips just before making a lift.

At the office, Mr. Lin had initiated the changes in inventory control suggested by Adam. Lucy had eyed him warily for a few days, but when he made no further move she gradually returned to her former attitude of casual familiarity. The weeks slipped by. Sister Louella complained intermittently of the expense of Adam's training program and special diet, but without conviction. She continued to gain weight.

[4]

In the third month of his program, Adam discovered one morning that he could no longer button his shirt collar.

"Land sakes, Adam," Sister Louella said querulously as she reset the button. "This shirt's brand-new, only a few months old, shrinking like that, we should get the money back."

"My coat is tight under the arms," he said. "Perhaps you could alter it."

"Adam"—Sister Louella stepped back to look appraisingly at him—"I do believe you're putting on flesh. Hmmmp. The way some people talk, and then. . . ." She clamped her jaw. "It's the fancy diet you been on. You'll have to cut down, we can't afford to go buying you all new clothes."

"No, I can't deviate from my diet," he said seriously. Sister Louella contested the point, cautiously, but Adam was adamant. That afternoon he priced a new wardrobe at Balani's. Afterward, he informed Mr. Lin that he would have to have a raise in pay to one hundred dollars per week.

"Out of the question, Mr. Adam," Mr. Lin told him emphatically. "Why, I gave you a handsome increase only a few weeks ago—not that it wasn't deserved, of course—"

"In that case, I'll have to seek employment elsewhere," Adam said absently. "Good-bye, Mr. Lin. . . ." He was listening to a voice some blocks distant, that of a Mr. Goldman, who was wondering disconsolately where to find a reliable manager to take over the running of his wholesale produce business on his retirement. The details of vegetable merchandising flowed into Adam's mind. . . .

"Just like that—you'd go off and leave me, with no notice?" Mr. Lin expostulated.

"Yes," Adam nodded in confirmation. "I must have the money, you see, Mr. Lin."

Mr. Lin waved his hands in surrender. "Ah, well, if it's like that. . . ."

[5]

Sister Louella exclaimed joyfully at the news of Adam's increase in salary.

"Why, Adam, you see, things are working out just like I told you! Lordy, at this rate, in another couple months we'll be ready to bring your gift to the public!"

"I'll need most of the money for clothes, dancing lessons, and a sports car," Adam explained absently. "I also expect to require a substantial amount for restaurants and theaters."

"Adam—what in the world are you talking about?" Sister Louella looked at him with an expression of astonishment as slack as her bloated face would allow.

"All these measures are necessary before Lucy will consent to take off her clothes and lie in bed with me," Adam explained matter-of-factly.

Sister Louella uttered a choked cry and recoiled as if he had struck her in the mouth. She made gobbling sounds. She sputtered.

"Sister Louella, are you ill?" Adam inquired solicitously.

"The idear—to be insulted, talked filthy at, mocked in my own home—"

"I wasn't mocking, Sister Louella," Adam cut in. "I have a great desire to lie naked with Lucy."

Sister Louella opened her mouth to scream her outrage; but no words came. She whirled to flee to her bedroom, caught her foot in the threadbare rug, and fell heavily. She cried out sharply, began to sob. Adam bent over her.

"Oh, Lord God," she wept. "I'm hurt, hurt bad. Oh, Lord, my back's broke, I'm paralyzed, I'll never walk again. . . ." As she continued to moan, Adam touched her thoughts, scrupulously avoiding her *voice,* seeking out the extent of her injuries.

"It's all right, you can get up, Sister Louella," he said, relieved. "You're not hurt at all."

"Not hurt? I guess I know if I'm hurt! You're heartless, along with all the rest! To think I nurtured a foul-minded, thankless creature like you all these months, doing without to give you the care and help you needed—"

"Your fat served a useful purpose," Adam said consolingly. "It padded your fall; otherwise you might have been bruised—"

Sister Louella cut him off with a screech of outrage.

"That's right, insult me, revile me, then run off with your scarlet woman! Not even a white woman, a dirty, smelly Chinagirl—"

"Be silent," Adam said. Louella gasped, cut off in midspate. "Don't speak that way of Lucy ever again," Adam said firmly. He turned away. Louella heaved herself to her feet.

"Where are you going, Adam? Going off to your fancy woman, are you?"

Adam turned on her sharply. "Sister Louella, you know that the ideas you're expressing are untrue. Also, they give me an unpleasant feeling." He put his hands on his lower chest. "When you speak like that, I have a desire to injure you. . . ." He paused, considering his own feelings wonderingly. Sister Louella had fallen back against the bed, uttering shocked gasps.

"You wouldn't dare lay a hand on me. You stand back now, Adam. . . ."

Adam took a deep breath. "It's all right now," he said calmly. "The impulse has passed. But you mustn't voice any further lies regarding Lucy. I . . . I don't like it." He savored the conception. It was the first time that he had consciously made a subjective judgment of an abstract personal preference, and the sensation was strange. He looked around the squalid room as if seeing it for the first time.

"This room displeases me," he said. "I'd prefer larger quarters, with better facilities and more comfortable furnishings." His mind reached out, touched that of Romona Ribicoff, an interior decorator occupying a handsome apartment on the other side of the city; for a moment he scanned the array of idealized dwellings present in the woman's thoughts.

"You think *I* like it?" Louella cried.

Adam considered the proposition. "You dislike living here also?"

"I hate it, Adam! The heat, and no room, and the smells, and these Chinamen just outside my door all the time—never know what hour of the day or night they might break in here with a knife—"

Adam disengaged his arm from her clutch. "I see you're fantasizing again, Sister Louella," he said calmly. "It's difficult for me to assess your actual wishes when you blend the unreal and the real in this way—"

"I'm sorry, Adam," the woman blurted. "I didn't mean to say the wrong thing, don't go off and leave me—"

"You may accompany me if you wish."

Louella slumped against the door frame. "I knew you wouldn't really run out on me after all I done—I've done for you—"

"Sister Louella, if you knew I wouldn't abandon you, your apparent anxiety was spurious; and as for assistance rendered to me, after your first kindly impulse, your intent has been in exploiting what you consider to be my unusual abilities."

"But, Adam—where—where're we going? You—you haven't gone and rented a new place, have you, not telling me? I'll bet that's it. It's a surprise. Isn't it, Adam?"

"No. But I perceive that much more desirable residences exist, and to procure one, it will be necessary for me to obtain money," he said briskly. "A great deal of money."

"But—then—you mean . . ." Louella sounded disappointed. "Guess I might's well fix supper," she said flatly, and turned away.

"As you wish," Adam said. "I'll return when I've acquired the necessary funds."

"Adam—what . . . how you going to get the money?"

"I shall devise an appropriate method, dependent on the circumstances that arise."

"You wouldn't—wouldn't rob the money, Adam?"

"Your grammar is incorrect, Sister Louella. One may

111

rob a man, but one steals money."

"Adam, don't do nothing—anything, illegal—anything you might get caught at."

"I'll conduct myself with circumspection," Adam said, and left the apartment, closing the door carefully behind him.

10

[1]

It was twilight in the city. Adam moved along the crowded sidewalk, monitoring the thought patterns that impinged on him from every direction. For a time he became engrossed in a study of the manner in which he instinctively assessed the direction and distance of an incoming *voice,* deciding eventually that the source vector was determinable by the reception lapse between the two sensitive cell-clusters in his cortex, one in each lobe of his brain. Range was easily determinable by signal strength. He probed, tuning for distant signals . . . a faint, excited voice came through the static.

"*. . . you! Where are you? Don't break contact, this is Arthur Poldak, tell me where you are! What city? Answer me, don't break off—*"

Adam brushed aside the insistent voice, noting in passing that Arthur Poldak was now only two hundred and twenty-four miles distant, on a vector of 035 degrees. . . .

He returned to the question of obtaining money in large quanities. Quick probings indicated that large sums were available in the vicinity. Here a merchant mused over the day's gross; there a gambler added his winnings; near at hand an unshaved derelict in a ragged overcoat three sizes too large lovingly fondled the thought of his hoard, safely tucked away at the bottom of a coffee can filled with rice, in the shack he had constructed of packing-crate material at the edge of the municipal dump area on the other side of the river. . . .

Adam set off at a brisk walk. It took him an hour and twenty minutes to reach the approximate spot the panhandler had visualized. Another ten minutes' search brought him to the tumble-down hut, half-concealed behind a growth of willow, at the rim of a drift of broken glass, rusted cans, and perished automobile tires. He circled it, found the entry—a hank of rotting tarpaulin nailed over an irregular opening—and stepped inside.

It was dark in the hut, and it stank vividly of sardine cans, human excrement, sour whiskey, organic decay. Adam reached out to touch the mind of the owner. . . .

"*. . . don't like it; worried,*" the voice came, unexpectedly strongly. "*Something's wrong, robbers—*"

Adam turned in time to see the tarpaulin flung aside, the man in the decayed overcoat burst into the shack. In the gloom, he did not see Adam. Muttering aloud to himself, he stooped over a table made from an apple box—and straightened suddenly, whirled, bringing a long-bladed knife into view.

"You're in here—I can smell you," he blurted. "Come out, damn your devilish soul! I'll cut your heart out!" The man lunged suddenly at a spot six feet to Adam's left. In instinctive response, Walter Kumelli took over, struck down at the exposed arm, chopping simultaneously at the hut-owner's neck. The man fell forward with a choked cry.

"Don't move and you won't get hurt," Walter snarled, and aimed a kick at the bum's head as the latter scrabbled, attempting to rise.

"It's up to you, crumbum," Walter grated as the man fell back, slack. "I'd as lief kick ye'r brains in as look at ye." He went to the apple box, groped, found the coffee can, dumped it. The roll of bills spilled out, fell to the dirt floor. He picked it up, pried away the perished rubber band, ruffled the curled bills. They were mostly hundreds, with a few fifties and twenties.

"Tricky old devil aren't you? Walter muttered. "Five grand plus—and living like a dirty animal."

With an effort, Adam forced the *voice* to relinquish control of his body.

"My money," the man on the floor said blurrily. "Damn

113

thief. Give me back my money. . . ." He tottered to his feet, but hesitated to attack the man the weight of whose blows he had already felt. "You got no right—no right. . . ."

"You make no use of the money," Adam said reasonably. "You merely accumulate it. I have need of it."

"You don't understand. They all want to get at me, kill me, see? I'll starve—die of cold, no food, no coal. But not if I have the money, see? I have more than they think, I'll fool them, some day. . . ."

"Your thinking is confused," Adam said, studying the other's mind patterns. "Your value system does not represent a one-to-one relationship with external reality." He saw the breaks and discontinuities in the other's rationality as noisy fracture lines crossing the misshapen world image that occupied his mind. Impulsively, he reached out, brushed away the obstructions, sealed the wounds in the other's psyche.

The derelict cried out, stood for a moment weaving on his feet. He said, "Ah!" and put his hand to his forehead. He looked around the hut.

"My God," he muttered. "What—what am I doing here? This foul place—cold—vermin . . ."

"I suggest you return home," Adam said. "I believe you will be able to function successfully now."

"Wait—who're you? What . . . how. . . ?"

"My name is Adam Nova, but that is an extraneous fact of no importance." He turned to go.

"My family—my law practice . . . how long? Years. . . ." The man's audible voice mingled with his silent one, groping to understand what had happened to him. Adam followed his thoughts as they flashed back over the years of drunkenness, privation, mental and physical anguish endured in response to the compulsion to hoard each dollar earned, begged, stolen. . . .

Adam took the money from his pocket, replaced it in the coffee can as the man gaped at him blankly.

"I acted in error," Adam said. "I see that I must devise another method of becoming wealthy."

[2]

Louella was waiting up for him when he returned to

the rooms. She recoiled from him, snorting.

"Adam, where you been? You smell like a hog pen. And just look at your shoes—and—"

"Obtaining money is more complex than I thought," he said, paying no attention to her expostulations as he sat on the bed. "All funds in existence have an owner, who has a vested interest in his possessions. To appropriate money without the permission of the owner is inequitable."

"You mean stealing's against the law? I told you that," Louella said sharply.

"Accordingly, it will be necessary to acquire money in a way which will offer a commensurate recompense to the donor."

"Well, what have I been working and planning for all along but setting us up in a legitimate line, doing readings and character studies, and maybe some business and marriage counseling? All we need—"

"No. In retrospect, I see that those who pay for such services expect the miraculous; to extract their thoughts and play upon them is mere trickery."

"Well, who are we to question the judgment of folks that want readings? We're providing a service that's in demand, and—"

"This is feckless thinking, Sister Louella, limited in scope and lacking in a realistic assessment of circumstances."

"Realistic assessment of—looky here, Adam, you're getting pretty high and mighty all of a sudden for somebody I practically lifted out of the gutter with no more brains than a newborn lamb! When it comes to business, you can listen to me! It's dog eat dog, don't tell me—"

"Do you approve of this state of affairs, Sister Louella?"

"You mean the way the world is? Lord, no, if it was up to me I'd have everything on a basis of love thy neighbor, do to as you'd be done to—all that. But—"

"Then why contribute to the very conditions you decry?"

"Look here, Adam, it's fight or go under in this world. I might have all these beautiful idears, but try to live by 'em, and they'll run you over like a stray dog."

"You base this conviction on personal experience?"

Louella laughed patronizingly. "Don't ask me about personal experience, Adam. Lordy, the things I done—I've done for others, only to be slapped down for my pains. Why, I mind once, back in 'fifty-two—or maybe 'fifty-three—after the war, anyways—out of the goodness of my heart I loaned out my back bedroom to my sister and that no-account waster she married—for just bare minimum board, you understand—and what kind of thanks did I get? Moved off owing me three weeks' back rent, and took my portable sewing machine along to boot!"

"You consider this an adequate test of the theory?"

"It's not just that! I done—did a hundred things for others in my time, and ended up on the short end every time! Why, the tales I could tell you—"

"That won't be necessary," Adam said. "My examination of the societal patterns indicates that only by offering value received can we produce a substantial long-term gain. The concept of sharp practice is fallacious—"

"Your societal studies! What in the world are you talking about, Adam! You're as ignorant of the world as a child of three!"

"I agree that my conceptions are tentative, based on superficial theoretical analysis of limited samples of experience," Adam said. "But I must act on the assumption that my conclusions are valid."

"Then what are you going to do?"

"The matter requires thought," Adam conceded. "But I'm certain there is an appropriate solution. However, I find that I'm fatigued at the moment. In addition, places of business are closed for the day. Accordingly, I shall sleep now, and make my fortune tomorrow."

[3]

Louella was still asleep when Adam left the apartment the following day. He went directly to the Dragon Import Company, found the doors locked, waited nearly three-quarters of an hour before Mr. Lin arrived.

"You're here early, Adam," the importer greeted his employee. "Out to earn your salary increase, eh? Your zeal is commendable, I must say."

"I've realized that my requirements for money greatly exceed any reasonable salary I might receive in my present

116

capacity, Mr. Lin," Adam said. "I must take action to earn a large sum at once."

"As simply as that, eh, Adam?" Mr. Lin said, sounding annoyed. "You're a capable bookkeeper, as I'm quite willing to concede; but there are times when I feel perhaps you've not quite grasped the realities—"

"Excuse me, Mr. Lin—I have no time to waste this morning. I need your help with an undertaking which will produce a large and legitimate profit for me very quickly. Do you wish to hear it? If not, I—"

"Adam, slow down, slow down," Mr. Lin cut in, frowning. "You've never before spoken discourteously to me, from which I judge that you feel strongly about whatever it is you're speaking of. A large and legitimate profit, you say?"

"That's correct," Adam said. "I must set to work at once, as I wish to complete all transactions in time—"

"What's this, Adam—some get-rich-quick scheme someone's sold you? Gold mine stock? The Spanish Prisoner swindle?"

"No, I merely propose to take advantage of the normal opportunities offered by commerce," Adam said, somewhat surprised. "I wasn't aware that conventional methods of getting rich quickly existed. Perhaps—"

"Never mind that—just what do you have in mind, Adam?"

"A business such as yours is based on the purchase of commodities at the lowest quoted prices, and resale at higher prices, the differential, after overhead, salaries, spoilage, and so on constituting the merchant's payment for his services in making such goods available at retail to the public. I propose to increase profits by two means: an increase in volume, plus an increase in the rate of profit."

Mr. Lin sighed and nodded. "Very ingenious, Adam. I have not been unaware of the concept, let me assure you. There are, however, certain difficulties which are insurmountable. First, the market for my rather specialized stock is limited, and my available funds for increasing inventories are equally limited, as is my warehousing space. Also, since I now buy at the best prices available and sell at the greatest resonable margin of profit—"

"Excuse me; I understand these factors. I propose to

purchase very large amounts of a wide range of goods at bargain prices and resell them to other merchants, who will in turn offer them at retail."

"You want to go into the wholesale end, is that it?" Mr. Lin said patiently. "But, Adam, this takes great financial resources, and a knowledge of the market—"

"Precisely. I've come to request that you provide the initial financial backing."

"Indeed, Adam? And who, may I inquire, will provide the market expertise?"

"I will," Adam said.

Mr. Lin stared at him. "Adam—you astonish me."

"From my knowledge of your books, I calculate that you can make the sum of twelve thousand four hundred and sixty-one dollars and nine cents available to me immediately for this purpose."

"Can I indeed? And why, please tell me, should I do such a thing?" Mr. Lin looked more amazed than outraged.

"In order that I may become wealthy, as I explained."

"Oh? And what about me? Do I become wealthy too, Adam."

"If you wish."

"If I wish!" Mr. Lin waved his arms, speech failing him for the moment. "Why do you suppose I spend the golden days of middle life buying and selling, if not to provide the wherewithall for a secure senility—a senility I appear to have entered somewhat prematurely, engaging in this fantastic conversation as I am! Good morning, Adam. If you wish to take up your duties with the books, please enter. If not, I must excuse myself."

"Very well, Mr. Lin." Adam turned away.

"Where are you going?" Mr. Lin called after him.

"Clearly I must employ another method to procure the money I require."

"Are you serious, Adam? Where? How?"

Adam considered for a moment, monitoring the voices murmuring around him. "Mr. Stan Obtulicz has a vehicle for sale; Mr. S. Hyman has need of just such a vehicle. I shall offer this information to the interested parties for a fee. This is a legitimate service, is it not?"

"Of course, certainly, but—what do you know of the

needs of Mr. Obtulicz, whom I have met and remember as a most incommunicative gentleman?"

"I feel that it would be unwise to answer that question, Mr. Lin. Sister Louella cautioned me—"

"Is this some idea of your sister's, Adam? I must say—"

"Not at all; she has just awakened and is wondering where I am . . . but now I must hurry along. Good-bye, Mr. Lin."

[4]

Mr. Obtulicz was skeptical at first, suspecting trickery; but in the end he cautiously agreed to pay a fee of 6 percent of the price if Adam did, indeed, produce a cash buyer for his four-year-old pickup truck. Mr. Hyman listened with his head tilted to one side as Adam described the vehicle, nodded, donned his hat and coat, and accompanied him to the garage where the truck was housed. Half an hour later, Sid Hyman signed a check for nine hundred and twenty-five dollars and took possession, and Stan Obtulicz handed over to Adam sixty dollars in cash.

"I got to admit you came through with the goods," he said. "Say, you don't know anybody needs a good used produce cooler, I guess?"

Adam reflected, scanning the mind patterns for the information.

"Yes," he said. "I can offer a number of possibilities. . . ."

An hour later, Adam, having midwifed the sale of the cooler, plus a thirty-six-inch window fan, accepted a commission from the purchaser of the latter items, a Mrs. Krase, to locate a commercial-model vacuum cleaner. A Mr. Brockman supplied the needed item, and lingered to purchase a cup of coffee for the lady, Adam collecting a handsome fee plus tip from both parties.

It was now five minutes after 10 a.m. and Adam had garnered ninety-one dollars. A quick mental calculation indicated that his present rate of accumulation was too slow. He scanned the voices, noted that an auction was in progress some six blocks distant. He hurried in that direction.

A large chair was being offered for sale on the cluttered

119

platform when he arrived at Baturian's Auction Sales. It with an unhandsome piece, bulky and ornate, with carved armrests and feet, and faded upholstery. The bidding had stalled at four dollars.

Adam reached out gently, found a mind voice with the knowledge gestalt he needed; through the eyes of one George Brice Whitby-Smith, a department-store buyer, he studied the chair, identified it as a basically sound early nineteenth-century piece, of German manufacture, worth perhaps two hundred dollars—to the right party.

Adam scanned on, the image of the chair in his mind like a complex piece of an elaborate jigsaw puzzle for which he sought a matching space. . . .

And found it: Mr. Irv Hammacher, bachelor, occupying a gloomy apartment on the second floor of a somewhat run-down residential hotel on Andrews Street.

Adam raised a finger, automatically abstracting the correct bidding technique from the mind of the auctioneer.

His seven-dollar bid took the chair; he paid at once and asked that his new possession be set aside until he could arrange to collect it.

The next item was a grandfather clock, minus the works. Bidding opened at two dollars, went quickly to twenty.

"Twenty-one," Adam offered. This inspired another spurt of bidding. Adam dropped out abruptly at forty-one dollars; the successful bidder, an elderly woman, shot him a venomous look as she went forward to collect her prize.

Thereafter Adam bought a matched pair of five-inch Dresden figurines, both badly mended, which he had wrapped to carry with him; a brass fire-screen and matching poker; and a heavy book bound in tattered leather, minus the first dozen or so pages. He spent his last four dollars on a hand-carved twelve-inch temple dragon of Burmese origin, and rose to depart. There was a lull while a massive player piano was being wrestled onto the platform; the auctioneer sauntered back, mopping at his forehead.

"Warm morning," he observed to Adam, intercepting him at the door. "You've been buying intelligently; I have some choice numbers coming up; why not stick around, and—"

"I have no more money," Adam explained. "However,

I'll return as soon as I've sold the items I've bought."

The man nodded thoughtfully. "That might take a while he said. "A proper appreciation of valuable antiques isn't so common, and—"

"These are not valuable antiques," Adam said in the rather lofty manner of Whitby-Smith. "Mere attic lumber, actually. But there is always a buyer for special-interest items."

Mr. Baturian's eyes narrowed; he pulled at his lower lip. "You're acting as an agent?"

"No. I must be going now—"

"I'll tell you what, mister. You look OK to me. You want to bid a few more numbers, I'll trust you for the money. Twenty-four hours only; I'll hold your purchases for security."

"Impossible. I must take delivery at once."

"All right, tell you what—"

"I must go now, Mr. Baturian." As Adam edged past the auctioneer, he caught his thoughts: ". . . funny sort of fellow—looks like a rube, but knows his merchandise . . . wonder if I'm making a mistake. . . ."

"My bidding gave you your optimum available profit," Adam said in Armenian, the language of Baturian's thoughts. "Though of course I'll resell the items at a considerable gain to myself, to the specific individuals who most desire to own them."

"You're Armenian!" Baturian said in surprise. "Funny—I'd never have guessed it. What was the name?"

"No, I'm not Armenian—insofar as I know," Adam added, realizing as he spoke that he was totally unaware of his ethnic origin.

"You talk it like a native, you sound exactly like my brother Aram—"

"Good-bye, Mr. Baturian." With the figurines under his arm, Adam hurried away toward Andrews Street, followed by the other's curious thoughts.

[5]

Mr. Hammacher was not at home. Adam *tuned,* located him at a quiet tavern two blocks distant. The man looked up from a plate of steamed sausages and sauerkraut as Adam approached his table.

"I have a chair for you, Mr. Hammacher," Adam said. "The price is two hundred dollars."

Hammacher looked him over, chewing the while. He swallowed, took a swig from his pewter beer tankard, grunted.

"I'm eating. I don't talk business while I eat. Gives a man indigestion. Mel sent you, eh?"

"Good-bye, Mr. Hammacher." Adam turned away.

"Two hundred dollars," Hammacher called after him. "Ha. Mel must think he's got hold of a live one. Wouldn't pay over fifty if it was just what I had in mind."

"I understand," Adam said, again starting for the door.

"Hold on a minute, what's your all-fired hurry? What's this chair like?"

"It's a very ordinary piece, quite ugly actually, of no special value. Approximately eighteen-forty. German; Munich, I surmise. Sound, and original."

"Some sales talk. I might go fifty if it suits me."

"The price is two hundred dollars, Mr. Hammacher."

"Go jump in the lake!"

"For what purpose?" Adam inquired gravely.

"Who does Mel think he is? Think I'm made of money? Some kind of sucker? He knows me better than that, you tell him—"

"I don't know Mel," Adam said. "I purchased the chair to resell to you on my own initiative."

"How'd you know I was in the market?"

"I can't divulge that. Will you come with me now to inspect the chair, Mr. Hammacher?"

"Where's it at?"

"At Baturian's Auction House, approximately one and three-quarters miles north-north-east of here."

"Wait'll I finish eating. I'll take a look. But I'm not going over fifty."

"On the contrary, Mr. Hammacher, you'll readily pay two hundred dollars for this chair, since it's precisely what you—"

"Oh, I will, will I? Think again, smart guy. Go on, get away from me—and you can tell Mel I said forget it!"

"You won't pay two hundred dollars for the chair?"

"Beat it—before I call a cop. What are you, some kind of con artist? I got a good mind. . . ." Adam fled.

Back in the street, Adam *tuned*, found an alternate buyer for the chair. He walked the ten blocks to the apartment house where his new client, a Mrs. Dowder, occupied the first-floor front suite.

His sales technique, he realized, had been faulty. He could afford to waste no more time. As he rapped at the apartment door, he scanned, opened a portion of his mind to that of Mr. Norm Abrams, a pawnshop proprietor on the South Side.

The door was opened by a fat woman of indeterminate years, dressed in a shiny black uniform with a white apron, who grumblingly ushered him into the presence of a thin, elderly woman who sat with crossed ankles on a massive divan which might have been a product of the same factory that had produced Adam's chair.

Mrs. Dowder listened attentively, asked a few questions as to details of the chair. Her interest increased visibly.

"And what are you asking, Mr. Adam?"

"Three hundred dollars," Norm Abrams replied promptly. "A rock-bottom price for a lovely piece."

"My, that seems very high." Mrs. Dowder's visible interest faded equally visibly.

"But frankly, I've got no place to store the piece," Abrams went on, with a disarming smile. "So I'll let it go for . . . two-fifty."

"I might pay as much as one hundred dollars for something just right," Mrs. Dowder murmured, "but above that . . ."

"Only take a look," Abrams urged. "Once you see this outstanding piece you'll see I'm not overpricing it a dime."

After ten minutes' discussion, Mrs. Dowder agreed to meet Adam at 3 p.m. to inspect the chair, it being understood that she had no intention of spending two hundred and fifty dollars. . . .

Adam's next call was on a used-furniture dealer occupying shabby premises at the edge of the clothing district. He unwrapped his damaged Dresden pieces and placed them on a table before the proprietor, a tall, lean man with a face of wrinkled leather perched on a scraggy neck.

"I'll take one hundred dollars for the pair for a quick sale," Norm Abrams said.

"They're valueless, only curiosity value, ten dollars maybe, not more," the dealer responded.

Adam haggled enthusiastically for ten minutes, accepted fifty-five dollars, refused a cup of tea, and went on his way. The fire screen and poker he sold for thirty-one dollars to a man with an interest in Shaker metalwork.

While at the auction house to make delivery, he picked up the leather bound book, sold it forty-five minutes later for fifty dollars to a rare-book dealer on Johnson Street. Pausing at the auction house long enough to collect the Burmese [Chinthe], he hurried across town, called at a large white house in the city's best residential section.

"Why—it's fantastic," the middle-aged householder exclaimed as he studied the wood carving. "If this isn't a perfect match . . . oh, Martha . . ." He hurried away to summon his wife. The lady studied Adam's offering.

"Well, I'll be darned," she said, and gave Adam a perplexed look. "Where did you get this?"

"I bought it this morning," Adam said. "I believe I'm correct in believing you wish to own it."

Her husband reentered the room, carrying the twin to the carving.

"Remarkable. A perfect match: nose-to-nose, the four feet, tail tip—the rosettes on the side. Even the grain. Martha, I believe they were carved from the same block!"

Adam parted with the carving for one hundred and ten dollars, hurried off to his rendezvous with Mrs. Dowder at Baturian's.

"I'm surprised, Mr. Adam," she said. "I believe I've fallen in love with your chair. I'll pay one hundred and fifty."

Adam (or Norm) settled for one seventy-five. When the transaction was completed, Baturian came up to him.

"You're full of surprises," he said. "You know your stuff, sir. I could use a man with your knack." He pulled at his lower lip. "It's just a small business, you understand," he said. "I operate on a small margin. I could start you at . . . say sixty-five. Plus commissions," he added quickly.

"I'm not interested in employment," Adam said. "How much money would you require in exchange for your business?"

"You want to buy the business? Smart man!" Baturian responded with enthusiasm. "A real money-maker, believe me, you wouldn't go wrong—"

"How much?"

"Fifty thousand; store, stock, fixtures, assets, and good-will."

"I estimate its worth at no more than thirty-five thousand eight hundred and fifty dollars," Adam said, using the figure in Baturian's mind.

Baturian expostulated, but quickly agreed on the price. Adam nodded. "Unfortunately, I don't possess that sum at present." He turned to go.

"Wait a minute! I can give you terms! How much cash can you put down?"

"At present, my funds total three hundred and ninety-three dollars and forty-five cents," Adam said.

"Three hun—what is this? You think I'm crazy? I'll take five thousand down, minimum—"

"Will the offer be good until close of business today?" Adam inquired.

"Yeah, sure, three hundred bucks, must think I'm out of my mind . . ."

"I'll return before five o'clock," Adam said. "Good-bye, Mr. Baturian."

"Another kook," Mr. Baturian said.

[7]

Following the voices, Adam used three hundred and fifty dollars to buy a player piano and three burst-out cardboard cartons of music rolls from a young woman intent on cleaning out the clutter from the house she had recently inherited from an eccentric uncle. For another twenty dollars he had the instrument hauled to a handsome house in the suburbs where he sold it for twelve hundred dollars to an elderly woman who wept when she found her initials on the back of the music stand, where she had carved them sixty-one years before. He invested the twelve hundred in a 1930 Duesenberg sedan housed in a long-locked garage in the same block, resold it to an ardent collector two streets away for a round five thousand. He was back at the auction house at four forty-five.

11

[1]

"Bought a business?" Sister Louella gasped. "Adam—you haven't went and throwed away—thrown away my hard-saved money?"

"I bought it with funds I acquired during the day," Adam explained calmly. "On reflection, I thought it best to secure a source of capital prior to the acquisition of a new apartment."

"Adam—it's happening too fast for me." Sister Louella sank into her chair and fanned herself vigorously with a Chinese menu. "What's come over you all of a sudden?"

Adam considered. "I've acquired new motivations as a result of which a number of deficiencies in my life pattern have become obvious. I've set about rectifying them."

"Sometimes you plumb scare me, Adam. You don't seem like the same feller I rescued in out of the storm—"

"I don't recall that the weather was inclement on the night we met," Adam pointed out.

"You know what I mean. Used to be I thought I knew you; now I never know what you'll do next."

"Is predictability of my behavior an important consideration?"

"Well, land sakes, a body likes to know what's going on—what tomorrow's likely to bring. Here I was saving up, planning on starting the readings and all—and now we're in business." Sister Louella shook her head. "I s'pose you'll

126

want me to manage the store; I've had selling experience—"

"No, that won't be necessary."

"Well, I'm willing to do my part like always, Adam. The cleaning, now—I was never much of a one for housekeeping—but I'll attend to the cooking for you—and that reminds me: what did you bring for supper? We're fresh out of most everything."

"Nothing," Adam said. "I spent all the money purchasing the business."

"Then it's beans and bologna sandwiches," Louella sighed, then managed a laugh. "You do beat all, Adam. Make and spend five thousand dollars in a day, and end up too broke to buy our dinner."

[2]

On the following morning, Baturian showed Adam over the premises, explained the vagaries of the heating system, advised him of the understandings with the building inspector, the police, the licensing commission, the union, the local Cosa Nostra representative, warned him of the tactics of his various competitors, mentioned the lease, and went his way. Adam spent an hour going over the books, determined that the monthly rent was four hundred and fifty dollars, and was two months overdue; that the stock consisted of approximately fifty thousand cubic feet of dusty warehouse air, plus a drift of assorted items that not even an auction *aficionado* would consent to own; that the fixtures were minimal and in need of repair; that assets were nonexistent; and that the goodwill resided in the bosoms of a few dozen impecunious junk dealers who regularly bid on the least undesirable of Baturian's acquisitions.

Sister Louella was appalled. "Why, you've been took, Adam! Skinned to the teeth! Four hundred and fifty dollars a month for this dirty, run-down barn? Why, we're going to the police and get the money back!"

"That won't be necessary," Adam said in his absent way. Mentally, he was cataloging the remnants of stock, matching each item with a likely buyer. By the end of the day he had sold 80 percent of the merchandise: broken pots, worn galoshes, balls of tinfoil left over from a World War II scrap drive, odd lots of spare parts for obsolete machines, mothballed clothing, chipped bric-a-brac, a brass lamp in the shape of a pregnant alligator. . . .

"Land sakes," Louella gasped, counting the take. "Four hundred and sixty-three dollars cash money—in one day! Adam, we got—"

"We've got," he corrected.

". . . a gold mine!"

"Have someone haul away the rest," Adam said, indicating the scattering of ultimately unsalable debris. He paused a moment. "Call Tony Pelucchi at 234-0987."

"You got—you've got a real head for telephone numbers, Adam. Me, I could never remember 'em."

There was a small, musty apartment at the back of the old building; Louella agreed with Adam's suggestion that they defer the rental of better quarters until the business was on its feet.

Happily, at Adam's direction—who in turn drew on various sources for the necessary lore—Sister Louella contracted for the services of a cleaning crew, carpenters and electricians and repairman and painters. For the next week Adam busied himself with buying and selling single items, personally picking up and delivering on foot, always unerringly to an interested party, and for a tidy profit. The following Monday, he purchased a small, second-hand pickup truck and employed a slack-jawed youth named Elmer as driver. Together they scouted the city, Adam directing their route first to a moldering tenement where he purchased a rusting iron stove, next to a prosperous suburb where an attic disgorged bundled magazines, then to a pawnshop on the South Side for a stuffed owl, an antique microscope, a tarnished gold watch, a defunct umbrella, a rococo walking stick, and less apparently desirable items. A full day's buying exhausted the available funds and crowded the refurnished store with a variegated clutter of cast-off goods. Louella grew more nervous as she inspected each arriving load.

"Lordy, Adam, who's going to pay good money for a busted Indian water pipe? And I wouldn't give house space to this here—to this indecent picture of a nekkid woman; and—"

"Buyers exist," Adam replied calmly. "Please call the following numbers and advise the persons you contact that the indicated items will be on sale tomorrow." He proceeded to dictate a list of names, numbers, and articles which reached a total of over three hundred before Sister Louella begged off. "Lord, Adam, this'll take me all day! We got to have—"

"We must have," Adam interjected.

". . . some better way than this to spread the word! How about getting some handbills printed up, and mailing them out?"

Adam responded with interest. The concept of direct-mail advertising was new to him. He immediately designed the campaign, with the assistance of Mr. Fred H. Yost of Yost, Peabody, Goldblatt, and Yost, and at once set the wheels in motion.

The first day's sale at the auction house was the liveliest that had ever occurred there. There appeared to be at least two determined bidders for every lot. A former British Indian Army officer and a professor of Psychedelic Science from a local one-room college contested hotly for the ownership of the hookah; a pale little man in a black velvet jacket competed doggedly with a fat, whiskery, tweedy fellow for the nude. Dealers, attracted by rumors of unwontedly furious activity at Baturian's former premises, arrived to scoff and stayed to bid. By nightfall, the building was stripped of everything, including the long-unused gas fixtures that had been attached to the wall.

In the now-clean apartment, Louella made small sounds of incredulity as she totted up the receipts.

"Over three . . . thousand . . . dollars," she cried. "Adam, we're going to be wealthy! Lordy, we can have that fancy home now—and some clothes for me—"

"Not quite yet," Adam said. "I owe over two thousand to the printer."

[3]

For the next two weeks, auctions were staged on alternate days, Adam employing the intervening days in purchasing the merchandise for the following day's sale. At the end of the second week he turned the buying over to a newly employed assistant, a malleable young man named Alvin, providing the lad with a list of addresses, items, and prices, thereafter maintaining *voice* contact with him as he made his rounds, reaching out to supply guidance as necessary, placing the thoughts, unnoticed, in Alvin's mind. With profits now standing at over thirty-two thousand dollars, he agreed with Louella that the time had come to lease a more luxurious apartment. He selected a tower suite half a mile from the store from the mind of Miss Ribicoff, appeared at the agent's office to pay six thousand dollars cash for one year's rent. A telephone call brought a crew who, the same afternoon, installed a complete gymnasium in one of the four bedrooms.

"I find these surroundings far more conducive to constructive thought," he commented to Louella that evening as they stood by the wide windows looking out on the sweeping view across the city and the river beyond.

"Adam—now we can start the readings," Sister Louella exclaimed rapturously. "With a setup like this—I mean, in these lovely surroundings—"

"No readings," Adam said absently. "I can become wealthy much more quickly by pursuing trade."

"Adam, you talk about getting wealthy as if it was the easiest thing in the world!"

"I find it quite simple, though tedious," he said.

"Adam, I've always dreamed of my own limousine," Louella blurted. "Big, shiny, black, with all the gadgets, a chauffeur to drive me around to all the smart little shops and I'll just stroll in and buy whatever I like. . . ."

"You require a large automobile merely for the making of purchases? To telephone is much simpler—"

"Lordy, Adam—the best part of shopping, is going in the better shops, looking at the things! I just *have* to have a car!"

"Very well, if this is necessary. What sum will be needed for the purchase?"

"Land sakes—you mean I . . . I can really have it? My own limousine?"

Adam looked puzzled. "I understood you to say it was essential that you own such a machine; accordingly, I agreed to its acquisition. Why does this surprise you?"

"Never mind, Adam, I'll take care of it, it'll cost a deal,

but the rate we've been coining cash you won't hardly notice; maybe six—eight thousand. And o' course we can charge it to the business, for taxes, I mean; and naturally, you can use it—"

"That won't be necessary. I purchased an auto for my own use this afternoon."

"Adam—you didn't!"

"Yes, I assure you I did."

"But—can we have—I mean, are you sure—two cars—"

"You will need a limousine in order to pay calls at shops; I require a small red car of the sports type to fulfill Lucy's requirements."

"Lucy—you mean that China gal? Adam—are you still—I mean, I thought you'd forgot all about all that craziness!"

"Forgotten," Adam corrected. "By no means, Sister Louella. My efforts during the past weeks have been directed specifically toward bringing about the physical juxtaposition I desire—"

"Don't tell me!" Louella covered her ears. "I don't want to hear another word about it!"

"Very well," Adam said. He went into the room Louella had selected for him, showered, dressed in one of his new outfits from Balani's, and left the apartment.

[4]

Lucy was surprised to see him. She looked him up and down, then stepped back to usher him into her apartment.

"Is it really you, Adam? You've bought new clothes —you look almost—you look very nice!"

"Thank you, Lucy. As you know, I've improved my musculature by a program of regular weight training, and in addition I've adopted a more nutritious diet, with a consequent improvement in my overall health, basal metabolism, and digestion—"

"There you go, still talking like a book," she laughed. "I admit you've gained weight—and in the right places. And your color's better. Your new job must agree with you."

"I own my own business. I have also acquired a sports-model automobile."

"My—you're really making progress, aren't you, Adam. Would you like a drink?"

"No, I consume no alcoholic beverages, as they tend to be injurious to the health."

"I see. Well, then, coffee?"

"I also avoid caffeine-containing beverages."

"You're not leaving yourself much room to swing, are you Adam? Well, if you don't want a drink, then what . . . I mean—well, why are you here?"

"Having met at least the material portions of your criteria, I entertained the hope that you would now be willing to engage in intimate physical contact with me." He took a step toward her. She yelped and ran behind a chair.

"Adam, you stop that! You're talking more like an idiot than ever!"

"You still don't return my desire for you?"

"No! Forget it! I already told you you don't turn me on, Adam! Sorry and all that, but that's the way it is."

"I . . . I find that very disappointing," Adam said. "It causes a most distressed sensation . . . here." He put his hands on his chest.

"Adam—I don't know whether to laugh or cry." Lucy stared at him incredulously. "Are you serious, Adam? You came up here all dressed up in your new suit thinking I'd fall into your arms?"

"In addition to the clothing," he reminded her seriously, "there is the improvement in my health, my sports-model auto, my new apartment at the Buckingham Arms, ownership of a profitable business, plus fifteen thousand four hundred and twenty-one dollars in cash. I estimate that I will have accumulated one million dollars at the end of approximately six months."

"You've got all the answers, haven't you, Adam?" Lucy said faintly. "Except the right ones."

"I don't understand."

"I believe you, Adam. You're the strangest human I ever met. In your way, you're smart—I wouldn't doubt you'd make a million, just like you said. But at the same time you're dumber than a three-year-old kid about some things—a lot of things. Too many things. You give me the creeps, Adam. I wish you'd . . . go. I . . . don't want to see you again. I don't want to hurt you, but—go, and don't come back."

Adam nodded, turning away. He groped for the door knob, but was unable to find it, due to a curious blurring of his vision. Lucy came forward to open the door.

"Adam—you're—you're crying," she wailed. He tried to speak, made a broken noise. He touched the tears that were running down his face.

"A very strange sensation," he managed to say. "Not at all pleasant."

"Oh, Adam," Lucy said. "Just go."

"Good-bye, Lucy," Adam said.

[5]

"Well, serves you right," Sister Louella said when Adam reported that Lucy had instructed him never to seek her out again. "Chasing after that heathen woman." She gave him a sidelong look. She was wearing a tentlike garment with a pattern of giant blossoms in unlikely colors.

"I don't see why you need to go running off after some strange woman anyway," she said. "Some folks'd think what they had at home was plenty good enough."

Adam turned to gaze at her curiously.

"I don't understand."

"Well, it's plain enough. I'm a woman—as much woman as that Lucy What's-her-name—maybe more!"

"Yes—I realize that you're a female . . ."

"Do I have to spell it out for you, Adam? Well, yes, I guess maybe I do. Some ways you're still as innocent . . ." Sister Louella took a deep breath and fixed Adam with a determined eye.

"I been thinking, Adam—"

"*I've* been thinking—"

"Never you mind my grammar! I've been thinking, and it ain't right—it's not right, me and you living together in this unchristian way, and not even . . . not even married."

"Married?"

"You know what married is, Adam."

"A legal relationship such as you entered into with Mr. Knefter. Yes, I recall—"

133

"Don't you go looking in my brains, Adam!" the woman shrilled, blushing furiously.

"I never do, Sister Louella."

"Well, see you don't. And don't try to change the subject."

"To what subject do you refer?"

"You and me—getting married!"

"For what purpose?"

Louella tried to glare, then tittered. "For respectability, for one thing . . ."

"You imply there's something else."

"Well—lordy, how do you say it? You remember what you was—what you were saying about . . . about that China gal? About wanting to . . . to get close to her? About . . . about laying in bed with her?"

"I recall clearly. I still desire—"

"Well—like I said, she's not the only woman in town."

"That's true. You suggest that perhaps I could find another woman who would engender the same desires and who might feel the same desires?"

"I'm saying let's get married, Adam—you and me."

"Am I to understand that you feel a desire to place your body in contact with mine?"

"Well—lordy, I'm only human—and even though you're not much to look at—well—" She broke off. Adam was nodding his head slowly.

"I understand now what Lucy meant. I desired her, but she didn't desire me. You desire me, and I don't desire you."

"Adam . . . you . . ." Louella looked stricken. She tried several expressions, settled on defiance.

"Well, why not, I'd like to know? There's some that consider me a fine figure of a woman—and who're you to go setting yourself up so choosy? You're not much, I'll tell you!"

"It's not that I consider myself superior," Adam explained. "It's merely that you're physically repulsive."

Sister Louella emitted a screech. "How dare you speak to a decent lady that way! Here I went and got a hairset and a new dress just to please you, and this is the thanks I get! You get out of here this minute! You crawling worm, you get away from me—"

"You're free to depart if you wish," Adam pointed out politely. "I'm quite fatigued, and wish to rest now."

"Oh! You! You'd insult me and then throw me out in the street, after all I done—"

"Sister Louella, I find your voice particularly irritating at this moment, possibly as a result of the emotions I've felt today. I feel an impulse toward violence, directed toward your person. You must cease vocalizing in that manner, or go at once."

The woman stepped back, her face a mask of dismay.

"I'll go," she found her voice. "But I got to have money. I can't go back home empty-handed, after all—"

"Take all you wish," Adam said.

Louella's eyes went to the black metal box where the cash was locked.

"We've got over fifteen thousand dollars; I guess I earned my share. I want—I want my half, Adam."

"Take it all," Adam said offhandedly. "I have no further need of it."

Sister Louella's mouth opened and closed several times. "Got no need. . . ?"

"My intention in gathering money was to qualify for Lucy's affections. I failed, and therefore have no use to which to put the money."

"You'd really give it all to me?"

"Just as I said, Sister Louella."

"Oh, Adam . . . I . . . I don't know what to think! You're . . . so good—in your way. And at the same time, you can be so cruel!"

"I have no intention of being cruel. But—yes, I see now. I caused you pain, just as Lucy caused *me* pain."

"Adam—for Lord's sakes, Adam, don't look at me like that or I'll bust out crying. She really did—you really did care for her, didn't you?"

"Yes; I wanted her very much, Sister Louella. The sensation was not unpleasant while I entertained the delusion that I might have her. Now that I've learned that that's impossible, it . . . hurts me with a pain that transcends physical suffering."

"Poor Adam. This is all new to you, isn't it? You've never been in love before. Oh, yes, it hurts, Adam. But

135

you'll get over it. You'll live. And one day you'll be able to laugh at it."

"Indeed? That seems most unlikely."

"Take my word for it, Adam."

"Very well, Sister Louella. Can you tell me how long the pain will continue?"

Louella laughed a shaky laugh. "No, Adam, but don't you worry, you just go along and get interested in . . . in something else, and after a time it'll just fade away."

"I'll try."

"Adam—what . . . what did you mean when you said . . . you said I was repulsive?"

"Is the word incorrect? I selected it as the antonym for attractive, attraction and repulsion being opposite forces."

"Then you didn't mean—I don't make you sick or anything, just to look at?"

"No," Adam said judiciously. "But I would not like to view your unclothed body."

"I never offered to show you my nekkid body, Adam! Don't you go talking dirty again!"

"Possibly I misunderstood."

"Well, indeed you did! Anyway, I always thought you men—that all you wanted was to get a woman's clothes off her." She looked at him defiantly.

"I've given this matter some thought," Adam said. "I deduce that the wish to disrobe a member of the opposite sex is analogous to the pleasure of unwrapping a gift; one hopes that what will be revealed will be a fulfillment of one's utmost desires."

"Well? How do you know—"

"In Lucy's case," Adam continued, deep in introspection, "the pleasing nature of her face and figure suggested that to observe her entire and unadorned would be an aesthetically satisfying experience."

"Well, maybe I'm not quite as—"

"In your case, by analogy with the exposed portions of your body, I would expect to find the concealed portions repugnant, particularly, I now see, by reason of the fact that the unveiling in itself constitutes an implication of physical intimacy—"

"Repugnant!" Louella found her voice. "Repulsive! Is that all you can say about me? You make me feel crawly, like something that ought to be hid out somewheres, not fit to look at!" Sister Louella burst noisily into tears. "You're a mean man, Adam, to talk to a body that way. I can't help it if I'm not as young as I used to be—"

"How old are you?"

"There you go, always prying, asking personal questions! Well, as it happens, I'm . . . thirty-one years of age."

Adam gazed at her.

"All right, damn you, Adam—I'm thirty-eight! And that's not old; lots of women—"

"I assumed you were much older," Adam said. "By comparison with other individuals of the same age you seem rather more advanced in the process of physical senescence."

Sister Louella uttered a faint cry. "I guess I've got no call to be surprised at anything you say now, Adam. You don't care a thing about a body's feelings." She sagged in her chair, dabbing at the streaked mascara on her cheeks.

"I had no intention of injuring your feelings," Adam demurred. "Surely nothing I've said comes as a surprise to you. You frequently examine your reflection in a mirror; you must be quite aware of your appearance."

"Well, I know I've put on flesh—" the woman began defensively.

"Sister Louella, I sense you're fantasizing again," Adam said. "I find the motive for this difficult to grasp. Like other members of the culture to which you belong, you've absorbed society's standards of beauty. You're aware that obesity, sagging breasts and stomach, thick ankles, extra chins, flabby muscles, clammy, toneless skin with blemishes, and so on are considered unsightly. I deduce that this is due to a possibly subconscious awareness that these are indications of ill health, and as such are particularly objectionable in the biological context of sexual mating, since unhealthy specimens suggest inability to breed successfully and to produce superior offspring. Yet you evince injured sensibilities if this fact is acknowledged by others."

"Well, I never," Sister Louella said with a faint attempt at indignation.

"You must, logically, be aware that you depart widely from any definition of the beauty you admire. Yet you take no steps to bring your image closer to that ideal, and in fact, continue in habits that accelerate your deterioration."

"Why, what in the world do you mean? I dress as well's a body can be expected—"

"If you reduced your weight, for example, your proportions would more closely approximate the ideal. Yet you continue to overeat, indicating clearly that the physical sensation of ingestion outweighs the theoretical pleasure of improved appearance. A most interesting paradox."

"Why, it's natural for a body to put on weight with time!"

Adam gazed at Sister Louella interestedly. "You offer justifications, or rationalizations, for this behavior, apparently in the belief that the negative response to your unsightliness will thus be neutralized, though that is, of course, contrary to logic."

"You're not even human, Adam!" Sister Louella screeched. "You're like some kind of mechanical man, a robert or whatever they call 'em! You set there and tell me all the things wrong with me, but what about you? You think you're perfect? Lordy, the things I could say to you if I had a mind to!"

"On the contrary, I've realized I was imperfect since Lucy pointed the fact out to me."

"Her again! I'm glad she threw you out! You deserved it!"

"Apparently you're directing your resentment at your lack of physical appeal—a lack exacerbated by your own life habits—against me. I find this most insequential. Wouldn't it be more satisfying, Sister Louella, to take some direct steps to improve your appearance?"

Sister Louella started a sharp retort, then clamped her mouth shut. "It's late," she snapped, "and we got to get up early; big day tomorrow, and—"

"I won't be going to the store again," Adam said.

"Won't . . . what did you say, Adam?"

"Inasmuch as your hearing, insofar as I know, is unimpaired, I assume that question is rhetorical, another strange habit—"

"What do you mean, you're not going to the store? You know you got to be there, to handle things—run the sales, and—"

"That won't be necessary now. I have no further motivation for amassing wealth."

"Then—what in the world—Adam—you don't mean—what will you *do?*"

Adam shook his head vaguely. Louella uttered a wail and fled the room, slamming her door. Adam sat awhile, staring at the wall before falling asleep in his chair.

12

[1]

"You've got to do *something,* Adam," Sister Louella stated positively the next morning. "You been advertising, built the business up; folks'll've come for miles around to attend the sale. And what about Alvin and Elmer? They're depending on you, not to speak of me. You can't just walk off and leave it."

"Very well; I'll continue with today's sale, and divide the proceeds between the men. Will that be satisfactory?"

"Satisfactory," Louella yelped. "Giving up a million-dollar business and he says, is that all right!"

At the store, Adam, assisted as usual by the *voice* of one Harry "The Hammer" Hirshfield, conducted the sale briskly, but with a somewhat absent manner. Prices were off a bit; the crowd thinned earlier than usual. By mid-afternoon, the shop was deserted, while a handful of items remained unsold.

A tall, gray-haired, conservatively dressed man came up to Adam as he paused to eat the sardine sandwich Louella had provided.

"You're the fellow that bought Baturian out?" he inquired.

Adam confirmed the statement. The man nodded casually, glancing around the big sales room. His eyes came to rest on Adam. They were sharp, pale blue eyes.

"Your volume of business has picked up, from what I hear."

"That's correct," Adam said.

The man nodded again, as if well satisfied. "Naturally, we'll have to bump your fee on the same scale." He gave the room another shrewd glance. "I'd say five hundred would be about right."

Adam chewed his sandwich, gazing blandly at the man.

"Better let me have about a week in advance," the man went on, "just as an earnest of goodwill."

Adam considered this. "You seem to be proposing that I make you a gift of time," he said. "Inasmuch as this would appear to be outside the scope of human capability, I suspect that a semantic difficulty exists."

The man frowned. "Don't get me wrong," he said. "You being a Jew's got nothing to do with it. But you don't look like a Jew."

"That statement would appear to be a non sequitur," Adam said.

"Huh?" the man said. "What is this, a stall?"

"No; it's a converted warehouse now in use as a retail sales store."

"Oh, a funny one, eh? Remind me to laugh."

"On what occasion?"

"Listen, chum—and listen good. I'm not here to make with the boffs. I deal in cash. Get it up—now."

"You have something you wish to sell?"

"Insurance."

"No, thank you. I have all legally required insurance now in force."

The man's face set itself in a grim look. "You got a big investment here, pally," he said softly. "You want more coverage."

"No," Adam said; he swallowed the last of the sandwich and turned away; the man's hand fell on his shoulder, spun him back. Adam was fleetingly aware of an impulse on the part of the Walter M. Kumelli voice to take control of his actions; but he had learned now to suppress such intrusions automatically. He waited quietly.

"Your attitude's not good, friend," the man said in a low, harsh voice. "I think maybe I better have a couple weeks' premiums instead of just one. Let's you and me go in the back and settle up."

"I have nothing to settle with you," Adam said calmly. "Please excuse me now; I have work to do." He tried to pull away, but the man's grip on his sleeve held him. The man looked angry now, no longer the urbane and civilized type he had appeared a moment before.

"Kick through—or we'll be seeing you later."

"That won't be necessary," Adam said. "I don't intend to purchase any insurance." Suddenly he dropped his forearm, brought it sharply up inside the other's arm, breaking the grip, then chopping hard at the pressure point in the forearm. The man stumbled back, grabbing at the paralyzed member.

"I'm sorry to have been forced to strike you," Adam said. "But I dislike being restrained by force." He turned and walked away; Elmer, who had been arranging empty cartons at the back of the room, came to meet him, his face registering strong emotion.

"My God, Mr. Adam—I seen that. You know who that was you slapped down, for chrissakes?"

"An insurance salesman; he didn't introduce himself—"

"That was Art Basom."

"I recall that Mr. Baturian mentioned a person of that name."

"Don't you know who he is, Mr. Adam? He's with the, you know, organization."

"What organization?"

"The Mafia, for godsakes!"

"Curious; he stated that he was selling insurance."

"Look, Mr. Adam—you don't mess with those guys. You don't know 'em; my old man's dry-cleaning place—"

"Excuse me, Elmer; I don't have time just now to listen to your anecdote. I would like to conclude the day's business—"

"Mr. Adam—you maybe concluded more than a day's business. Those guys mean trouble. You got to do something."

"You have some specific action in mind, Elmer?" Adam asked, genuinely puzzled.

"Mr. Adam—take my advice: go see the man; say you

141

were just horsing around, pay up—"

"I have no intention of giving money to Mr. Art Basom. I intend to make an equitable distribution—"

"Then I quit, Mr. Adam." Elmer pulled off his work gloves and slapped them down on an empty packing case. "I like working for you; you're nuts, but you treat a guy right. But this is asking for it. So long, Mr. Adam. Good luck." He walked away, passing Sister Louella with a muttered farewell at the door.

"What's got into Elmer?" she inquired, patting her back hair. She gave Adam a sidelong glance. He noticed that her hair had assumed a new color—a chemical russet—and that chemical pigments had been applied to her face; also she wore a dress Adam had not seen before, of different cut than her usual voluminous garment.

"Elmer has resigned his position," Adam said.

"Land sakes! Why?"

"He feels that my handling of Mr. Basom's offer of additional insurance was inappropriate."

"Hmmph. We got all the insurance we need. That Elmer was getting too big for his britches, anyway." Sister Louella placed a hand on one hip, almost indistinguishable against the bulk of her body, and gave Adam a lingering glance.

"Well, how do you like it, Adam? I taken—took your advice. . . ."

"Of what, precisely, are you soliciting my opinion?" Adam asked innocently.

"Well, how do you like that! I'm wearing makeup, a new girdle, just had my hair done, bought a new dress—just like you said."

"I believe you misunderstood me, Sister Louella. Applying artificial color to unhealthy skin and hair merely adds the element of artificiality to an already unappealing composition. Compressing fat by means of reinforced garments, or adding apparent bulk by means of padding seems a most ineffective substitute for correction of undesirable conditions."

Louella registered shock, indignation, then resorted to tears.

"I tried diets, Lord knows. They just don't work for me.

142

And I could never go in for them—those hard exercises; they make my head swim something awful. And—"

"I see that the desire for physical beauty is a far weaker impulse than the wish to avoid abstinence and physical effort," Adam commented, turning away.

"There you go, changing everything around! You know perfectly well I work myself to death keeping house for you, fixing meals . . . and as for doing without—"

"Sister Louella, I have no desire to influence your life habits. I was merely pointing out certain obvious anomalies. Now I must attend to the details of liquidating the enterprise before Mr. Basom returns."

"What's he coming back for? Didn't you tell him 'no'?"

"Mr. Basom is associated with an organization known as the Mafia. They wish to extract money from me, presumably. However, since I indicated my unwillingness to cooperate, Elmer feels that violent reprisals may be taken."

"What you going to do, Adam?"

"I'll proceed to distribute the funds on hand and discontinue the operation here—"

"Ain't you going to fight back, Adam? You going to just let them hoodlums do you out of house and home?"

"I have no further interest in the business," Adam explained. "There therefore seems to be no reason to interpose obstacles to Mr. Basom's plans, whatever they might be."

"So we'll all just starve—cause you got no backbone!"

"That would seem to be a highly emotional statement without a functional relationship with external reality," Adam commented thoughtfully.

Sister Louella caught Adam's hand. "Adam—go to the cops—right now! Tell 'em to send policemen here to arrest that Mr. Basom when he comes back! Do it for me, Adam! You can't let me down now!"

"Very well, Sister Louella," Adam said, disengaging his hand. "Since it appears to be a matter of emotional urgency to you, I'll do as you ask."

Adam drove the five blocks to the nearest precinct house. Inside, a uniformed man wearing sergeant's stripes watched him from behind a desk as he came across the room.

"I've come to request protection for my employees," Adam said.

The policeman eyed him neutrally. "Yeah? From what?"

"I've been advised that members of an organization known as the Mafia are likely to attempt to injure me and those associated with me."

The sergeant leaned back in his chair; his eyes were careful now.

"What are you talking about, Mister? You've been kidded. We got no Mafia in this town."

"That was my opinion. Thank you." Adam turned away.

"Just a minute!" the cop barked. "Who told you to come down here and stir up trouble? What's your name?"

"Sister Louella urged me to report the situation to the police," Adam replied. "My name is Adam." He turned again as if to go.

"Hold it, Mister; I'm not done talking to you." The policeman pulled a pad toward him. "Adam, hah! First name?"

"Yes."

"Let's have the rest of the handle."

"I don't understand your proposal."

"Your name, Mister—first, last, and middle."

"Occasionally Sister Louella addresses me as Adam Nova; however, I am usually called Adam, or Mr. Adam."

"No games, palsy. Just the name—or have I got to get tough?"

"I have no further data to give you on the subject of my name."

"Like that, huh? How'd you like to spend the night in the tank?"

"I would find that inconvenient."

"You bet you would. Now give—before I get mad."

"I assume you use the word in the sense of 'angry,'

rather than 'insane,' " Adam commented. "Am I to understand that you can anticipate emotional states?"

"Another nut," the sergeant said. "Go on—get out of here. Beat it—fast."

Adam left without further conversation.

[3]

A man was waiting for him as he approached the store; he stepped into Adam's path, blocking his way. He was a large, youngish man with heavy black eyebrows and numerous small scars on his cheekbones and chin and around his eyes.

"You and me want to talk," he said.

"Are you a representative of Mr. Art Basom?"

"You could say that."

The man locked a large hand on Adam's arm and exerted a painful pressure.

"But I ain't such a pushover like Art," he said, smiling into Adam's face. "He said you had a couple fancy tricks; try 'em on Tod Marduk and see what it buys you, chump."

Adam attempted to free himself by the same maneuver by which he had numbed Basom's arm; but the smiling man's grip held firm, the fingers digging in painfully. Without conscious volition, Adam's knee came up, only to encounter a hipbone as Marduk pivoted to the right. Continuing the same motion, Marduk twisted Adam's arm deftly behind him, bringing his wrist up to the small of his back. The pain made him gasp. He felt the Kumelli voice assuming control; this time he allowed it.

"We just take a little walk, chump," Marduk was saying. "Back this way where I got my heap parked."

Adam bent his knees suddenly; violent pain shot through his shoulder. Marduk, surprised, loosened his grip. Adam spun, caught the man solidly across the cheekbone with his elbow, chopped down on the pressure point at the base of the neck, chopped again at the temple, then doubled his fist with his middle knuckle protruding and struck Marduk solidly at the base of the sternum, at the same time delivering a stamping kick to the right leg just above the knee, bringing the side of his shoe down across the kneecap, raking the shin, to smash down on Marduk's arch.

145

Adam/Kumelli stepped back as Marduk fell to the pavement and lay inert. A pair of passersby gaped, skirted the scene, and hurried away. Adam went on to the store, holding his right wrist with his left hand.

Louella stifled a scream when she saw him.

"Adam—what's happened? Your face is white as a sheet! Your arm—what—?"

"The shoulder is injured," Adam said. He was seeing the woman through a thickening haze of light-shot, silvery blackness. "The pain is . . . indescribably intense. . . ."

He was lying on his back. Sister Louella was bending over him, her face swollen and blotchy, her mascara dissolving, her rouge smeared.

"It was my fault, I never should of sent you down there," she was wailing. "You just lay quiet, Adam; I'll get a doctor to that arm. . . ."

She was gone. Adam was only vaguely aware of time passing, of his consciousness wavering in and out of awareness. A man was there, a thin, bald, perspiring man who gently manipulated his injured arm.

"It's badly dislocated," the doctor was saying to Louella, who was sobbing and sniffling. "I'd like to do X rays . . ." The voices faded away, points of multicolored light winked and flickered.

". . . his hand," the doctor was saying from far away. "Broken bones . . . don't understand . . . report this to the police . . ." His voice was gone. Adam concentrated on the lights; watching them seemed to make the pain more remote, as if it were an unimportant sensation happening far away, to someone else. . . .

One light swam closer, evolving into an intricately convoluted pattern that pulsated like a living thing. Adam reached out to it, touched it—

"Adam! don't break contact! Tell me where you are! You must answer me!"

Adam recognized the voice of Arthur Poldak. He did not answer, but moved on to other voices, touching one here and there . . .

". . . *hát itt mi mergy végbe. . . ?"*

". . . *shouldn't have done it, should have said no, should* . . ."

". . . *men ju var min farfar skeppare acksa . . ."*

146

—something was shaking Adam. He opened his eyes. Louella was bending over him again.

"Adam . . . wake up! The doctor left you; ran off, there's men here—they—" Her speech ended in a shrill squawk as she was flung roughly aside by a man with a broad, swarthy face with a texture like old leather. Adam started up; a blow to the side of the head knocked him back. Hands caught him, pulled him from the bed, thrust him across the room. He staggered, then caught his balance. Waves of pain radiated from his strapped-up arm as he was urged forward through the door, down the stairs.

[4]

Adam sat in a straight wooden chair under an exposed sixty-watt bulb in a windowless room. The concrete floor was cold to his bare feet. He was naked; he shivered in a chill draft. Someone laughed. The swarthy man sauntered around from behind him and stood looking down at him, smiling a crooked smile. He took a leisurely puff from a cigarette and dropped it on the floor. The concrete rasped under his sole as he extinguished it.

"I'm Detective Sergeant Fedders," he said in a gravelly voice. "I've got information you're a receiver of stolen goods. I want names, dates, amounts. Start now."

"Your information is incor—" A slap delivered from the side rocked Adam's head. His ear rang. He blinked away pain tears.

"Talk it up feller. No stalling. I've got no time to waste."

"In that case, I suggest you discontinue this conversation," Adam said. His words were blurry; he tasted blood inside his mouth. A tooth seemed to be loose.

Fedders leaned close. "A grand larceny felony can get you three to ten just like that." He snapped his fingers with a sound like breaking bone. "Now, if you act nice, give me what I want—maybe I can give you a break."

Adam said nothing. The unseen hand slapped him again. Ungentle hands thrust him back upright. He felt Kumelli attempt to take control, but automatically suppressed the *voice*.

Fedder caught Adam's chin in a painful grip and tilted his head back.

147

"I haven't checked your prints out yet, feller," he said in a confidential tone. "No reason to—yet. Could be it's all a mistake. Depends on how you cooperate. Now, you give me a nice confession, with all the details, and maybe it won't have to go any farther; after all, I like to see an old con make it on the straight—more or less."

"Your remarks seem to be meaningless," Adam said. "As well as contradictory in their implications—"

A slap cut that off.

"Don't rib me, Jake; I know cuff burns when I see 'em. And some of these hick sheriffs make scars on a man's skull a lot like the ones you're carrying. Don't tell me you haven't done time, I know better."

"I have been incarcerated, yes—"

"You use too many fancy words, Jake. Keep it simple; I'm just an ordinary college graduate, not one of these smart cops. All I want from you is a list of jobs you've fenced, say in the last two weeks."

"Please define the word 'fence' in this context."

Fedders snapped the cigarette aside and folded his arms. He sighed. "Look, feller; here's how you've been working it: the stuff is heisted—by you or somebody else. You boys contact the owner and tip them how to get it back—and the price. Neat, open, and almost legal. OK? Now—"

"If by the interrogative 'OK' you mean to solicit my agreement in your hypothesis, I demur," Adam said.

"Keep it simple," Fedders said in an ominous tone. "I told you once."

"I employ the minimal locution consonant with precision," Adam said. "If you wish me to speak in a more cumbersome dialect, please specify the parameters."

"Geeze, the guy ain't human," a voice said behind Adam.

"Get this, Mr. Adam," Fedders said. "You can play dumb—or you can play smart, I admit it's a switch—but before you leave this room you open up like a cargo hatch, got me? So you might as well start talking."

Adam opened his mouth to speak; as he did, he was aware of a movement behind him; a tensing. He *reached* then, touched the mind of the man poised behind his chair—a patrolman named Kowalski, he saw, absorbing the man's personality gestalt in a swift glimpse. Kowalski's hand was raised, ready for a blow, waiting for Fedders' signal, his thoughts totally concentrated on the pleasurable anticipation of the impact. Adam *groped,* found the operative point, suppressed nervous activity in certain neural circuits in Kowalski's brain. He *felt* his ferocity drain away. He withdrew the contact.

"Your remarks are meaningless to me, Mr. Fedders," Adam said. "I wish to go now." He stood. Fedders stepped back, his eyes going past Adam. There was a strangled grunt from Kowalski.

"Boss—I been thinking—I don't like the job. I quit."

Fedders snarled and reached for Adam as if to take him by the throat. Adam *thrust* at him—

Fedders fell as if he had been shot through the brain. Kowalski made a distressed sound and scrambled to kneel by his chief. Adam headed for the door. As he reached it, he became aware of the chill.

"Where are my clothes?" he inquired mildly of Kowalski; the latter, fully occupied in chafing Fedders' wrists, failed to answer. Adam probed past the intangible barrier into the interior of the policeman's mind, scanned for the information he needed. . . .

He saw a jumbled panorama of hopes, fears, compulsions, taboos. He saw the intangible form that was Kowalski's naked being, cramped, twisted, distorted by the forces that had acted on it since the traumatic moment of his birth. And beyond it he saw the convolution skein of pressures applied by the society of which Kowalski was a part and a reflection, saw the looming dominance of Fedders.

He switched to Fedders' unconscious brain, probed for the same level of subconscious motivation that he had discovered in the other man—

And burst through into an even more bewildering structure of conflicting ambition and ideal, of self-love and self-hate, of anxiety, aspiration, cowardice, steely courage, of secret vice and secret shame, of unremembered heroism and an abiding drive toward a goal that was nebulous, distant, but wreathed in an aura of the ultimately desirable, eternally beyond reach. . . .

He saw the intertwining threads of motivation, followed them back to their sources in illusions, promises, threats, fears. Orders from superiors, pressures from influential individuals, offers of financial and political gain—and regrets for early idealisms abandoned, tarnished integrity, disappointed dreams. He saw the naked ego that was Fedders impaled on a dilemma of infinite complexity; tortured, but somehow, not broken; defiled, but not beyond the still faintly glowing hope of redemption.

He withdrew, shaken and dizzy.

". . . better just get out while the getting's good, Mister," Kowalski was saying. "Your clothes're in that locker—get 'em on and beat it—fast. I don't know nothing—ain't going to know nothing."

[5]

He found Sister Louella at the apartment, huddled on the bed, moaning. She heaved herself upright as Adam entered the room.

"I thought you was dead, I thought they'd taken you off to the pen and I'd never see you again, I thought—"

"You were mistaken," Adam interrupted. "I see no benefit to be gained from a recital of misconceptions of the state of affairs."

"What'd they do to you? You all right?"

"As you see. I was struck three times by a Patrolman Kowalski, but otherwise not physically assaulted. However, my arm is still decidedly painful."

"I'll pack, Adam," Louella gobbled. "We'll put what we can in your car and be on the way in half an hour."

"I hope you have a pleasant trip," Adam said. "I'm not going."

"Why not? What's happened to change your mind?"

"You're well aware of the incidents of the day, Sister Louella," Adam said. "I assume that the question is of the rhetorical type which presumably is asked in order to elicit verbal reinforcement of security feelings."

"All I know is that Art Basom hoodlum came around, and then the cops beat you up, and that's hint enough for me we ain't welcome!"

"A basically accurate summation of the dynamic elements involved in my decision," Adam concurred. "However, I've become aware of new factors which have

150

caused me to modify my intention."

Louella looked at him, her mouth sagging open. She laughed in a manner suggestive of incipient hysteria.

"Lordy, you're a caution, Adam! While we're making a mint and everything's rosy—you decide to quit, give it all up; but after the mobsters and the crooked cops jump you, you decide to stay on!"

"Of course," Adam said. "You find that remarkable?"

"No—not anymore," Sister Louella said, shaking her head. "I guess I'm learning not to be surprised at anything you do, Adam. Never again. What's next?"

"I've learned that certain inequitable conditions exist," Adam said. "I feel a strong urge to correct them, for reasons which are not clear to me. Accordingly, it will be necessary for me to amass a much larger aggregation of monetary wealth than I heretofore contemplated. I'll consider the matter and determine an appropriate course of action. In the meantime, we'll continue with business as usual."

13

[1]

On the following day, Adam composed a list of several hundred items for purchase, with sources and prices, and delegated the chore of acquisition to Alvin and Lester, a new employee. The time thus freed he devoted to a detailed examination of business methods and principles, extracting the data from the minds of a dozen assorted merchants, brokers, bankers, and stock manipulators. It was the activities of the latter group which most interested him, involving as they did the symbolic manipulation of commodities, rather than the actual handling of goods, equipment, and personnel.

After lunch he approached the offices of Rifkin, Katz, O'Toole, and Eisenstein, and secured an appointment with a Miss Gluck, a young woman with carefully arranged false hair and the title of Account Executive.

"I wish to invest in the stock market," he explained, having accepted a chair in the sterile, gray-rugged, gray-lit room.

Miss Gluck nodded, giving Adam a quick, assessing glance.

"Anything particular you had in mind, Mr. Uh—or may I suggest—"

"I intend to take a position in Seaboard Metals," he said.

". . . one of our mutual funds . . ." Miss Gluck's voice trailed off. "Seaboard Metals, did you say?" She pulled a book toward her, leafed through it, shook her head, closed the book.

"I wouldn't recommend it," she said. "Now, we feel that a small growth fund—"

"Am I to understand that it isn't possible for me to initiate my investment in Seaboard Metals through you?" Adam asked.

Miss Gluck smiled a pained smile. "As I was just explaining, Mr. Uh—"

"Why do you address me as Mr. Uh?" Adam inquired interestedly.

"Maybe I didn't get the name just correct," Miss Gluck snapped.

"Adam."

"Seaboard is a nothing proposition, Mr. Adam. Undercapitalized, no growth potential. Nothing I could recommend—"

"I haven't requested a recommendation," Adam explained. "I merely require an agent to handle the transactions."

Miss Gluck's lips thinned. "Well. And just what did you have in mind? We don't handle accounts under fifty dollars, you understand."

"My initial investment will be twenty thousand dollars," Adam said mildly.

152

Miss Gluck sat up straighter.

"We'd have to have a certified check, of course," she said in a voice from which much of the edge was gone.

"Oh. Then that will entail some delay," Adam said. Miss Gluck's lip lifted a tasteful millimeter. She smiled a sour smile.

"I had expected that currency would be acceptable," Adam added, rising. "I regret having wasted your time as well as my own."

"Did you say—currency? You mean money?" Miss Gluck's voice carried a rising note of incredulity. She laughed, a short cackle not in consonance with her polished exterior. "Well, I guess we could stretch a point and accept cash, Mr. Adam," she said.

"Thank you," Adam said, and extracted a fat sheaf of bills from his jacket pocket. He placed the money on the desk under Miss Gluck's wide-open eyes. She reached out to riffle the stack.

"Kindly purchase the shares I requested as soon as possible," Adam said. "I shall have further instructions for you as required."

"Wait a minute!" Miss Gluck called after him, scrambling to her feet. "Don't you even want a receipt?"

[2]

Twenty-five hours after Adam's transaction with Rifkin and Company, Seaboard Metals announced a three-to-one stock split on the basis of a newly perfected method of extraction of light metals from sea water. Adam ordered the sale of his shares at thirty-three thousand five hundred dollars and transferred his interest to Allied Minerals, an obscure firm, as Miss Gluck assured him, eking out a marginal existence via certain borax holdings in New Mexico. Within two days, Allied announced a merger with Southwest Chemical, and the new firm, Southwest Allied, quietly sold out to Standard Oil of New Mexico for a round ten million. Adam's new net worth was in excess of one hundred thousand dollars.

In the weeks that followed he shifted his interest almost daily, each time to a stock which almost immediately rose sharply in value; each time eliciting effusive congratulations first from Miss Gluck, then from a Mr. Rumbert, at last from Mr. Rifkin himself.

"You have a remarkable nose for the market, my boy," the senior partner told Adam in tones of warm congratulation. "I don't mind saying that even I didn't anticipate any such jump in sugar beet futures as we've seen in the last day or two."

"Yes," Adam said.

"Well." Rifkin looked a trifle taken aback by Adam's indifferent response to his effusion. "Just what, ah, did you have in mind now?" he inquired. "As it happens, the firm has been entrusted with the handling of new debenture issue—"

"I'm closing out my account," Adam said.

". . . which I think I can assure you . . ." Rifkin paused; his expression underwent a change.

"Closing your account?" He sat up straighter. "Mr. Adam, if our handling of your affairs has been in any way unsatisfactory—if any employee of mine has failed to maintain the standards of the firm . . ."

"I have no complaint," Adam said. "I would like to have cash; hundred dollar notes will be satisfactory."

"But—this is most unexpected! Haven't we done a job for you? Why, in less than three weeks we've increased the net worth of your holdings by an unprecedented five hundred percent."

"Your company has merely carried out my instructions, Mr. Rifkin," Adam pointed out. "I've now concluded this portion of my program, and wish to liquidate my holdings in order to accelerate the rate of earnings. No criticism implied."

"Accelerate! No legitimate brokerage firm could make a better showing than we have!"

Adam said nothing.

"You understand you'll have to expect to absorb a loss," Rifkin snapped when it was clear Adam did not intend to dispute the point. "Dumping over six thousand shares of a sensitive issue on no notice—"

"Mr. Rifkin, kindly telephone Mr. Harvey L. Platt of Des Moines and inform him that my block is on offer at twenty-five dollars."

"That's five dollars over the current quotation," Rifkin

said contemptuously. Adam said nothing. Rifkin managed a suggestion of a kindly smile.

"I suggest you allow me to sound out a number of contacts who may be willing to meet the market for a purchase of this size—"

"My block represents tie-breaking power and control of the company, inasmuch as opposing factions are each in possession of some forty percent of the total issue; thus it commands a price in excess of nominal value," Adam remarked mildly. Rifkin's face reddened.

"Well, since you're adamant," he muttered, and reached for the telephone. He gave terse instructions, hung up ungently.

"May I ask who'll be handling your affairs now?" he asked curtly.

"I will continue to handle my own affairs," Adam replied.

On Rifkin's face, outraged pomposity struggled with curiosity. He leaned on one elbow, arranged a shrewd look on his foxy features.

"If you're going into something," he said to a far corner of the room, "I might be in a position to swing some capital behind it. Real capital."

Adam considered this. He nodded. "That will be satisfactory," he said. "You may place thirteen million dollars at my disposal. I estimate a twelve percent profit within ten days."

Rifkin's mouth was open. "Thirteen million? Are you out of your mind?" He thrust himself upright. "I might consent to match your own personal investment. Might, mind you. But I'd have to know something about the venture, naturally."

"In that case, we'll be unable to work together," Adam said. He rose. "Kindly send the cash to me at my apartment this afternoon."

[3]

The money was delivered: one hundred and fifty-one thousand three hundred and forty-one dollars and thirty cents, twenty-five cents of which Adam gave to the messenger. Louella's eyes widened when Adam casually

155

replied to her query as to the contents of the steel box.

"All that money—here? Lordy, Adam—what if we're robbed? What if the place burns down? What if—"

"The cash will not remain here," Adam said.

"What you going to do with it?"

"First, I'll make distributions to certain persons in need," Adam said absently; his eyes were half-closed; he seemed lost in thought. Louella caught his arm.

"Adam—you're talking crazy again! Give it away, you said! What you think you are, God Almighty? That's *our* money, it's for *us* to use, to buy all the things we need—you and me!"

"Many individuals are in great need of the essentials of life," Adam said calmly. "A Mrs. Petrino, who lives at 3452 Agnes Street, urgently requires food, medicine, and fuel. Arthur Pomfer, residing at 902 Blite Avenue, Apartment 6, is in need of funds to defray his back rent—"

"What do I care about that?" Louella said fiercely.

"To me this seems obvious," Adam said. "Are you able to feel contentment while aware that corrigible negative elements exist in the societal matrix?"

Louella made a gesture of dismissal.

"What's come over you, Adam? All of a sudden you're all fired up to uplift the poor, going to be a big philanthropist, give away a fortune! Don't you know that's wasted effort, Adam? You pay somebody's rent, it just comes due again! You feed some ne'er-do-well, he just gets hungry next mealtime!"

"I intend to embark on a continuing program," Adam said mildly. "A young girl, Angela Funk, of 21 Parnell Road, needs immediate cash for the purchase of spectacles; she is also in need of a special diet, as well as corrective surgery for a deformity of the left foot."

"Adam—you go spreading yourself thin, throwing that money to the winds—pretty soon it'll be all gone—and what good will you do? Some good-for-nothing's got his rent paid up, somebody gets a free operation by rights she ought to go to work and pay for herself—and what have you and me got? Nothing! We'll be as poor as the rest of 'em—and then what can you do?"

"I intend to maintain the level of funds—"

"Charity begins at home! What about me? Have I got a

closet full of dresses? Have I got the back treatments I been putting off, trying to help you get on your feet? This Angela somebody—she needs an operation; what about my gall bladder condition, that I never complained about because I didn't want to worry you? What—"

"You are in need of surgery?" Adam cut in.

"Dern right," Louella confirmed, her face mottled with emotion. "That's not the half of it. I need a orthopedic foundation like I seen—"

"Saw."

"—saw advertised in the paper. And I need a good rest, at that health spa out west where Mamie Eisenhower went—and I need—"

"I will of course arrange for any needed surgery and treatment for you," Adam said.

"Then you won't be giving our money away?"

"Your needs will be provided for."

"I'll need expense money, Adam, you can't send me off in the desert with no cash on hand. And I'll need clothes—you wouldn't expect me to show up among them—those society women looking like a scrub lady. And—"

"Kindly prepare a list of your requirements," Adam cut in in the way that he had learned was necessary when conversing with Louella.

"I will, Adam. You just don't go off half-cocked and do something foolish, promise me?"

Adam gazed at her with a neutral expression. Louella put her fists on her ample hips and glared back.

"Promise?" she repeated.

"I will of course take no action which I recognize as foolish," he said. "I assumed the question was rhetorical."

"What *are* you going to do?"

"I intend to place a series of wagers with a betting agent named Louis Welkert."

"You're going to *gamble* that cash away?"

"By no means; I intend to augment the money at a much more rapid rate than was possible by dealing in securities."

"You'll lose it all! Anyway, you won't find no—any bookie in town'll handle that kind o' money!"

"Mr. Welkert customarily accepts bets in excess of one million dollars."

"On what?"

"On anything a client desires. Mr. Welkert offers odds, and the better may accept or reject them; but Mr. Welkert's policy is never to refuse a tender."

"I never heard o' any such thing!"

"His business is conducted in secret to avoid taxation."

"Crooks," Louella whispered. "You had a taste o' that—you know what that kind of men are like! They'll eat you alive, Adam!"

Adam looked thoughtful. "I assume this is a hyperbole, and does not actually indicate an anticipation of anthropophagy."

"Oh, lordy, Adam," Louella wailed. "I don't know what to do with you! You're going out there and—and . . ." Her eyes searched Adam's face, which was relaxed, reflecting no particular emotion.

"What you going to bet on, Adam?"

"Initially, the outcome of the vote on a proposed county zoning law."

"You think you'll win?"

"Of course." He looked faintly surprised. "Otherwise I shouldn't bet, of course."

"How much?"

"Mr. Welkert will accept one hundred thousand at even money."

Louella sucked in her breath sharply.

"Double your money," she whispered. "But if you lose. . . ."

"As I said," Adam said, "I do not intend to lose."

[4]

Louis Welkert was a plump, round-faced, mild-mannered man with downy white hair and a face that suggested a kindly old Swiss cuckoo-clock maker, with the exception of his pale blue eyes. They flicked over Adam, probed once into his eyes, then looked at his chin.

"What can I do for you, sir?" he asked in a soft, tired voice.

Adam placed the steel box on the chipped oak desk. Outside the not recently washed window, a neon sign advertising Used Car Bargains flicked on and off.

"Next Tuesday's zoning election," Adam said.

The pale eyes went to the strong box, back to Adam's chin.

"What about it?"

"The measure won't pass."

Welkert reached up and scratched his chin.

"Who sent you around?"

"I got your name from Mr. Clyde P. Walmont III."

Welkert nodded. "Nice fellow, Wally. Good loser." He sat forward.

"I have a little money says the bill will fly," he said diffidently. "Six-four odds."

"I wish to place one hundred thousand—at even money."

Welkert pushed his lips in and out. "Oke," he said. "We'll take it all."

Adam opened the box and counted out a hundred thousand-dollar bills. Welkert nodded.

"We'll go down the street to the bank. Safe-deposit box in both names."

[5]

Leaving Welkert, Adam drove to Agnes Street, found a parking space half a block from number 3452, a decaying former mansion of blackened stone with a curling scrap of plywood nailed over the broken fanlight. Inside, in a rank odor of organic decay, he found the name Mrs. B. Petrino inscribed in an uncertain hand under the sprung door to a brass filigree mailbox marked 14.

He went up one flight, explored along a narrow hall littered with papers, burst cardboard boxes, bottles, a broken tricycle. Aluminum numbers were nailed to the black oak doors. Adam rapped at 14. A hoarse voice cawed a reply.

"I've brought you some money, Mrs. Petrino," Adam called. There was a moment's silence. Down the hall a door opened and a woman's head poked out to eye Adam without friendliness.

"Nate?" the cracked voice called from behind the door. Feet shuffled. The latch rattled, the door swung in a cautious inch. One bleared eye and the tip of a sharp, pale noise came into view. A thin hand came up to brush back a lock of grayish hair.

159

"You ain't Nate," the woman accused.

"That's correct," Adam extracted a precounted stack of new twenty-dollar bills from an inner pocket, proffered it. The thin hand started to reach, jerked back.

"What is this? You a counterfeiter? Or what?"

"I'm providing the funds you need."

"Yeah?" the hand shot out and took the money. "About time," the thin mouth snapped. "And you can tell that SOB I got plans for him. Where's he at?"

Adam's eyes half-closed; there was a pause. "At the present moment, Nate Petrino is drinking a draft beer at a bar called Pearl's Place, on Twenty-second, in Omaha."

"Ha! A gut-buster! Take the air, creep!"

Along the hall, a dozen sets of eyes followed Adam as he left the premises.

[6]

Blite Avenue was a prophetically named street on the far south side of the city, where a few large, crumbling frame houses built eighty years before by rich retired farmers huddled like fallen gentlewomen amid the crudity of warehouses and small manufacturing plants. Number 902 was one of the smaller houses; its shiplap siding was warped and paintless; net curtains black with age hung at the high, grimy windows. Broken gingerbread decorated the eaves; the porch had been badly patched with battered two-inch planks.

A small man with moth-eaten hair and a puckered face answered the bell. He wore a flowered vest—once Burgundy, now greenish black—a lilac shirt with red and green armbands, baggy brown trousers, sharply pointed shoes with knotted string. He looked Adam over, looked past him, scanned the curb, saw Adam's car, its red paint incongruous in the gray street.

"Been years since a salesman been here," Pomfer said. "What you selling? Not that I'm buying."

Adam took out a stack of new twenties. "I've brought your rent money," he said. Pomfer looked at the money, at Adam, back at the money, back at Adam.

"It's a new approach, I'll say that for it. What's the angle?"

"I'd like to explore the implications of your remarks," Adam said, "but I have a great deal to do today. I find the process of correcting inequities more time-consuming than I'd anticipated." He was still holding out the money. Pomfer made no move to take it. He leaned out, looked up and down the street.

"You the Candid Camera man?" he inquired.

"No."

Pomfer looked thoughtful. He frowned.

"What's the story, pal?"

"I'm simply giving you money."

Pomfer grinned a wise grin and shook his head. "Oh, no. You don't catch me that easy. I been around too long."

"You refuse to accept the money?" Adam's expression reflected deep puzzlement.

"Damn right. You think I was born yesterday? I—"

"No, you were born October 5, 1921. But—"

"—seen 'em all, chum . . ." Pomfer paused. His expression hardened.

"What's the idea snooping around me? What's my birthday to you? Who are you, some government wiseacre? You got nothing on me. And you can keep your bait; I'm not biting." Pomfer stepped back and slammed the door.

Adam made three more calls, conferring two hundred dollars for a delivery bike on a newsboy who accepted the money in silence and ran; one hundred and twenty dollars on an elderly woman on a park bench, who immediately brightened and offered, for an additional hundred and twenty, to show him a few tricks he hadn't seen before; three hundred dollars went to a plump and pregnant young woman with a bad complexion and an ill-tempered child clinging to a baby carriage which contained a messy infant and a six-pack of beer. She took the cash and listened in apparent amazement to Adam's explanation that the money was intended for an operation designed to render the recipient sterile. Her jaw clamped; her meaty features assumed a mottle hue. She cursed Adam, damned the Welfare Board and all its works, and ran the buggy over Adam's foot on her departure, which was abrupt.

Angela Funk was not at home. Adam *tuned*, located her behind the counter at an establishment bearing a hand-painted sign identifying it as Chuck's Diner Eat. She was a thin, pale girl with dead-looking hair, crooked teeth, and sharply pointed false pectorals. She slapped a pad down before Adam when he took a stool at the counter, jerked a well-chewed red pencil with a large yellow eraser from over her ear, and gave him a look of pained patience.

"I don't wish food, thank you," Adam said. "I've come—"

"We don't serve drinks here. This is a restaurant, not a bar." Angela grabbed back her pad from the counter and turned away.

"You need glasses," Adam said. "As well as—"

Angela spun on him. "Oh, yeah? Says who? What're you complaining about? You got a nerve—"

"Excuse me," Adam cut in, holding up a hand. "I wish to give you the money for an eye examination and the purchase of spectacles, and for surgery to your foot."

Angela's head jerked. Her face stretched. A yell of rage came from her mouth. A man at the end of the counter, the only customer present, slopped coffee down his jacket front and began to swear.

"Get out of here, you bum!" Angela shouted. "You come in off the street and start insulting me, I never seen you in my life, some of you bastards think just because a girl works you got a right to treat her like dirt, but let me tell you—"

Adam held out a sheaf of bills; Angela, hardly glancing at it, struck at his hand. Money went fluttering. The coffee drinker gaped, scrambled from his stool, began picking up new twenties.

"I assure you, Miss Funk—" Adam started.

"What's that money . . ." Angela gasped. Her face contorted with renewed fury. She seized a plate and threw it at Adam; he ducked and it smashed through the diner window.

"You dirty, lousy sex fiend! Coming in here, making filthy remarks, propositioning a decent girl!" Angela wailed, and subsided in tears. The swinging doors from the rear burst open and a large man in a soiled apron crashed through.

"What the—" he saw the money, picked up a bill, held it before his face with both hands as if reading the fine print. Angela squalled. The coffee drinker, having sidled to the door, stooped, grabbed up another bill and slipped outside. The big man roared and started around the counter. Angela grabbed him and began to screech, pointing at Adam. The big man swore and struck Angela aside, charged around the counter and through the door in pursuit of the coffee drinker.

Adam fled.

[7]

A small, sad-faced man in a gray suit badly in need of replacement watched in silence as Adam conferred one hundred dollars on an aged man he had encountered rooting in a wire wastebasket near a statue of a mounted soldier.

"I see you're a practicing Christian," the small man commented to Adam as the old fellow scuttled away, looking over his shoulder. "Alas, brother, you're casting your bread on hostile waters. They'll not turn away from the ungodly life; what they'll do, they'll drink it up in cheap wine." He smacked his mouth and studied Adam's jacket intently.

"Many individuals suffer from conditions which can be remedied by cash," Adam explained. "My intention is to correct this state of affairs, which occasions me discomfort. I now perceive that I underestimated the complexity of the task."

"Amen, brother. Bringing Jesus' light to darkened souls is the hardest task a man can undertake. Now you're going about it the wrong way." The little man offered a small calloused hand. "I'm Brother Chitwood, and I think I can help you, praise His name."

Adam accepted the hand gravely. "That's very kind of you, Brother Chitwood. I'm Brother Adam. What recompense will you require?"

"Why, bless you, Brother Adam, there's no question of pay. An opportunity to do the Lord's work is recompense enough. Just, ah, how much—that is, what size program have you got in mind?"

"I've allocated a quota of ten thousand per day; however, so far today, I've succeeded in distributing only thirteen hundred and forty dollars."

The small man moistened his lips and swallowed. "You got it on you?" he almost whispered. "Let's see."

Adam extracted two half-inch-thick bundles of bills from two inner pockets. "As you see, I've fallen far short of my quota."

"Praise the Lord," the small man said with obvious deep feeling. "From whom all blessings flow. Tell you what: I'll take over for you and see that this bundle gets into needy hands, while you go back for more, OK?"

"Excellent. I'll supply the names of the intended recipients—"

"No need, Brother Adam; I know more deserving cases than you can shake a stick at. Just leave me have the cash, and it'll be gone before you know it."

"I regret my lack of experience in this work," Adam said as he passed across the bundles of bills, returned to his pocket for another, plus a sheaf of loose twenties. "I sought appropriate guidance, but to no avail. I deduce that the techniques of relieving distress are less practiced than techniques of acquisition of money."

"So true, Brother Adam, so true." The small man tucked the money away. "I'd best be on my way now, got lots of ground to cover." He waved a hand and hurried away into the gathering twilight.

14

[1]

Adam returned to Mr. Welkert's establishment on Tuesday. Mr. Welkert was glum but businesslike.

"You called it, Mr. Adam," he said.

"I'd prefer to allow the sum to ride," Adam said. "I wish to wager the full amount on the outcome of a boxing contest."

Welkert looked at Adam and rubbed the side of his nose.

"Two hundred grand—on what fight?"

"The Flyweight Championship bout to be staged on Thursday at the Municipal Arena. Kugel will win."

"A flyweight fight—I never heard of the guy," Welkert complained.

Adam waited. Welkert drew the phone to him, dialed, carried on a muttered conversation.

"Even money OK?" he inquired as he hung up.

"Quite satisfactory."

"You're on," Welkert nodded. He took a sheet of paper from the desk, wrote on it, handed it over.

"My marker, good as gold, ask anybody."

Adam accepted the paper. "The bout is scheduled for eight p.m. I'll call on you at ten."

"What for?" Welkert allowed himself a crooked smile. "Kugel's got about the same chance as a fifth of bourbon at an Elk's smoker."

"You're mistaken," Adam said. "Good afternoon, Mr. Welkert."

[2]

Welkert's good humor had vanished when Adam arrived at precisely 10 p.m. on the following Thursday evening. There was another man with Welkert, sitting in a straight chair in a shadowy corner, smoking a cigarette in an ivory holder. Welkert took a paper sack from the desk drawer, dumped out bundled cash.

"Two hundred grand. Count it."

Adam glanced at it. "Substantially correct," he said. "I—"

"What've you got, X-ray eyes, you don't need a count?"

"I can estimate the number of certificates to a close tolerance by gauging the thickness of a stack visually. However, I don't wish to collect the money at this time. I have another wager I wish to make."

"Another wager," Welkert said without enthusiasm. "What's it this time?"

"What odds will you offer on a man's death?"

"Hah?" Welkert leaned forward, thrusting his face toward Adam. "What you pushing at me now?"

"Mr. Lyman F. Bossman will commit suicide tonight."

"Bossman? You mean the Assistant DA?"

"Yes, Mr. Bossman is employed in that capacity."

"Where'd you get this from?" Welkert demanded. He no longer looked like an old Swiss clockmaker.

"From a source I don't wish to divulge."

"Just a minute," a quiet voice spoke from the dark corner. The man sitting there leaned forward to snub out his cigarette. "Before entering into any contract I think we need to know a little more about this source of yours, Mr. Adam." He was a dark, thin, elegant man with a long nose, close-set eyes, a glint of cufflink at his wrist.

"This is a firm condition to your accepting my bet?" Adam asked.

"Uh-huh." The thin man smiled. "If you don't mind."

"I was cautioned by Sister Louella not to divulge the information. She felt that it would prejudice my hearers, probably giving rise to a conviction that I am mentally unbalanced. But in this instance, the benefit to be derived is such that I feel justified in violating her ordinance. I'll therefore confide that I obtained the information from Mr. Bossman."

"Bossman told you he was going to do a Dutch?" Welkert asked in a tone reflecting skepticism.

"Not in person; it was merely his voice."

"His voice."

"That's correct."

"You heard his voice? How?"

"I attuned to it."

"You were eavesdropping outside his office, or his bedroom—or what?"

"No, I was riding an urban transit vehicle at the time."

"He was sitting beside you on the bus, talking to himself?"

"No, he was at his country club."

The two men eyed Adam for a moment; then both leaned back, visibly relaxing. They exchanged glances.

"And you want to bet the two hundred thousand Bossman pulls the chain tonight," Welkert said.

"I assume you're employing an idiom equivalent to self-destruction."

"Oh, yeah, I got two, three idiots working for me. What kind of odds you have in mind, Mr. Adam?"

"On the basis of statistical considerations, odds of one

thousand to one would of course not be excessive. However, since your resources are limited, ten to one will be acceptable."

Welkert looked at the thin man, who nodded.

"Sure, we'll go along, Mr. Adam. Tonight, you say. What time?"

"Mr. Bossman isn't sure yet. He intends to complete certain arrangements first."

"Oh, sure, a fellow would want to make some arrangements first. Well, nice talking to you, Mr. Adam."

"I'll return at seven a.m. for my winnings," Adam said. "If that's agreeable to you."

"Sure, seven a.m. whatever you say. Not going to let it ride this time, eh?"

"It would be pointless to continue, since your capitalization will have been wiped out by the payment to me of two million dollars," Adam pointed out.

[3]

In the apartment Adam prepared a simple meal of yoghurt, wheat germ, Pro-ten, and organically grown honey, and retired. Sister Louella had been in Denver for over a week now; Adam thought of tuning to her *voice*, but reflected that she would probably resent the invasion of her privacy. He listened idly to other *voices*, the incessant background babble which he had long since learned to tune below the conscious threshold at will. Adam did not think of the *voices* as people; they were merely disembodied entities, existing in a nebulous medium he had never attempted to visualize. They seemed usually to be in a state of excitement, arguing, pleading, haranguing. . . .

". . . *Adam! There you are! I was afraid I'd lost you for good! Listen to me, Adam! I want to know where you are! This is Arthur Poldak. Where are you, Adam. . . ?*"

The idea of making a specific response never occurred to Adam. The *voices* spoke; he listened. It was a one-way traffic. He tuned in, ignoring the urgent call as he ignored the content of the other *voices*. The fact that the *voice* of Poldak called his name seemed in no way remarkable to him. He remembered the Poldak voice dimly as one that had once invaded his mind and attempted to push the *me* aside. He harbored no resentment; but neither was he desirous of yielding control of his body to another.

He woke promptly at 6 a.m., dressed, ate another meal identical with his dinner, and repaired to the office of Mr. Welkert, where he found the door locked. He rapped, but received no response. He reached out, sensed that the building was empty.

For a moment he stood under the forlorn banners of the abandoned used-car lot, bleak in the chilly dawn, utterly confused. He turned again, probing at longer range, quickly located the intangible pattern gestalt that was Mr. Welkert. The betting agent, he perceived, was in a hotel room some miles distant, speaking on the telephone:

"... open the paper, and there it is! Front page! The garbage man found him, every bone in his body busted—and they're calling it murder!"

"Wait'll I check this out." Adam recognized the voice of the thin man from Welkert's office.

"Look, Siggy, I don't like this. What about that pigeon Adam? Did he knock Bossman off? Or what? I don't like it!"

"You don't have to like it. Stay by the phone. I'll be back to you."

It was a fifteen-minute drive through the early morning streets to the hotel where Mr. Welkert occupied a twelfth-floor suite. Adam went directly to the elevator and rode up, stepped off in a small foyer. Air conditioning murmured softly. He rapped at the door, an austere slab of oiled teak.

A man Adam did not know opened the door. Behind him Adam saw Welkert, pouring a drink.

"I've come for my money, Mr. Welkert," Adam called. Welkert spun, dropping the bottle, which gurgled forth onto the fawn-colored rug. Welkert swore.

"You know this bum, boss?" the door opener inquired. He was a small, wiry man with a crooked jaw, wearing black trousers and a white shirt, open at the neck.

"I know him," Welkert growled, coming forward. "Al, clean that up." Welkert glanced into the corridor, invited Adam in with a tilt of his head. Adam went past him, stood in the center of the room. It was an elegant apartment, decorated in pale brown and white and gold. Wide windows offered a view over the city.

"How'd you find this place?" Welkert demanded.

"I prefer not to divulge that information," Adam said.

"Oh, that gag again," Welkert said. He lit up a cigarette, blew out smoke, squinting through it.

"You're in plenty trouble, guy," he said. "Cops are on their way here right now."

Al's head jerked at the words. Adam regarded Welkert calmly. "I would like to have my money at once," he said. "I have a full day scheduled—"

"You hear what I said?" Welkert snapped. "Cops, buddy-boy. Cops that want to ask you some questions about Bossman."

"I know nothing of Mr. Bossman, other than that he took his own life at twenty minutes past two a.m. this morning."

"How do you know what time he pulled the plug? It wasn't in the papers."

"I prefer not to divulge—"

"Yeah, yeah, I know. You don't say much, do you, pal? You've got a nice angle working for you, whatever it is—I'll say that. But you're half-smart, punk. You blew it bad when you took me on. I don't know how you worked it, but it stinks from here to Sing Sing. You can dust now."

"You don't intend to pay me the money you owe?"

"Get going, chump. Do I look like I was soft in the head?"

"Your cranium appears to be of average permeability," Adam said. "But—"

"All right, out!" Welkert snapped. "Al, show this boob the door. And if I see you hanging around, I'll blow the whistle for real, understand?"

"No, I don't," Adam began, and was interrupted by a jab in the side. He turned; the man called Al was aiming a pistol at him.

"Lift 'em," Al said.

"Skip that," Welkert cut in. "He's not ironed. Just throw him out. Walk him down to the lot."

"Walk, you," Al said, and made as if to prod Adam again; Adam's hand came down in a hard chop at Al's wrist. The gun bounced away. Adam heard a muffled exclamation from behind him, sensed movement—

Blinding light exploded in his head.

169

4

Adam was dimly aware of being half dragged, half carried. His skull ached terribly. There was something he should do, but his limbs refused to answer his commands.

The light grew dimmer, then brightened. There was a sense of motion. Another sound, and motion ceased. Hands urged him forward.

His legs worked, after a fashion. He felt sick, but was able to see now. He was in a large, concrete-floored room, where rows of automobiles were ranked under hanging lights. His feet and those of Al rasped on the floor as the gunman urged him across toward a small door.

Outside, the air was cold. Adam shuddered, stumbled. Al cursed and heaved him erect, pushed him forward. They made their way along a narrow bricked alley between plain walls. Street sounds came from ahead. As they emerged into brighter light, Al gave him a final shove. Adam tottered a few steps, almost fell as he stepped off the curb. Someone shouted. Brakes squealed—

There was an impact, dull and remote. Adam seemed to be flying through bottomless space. It was almost a pleasant sensation until he smashed into a wall he hadn't seen.

5

Adam returned to consciousness in an airy, pale-green-walled room, lying on his back in a crisp, soft bed. A vase of roses was beside him. There were unfamiliar chemical odors in the air, along with the known smells of flowers and food and disinfectant. A woman in white was standing nearby with her back to him, filling a syringe. She turned, started when she saw that his eyes were open, watching her.

"Well, we're awake at last." She put a hand on his forehead. "How are we feeling?"

"I don't understand the use of the plural pronoun in that construction," Adam said. "I can state that I feel weak and nauseated. You are of course aware how you feel."

"Sure, you just go back to sleep," the nurse said, nodding. He watched as she swabbed his arm and gave him the injection; then he closed his eyes and let it all drift away.

. . .

The next time he woke a man was there, a plumply smiling man with thinning hair and pink cheeks, dressed in a short-sleeved collarless white tunic.

"Well, there you are," the man said, and reached for Adam's wrist. "You've had quite a rest, sir. Feeling better, are you?"

"By comparison with my condition at my last interval of consciousness, yes. However, by comparison with the condition I think of as normal, no."

The doctor looked startled, then managed a smile. "You've been a very sick man, sir. But you've made a fine recovery. You'll be on your feet—that is to say," he hurried on, seeming flustered, "you'll be fully recovered before you know it."

"That statement appears paradoxical," Adam said.

"Eh?" The doctor gave a forced chuckle. "Figure of speech," he said. "Now—whom would you like to have us call—to notify of the accident, that is?"

"That won't be necessary," Adam said.

"I see." The doctor looked blank. "Actually, sir, we don't know your name. You were carrying no identification. . . ."

"Adam."

"Well, you've had us wondering, Mr. Adam. No one you wish to call, you say. Perhaps your lawyer. . . ?"

"For what purpose would I require the services of a lawyer?"

"Well, there are some routine items, of course. The matter of, ah, payment, and so on. . . ."

"What payment do you refer to?"

"For your treatment. Your skull was fractured, you know, and amputations cost money, as I'm sure you're aware."

"I don't wish an amputation," Adam said. "But perhaps this is another figure of speech. . . ?"

"Your leg was badly mangled, Mr. Adam," the doctor said sternly. "I had no choice if I was to save your life. I did what in my considered professional opinion was best under the circumstances."

Adam raised his head, surveyed the length of his body beneath the pale pink blanket. Only one foot jutted up at the position where he had been accustomed to see two.

"I don't like to press you at this time, Mr. Adam," the medical man went on, "but for the hospital records we need certain information, as I said. The business office has its rules, you know." He attempted a smile, dropped it, waiting.

"I'll be unable to walk," Adam said.

"Now, Mr. Adam, let me ease your mind as to that. In a matter of a few weeks—as soon as the stump is healed—we can fit you with a prosthetic device. Some marvelous work has been done in prosthesis in recent years. Costly, of course, but I'm sure you'll want the best. Now, where do you bank, Mr. Adam?"

"I don't."

"You have a checking account, surely?"

"No."

"Mr. Adam, who handles your financial affairs?"

"I had some help, briefly, from a Brother Chitwood. Otherwise, I attend to the disposal of money personally."

"What I'm getting at," the doctor said sharply, "is how do you intend to go about paying your bill?"

"I have money in my pocket," Adam said.

"Yes—I know. Twelve hundred and twenty dollars. It was placed in the hospital safe."

"You may extract your fee from that sum," Adam said.

"Mr. Adam, twelve hundred dollars won't cover half what you owe," the doctor snapped. "Why, for four weeks you've occupied a private room, had round-the-clock nursing care—in addition to the cost of surgery, anesthetist, ambulance service, blood—do you realize you took twelve pints of AB negative, a very rare type—"

"I have no other money," Adam said.

"No other money?" The doctor's face darkened. "I assumed—that amount of cash in your pockets—your clothing was new and expensive—surely—"

"I gave it away," Adam said. "Except for the sum I wagered. And inasmuch as Mr. Welkert refused to pay, I have no further funds."

"I see." The doctor turned and disappeared. Five

172

minutes later two husky male aides lifted Adam from his
bed, deposited him on a cart, and wheeled him to a large,
noisy ward.

[6]

Adam was discharged two weeks later. His clothing
hung on his body; he had lost fifty-two pounds, including
the weight of one leg. The hospital supplied him with
crutches and ten dollars in cash. The doctor who had per-
formed the amputation was not present to bid him farewell.

It was a cold, blustery day. Adam—moving awkwardly
at first on his new crutches, but more surely after he bor-
rowed tips on technique from Henry Populous, an amputee
of fifty years standing—made his way half a dozen blocks
before he came to a small park. He sat for a while on a
bench, watching the wind blow leaves and candy wrappers
along the graveled path. A small man with a sad face,
wearing a new-looking but badly rumpled suit took a seat
at the opposite end of the bench.

"Good afternoon, Brother Chitwood," Adam said.

The little man started nervously, stared at Adam,
squinted his eyes, which, Adam noted, were badly blood-
shot.

"I know you from someplace, brother?" the small man
asked in a voice that wheezed. He coughed. He scratched
his chest through his shirt.

"You assisted me, some weeks ago, in distributing funds
to the needy," Adam said.

The small man jerked violently.

"Lookit here—what do you know . . . all I done . . ." his
voice trailed off. He stared at Adam with an expression
that changed from fear to horror.

"You're not—are you . . . my God, what happened to
ye?"

"My left knee was crushed by a lumber truck," Adam
said. "The surgeon in attendance, judging the member
damaged beyond repair, removed it."

"Jesus God. You look awful. You're nothing but skin
and bones. What you doing out of the hospital?"

"The last of my money was expended for the amputa-
173

tion," Adam explained. "Accordingly, it was impossible for me to remain."

"Them sons of bitches. What you mean, the last of your money?"

"I had allocated a portion of my funds to a program designed to produce income, while making immediate distribution of the remainder. With your assistance, I was able to dispose of the money allocated to the relief of suffering; but my income-producing plans proved to be unproductive."

"That's usually the way. Adam, you said your name was? Tough luck. I, uh, had some hard luck myself. Flat busted, like you. Where you staying?"

"I was making my way but grew fatigued. I'm unaccustomed to walking with the aid of crutches."

"Got any, uh, chow up to your place, Adam?"

"The pantry is adequately stocked."

"You got a funny way of talking, Adam," Chitwood said, rising. "But you're one of the boys at that. Let's go up and have a drink and talk over some ideas I got."

Adam accepted his acquaintance's proposal. Also at the suggestion of the latter, they hailed a cab, which deposited them before the imposing entry to the Buckingham Arms.

"Classy joint," Chitwood muttered, eyeing the doorman dubiously. "You sure you live here?"

"Quite certain."

The doorman stepped casually into Adam's path as he approached the quadruple glass doors.

"No panhandling around here, I told you boys before," he said carelessly.

"I have no intention of soliciting money, Clarence," Adam explained. "I merely wish to make use of my apartment."

"Yeah—sure. How'd you know my name? And it's Mr. Dougall to you, crumbum."

"You were introduced to me by Mr. Farnsworth, the manager," Adam said, "on the day I took possession of the apartment."

"What apartment?" Clarence demanded, uncertain now.

"Twelve oh two."

"You're nuts. Twelve oh two is Mr. Adam—" Clarence broke off. He stared at Adam. "You ain't—are you—"

"Wise up, dummy," Chitwood said, brushing past the doorman, "or Mr. Adam'll have Mr. Farnsworth cut your pretty buttons off."

They progressed as far as the elevator before being intercepted by a portly man in a Harris tweed jacket superbly cut to minimize his paunch.

"May I inquire—" he started, and broke off, staring. "Is it—Mr. Adam?" he whispered.

Adam confirmed his identity.

"Good God, Mr. Adam—your leg—what happened? We thought—we assumed—"

Adam explained.

"I'd concluded you were dead, Mr. Adam," Farnsworth said, mopping at his forehead with his show handkerchief. "After all, over six weeks with no word—no trace—"

"I understand," Adam said. "I'm tired, Mr. Farnsworth. I'd like to rest now, if you'll excuse me."

"Ah—but that's my point. We were forced to re-lease your apartment, you understand. Your lease specified—"

"Another apartment will do as well. You may transfer my belongings there, and—"

"Mr. Adam, you'll understand that I had no choice. Your, ah, possessions were sold, in part payment of the overdue rent. But of course I'm sure we'll be able to find space for you—but you'd like to clear up the balance, first, I'm sure. I'll have to check, but I believe six hundred will cover everything."

"I have seven dollars and fifty cents," Adam said.

Four minutes later, Adam and Chitwood stood on the sidewalk together, balefully eyed by Clarence.

"Tough luck," Chitwood said. "Where you going now?"

"I don't know," Adam said.

"Look," Chitwood said expansively, "you can come up to my place. It ain't much, you understand, but what the hell. I got a can of beans, and maybe we can come up with something . . ."

15

[1]

Brother Chitwood led Adam to a stone-fronted building on a narrow street devoted to pawnshops, beer bars, used-clothing stores, and tiny sidewalk markets featuring obscure vegetables of interest largely to recent arrivals from abroad. His room was on the top floor. Inside he motioned to a wooden chair, flopped himself down on the unmade bed. Adam removed an empty gin bottle and seated himself. He felt dizzy and weak. His hands were cold.

"I been wondering, Adam—where'd you get the dough you were handing out?" Chitwood inquired. He lifted an empty bottle from the floor beside the bed, frowned at it, tossed it aside.

"Various means," Adam said. His voice sounded weak. "Excuse me, Brother Chitwood; I'm too tired to talk just now. . . ."

"What was the angle—you handing out money like that?"

"I was attempting to relieve distress arising from the need for small sums of cash."

"Why?"

"I find . . . the existence of suffering . . . disturbing."

"Hey—maybe you better lay over here," Chitwood rose, assisted Adam to the bed, where he fell back, feeling weak and nauseated.

"Can you get more?" Chitwood persisted.

"Of course. But . . . at present I'm unable . . . to take effective action. . . ."

"All right, get some sleep. We'll talk later."

Lying on the bed, Adam assessed the sensations he was feeling. His body was trembling violently now. He felt icy cold. Brother Chitwood was standing over him, a frightened look on the pinched face.

"Adam—you all right? You look bad—like raw dough—and you're soaking wet and shaking like a leaf!"

"I'm not well," Adam managed to say. Automatically, his thoughts reached out, searched swiftly for needed information.

"Shock," he said. "Get blankets—keep my head low—call a doctor—Doctor Meyer Roskop, 234 Perry Street . . ."

"Blankets? You're sweating like a pig now! What you been drinking, fellow?"

"Doctor . . ."

"I got no money for doctors . . ." Chitwood's voice faded in and out. "Listen, Adam—the money—where'd you get the money? You got any more. . . ?" Chitwood was shaking him now, but he was far away, fading, dwindling, and the roaring in Adam's head rose to drown the persistent voice.

As Adam returned to consciousness, Brother Chitwood was saying urgently, "You can't die here. They shouldn't of never let you out of the hospital, the rats. Now, you got to get on your feet, see? I got to take you back to the hospital, understand?"

"I understand," Adam said. He rose shakily. "But I won't be welcome there. I have no money." He sank down again.

"You can't die here," Chitwood repeated. "Come on, Adam—you don't want to put me on the spot. Look at all I done for you, helping you hand out dough, bringing you up here—only I didn't know you were in this kind of shape—"

"I have no wish to cause you inconvenience," Adam said, and tottered to his feet.

"It'll inconvenience me plenty if I have a stiff on my hands," Chitwood declared with feeling, urging Adam toward the door. "Let's go. You sure you got no more money for me to help you pass around?"

"Quite certain; and you needn't maintain the pretense that you distributed to the needy the funds I entrusted to you."

"Hey—what kind of crack is that? You saying I stole the dough you gave me?"

"You expended the funds on an automobile, which you abandoned after wrecking it while inebriated, on six suits of clothing, on a gift for a woman employed as a hostess at the Ideal Bar and Grille, and on visits to a variety of restaurants and night clubs—"

"What are you, you crummy spy! If this is some kind of frame—!"

"If by that you imply an attempt at entrapment, it is not. I encountered you by accident—"

"Yeah—I'll bet you did. Let's go, you. Out. Now."

Five minutes later, Adam was alone on the sidewalk. He stood for a moment, attempting to think. It seemed more difficult to think now than it had before his accident—as though the medium he was employing to formulate his thoughts were no longer operating as efficiently.

There was a public telephone booth half a block away. Adam made his way to it, with frequent rest stops. In the booth, he deposited a dime and dialed. A brisk voice answered after the second ring.

"This is Adam, Mr. Lin," he said. "I wish to return to your employment."

"Mr. Adam! It's been a long time—months. How are you? I heard you were making a big success—then suddenly—you dropped from sight."

"I encountered a number of reverses," Adam said. "I'm in need of employment as I indicated."

"Yes; well, Adam—I have another man. Not as competent as yourself, of course, but adequate."

"I would accept a lesser position."

"Well—frankly, Adam—Lucy has a young man now; fine young chap. Musician. Benny Chin Lee and his Sweet and Sour Five. They're to be married next month. Under the circumstances—it might be . . . well, we both want to avoid awkwardness, eh?"

"You don't wish to employ me?"

"Adam, I'd like to have you—but after talking with Lucy—well, I'm sure you can find a splendid position elsewhere."

"Good-bye, Mr. Lin."

Adam remained in the booth, slumped half-conscious on the seat, until a plump woman with a face like a Pekinese rapped sharply on the glass. He proceeded to the next corner and rested there, leaning against the wall. A passing policeman gave him a careful scrutiny. It was a chilly day. His clothing felt clammy against his skin. The toes of his missing foot ached as if frostbitten.

"You waiting for something, bo?" a voice said beside him. It was the policeman.

"No," Adam said. "Nothing specific."

"Better keep moving, bo."

Adam complied. His vision was failing now: bright lights dawned in a darkening haze. In the next block he rested again, in the doorway of a restaurant. After five minutes the proprietor emerged and ordered him to find another place to freak out.

There was an alley in the next block. He entered it, found a spot behind a rank of garbage cans, sank down on the greasy bricks. He dozed, and awoke chilled at the bone. His thoughts seemed fuzzy and vague. He was here—and he was elsewhere, walking on a sunny beach, swimming through deep blue water, dancing to the sound of tinkling music, dining in a vast room filled with light and sound and aromas. . . .

. . . *ereszetek ki inét* . . .

. . . *kill that lousy mother* . . .

. . . *jag har inte gjört; jag har inte gjört* . . .

. . . *Adam! Liten to me! I have to find you! Where have you gone? I came to the hospital; they said you'd been discharged—where are you? Answer, Adam! Answer me!* . . .

Adam tuned out the intruding voices. It was time, he realized, to inform Sister Louella of his situation. He tuned, reached out . . . close—not five miles away, here in the city. He considered attempting to speak to her with his mind; but Sister Louella had commanded him never to intrude on her privacy in that way.

Slowly, painfully, Adam got his crutch in position, with the help of an overflowing can rose to a standing position. He hobbled back to the street, made his way to the curb, flagged a cruising cab, gave the driver directions. The cabbie watched him in a mirror.

"You know somebody over there, pal?"

Adam confirmed that he did.

"How'd you lose the pin?"

Adam told him.

"You look bad, pal. You OK?"

"I have little time remaining," Adam said absently. "I

suggest you drive quickly, to spare yourself the inconvenience of disposing of my remains."

"Wha . . . ?" The cab swerved as the driver looked over his shoulder. He drove silently and tensely across the city; before a lighted entry he braked sharply and pulled to the curb.

"This is the address you said. Two fifty."

Adam searched his pockets. With the exception of thirty-one cents they were empty.

"Skip it, pal. Somebody here expecting you?" The driver had gotten out, assisted Adam from the cab.

"No."

"You want to go inside?"

"Yes."

The cabbie helped Adam up the walk, through the door, and fled.

Adam scanned the building, located Sister Louella on the fifth floor. He rode the automatic elevator up, rested, then made his way along the softly carpeted hall to the door behind which he sensed the woman's presence. He rapped.

"Who's that?" Sister Louella's uncertain voice came muffled through the door.

"Adam," he said, half aloud, half with his mind.

There was a gasp.

"Adam? What you want?"

"I wish to speak with you, Sister Louella."

"What about? We got nothing to talk about anymore." A chain clinked, a bolt clacked. The door opened half an inch. Adam saw a glint of light on an eyeball.

"Why, you ain't—or—Adam?" The door opened wider. A slim, carefully coiffed and cosmeticked woman in a sophisticated black afternoon dress stared out at Adam. For a moment, Adam was taken aback; automatically, he reached out, touched the familiar contour of Sister Louella's personality gestalt.

"My God, Adam—what happened to you? You look as bad as you did the night I first saw you—worse! And—your leg . . ."

"The limb was removed due to an accident," Adam stated emotionlessly. "The organism has failed to rally, and will soon cease to function. Accordingly, it's necessary that I pass along certain information prior to that event."

"Adam—I guess you can come inside. What happened to you? I thought you was eating high on the hog." Sister Louella assisted him to a long, low couch before a meticulously laid fireplace in which an artificial fire burned briskly.

"I encountered certain reverses," Adam said, "due to a faulty assessment of the interpersonal dynamics involved. As regards the Baturian store, it now appears it will be desirable to continue its operation for an additional period. I will now dictate a list of commodities and potential purchasers, as well as prospective recipients of financial assistance."

"Adam—wait a minute. You talk like—like you wasn't—weren't coming back. Why, that's—"

"Please make note of the material I'm about to communicate," Adam said. "My strength is rapidly dissipating."

"Adam—if you—if you mean—maybe we better have a doctor—and a lawyer. Just a minute—I'll call Jerry . . ."

"Wait," Adam summoned the strength to say sharply. "Time is short. I have no wish for further ministrations from medical men. Kindly do as I request. . . ." His voice trailed away; he felt his thoughts slip from their path, wander away into realms of soft pink cloud and beckoning blackness. . . .

[2]

". . . who is this fellow?" a strange voice was saying; a testy, sharp voice. "What's he doing in your apartment? Looks like a derelict. Faw! He smells! What—"

"If you'd hush up a second, Jerry, I'd tell you," Sister Louella's voice cut in. "I told you about Mr. Adam, my . . . my former employer—"

"Adam! You said he was a well-to-do businessman!"

"I hadn't saw—seen him in months, I told you! He's been in some kind o' trouble, got hisself hurt, lost a leg—he didn't say how. He come to me. I couldn't turn him away like a stray dog, could I?"

"He looks like a corpse. You sure he's still breathing?"

181

Adam felt Louella's touch on his neck.

"There's a pulse. But he's slipping fast. But before he goes, there's things he's got to do. There's property. That's why he come here, he said so hisself before he passed out. Adam! Adam, you can hear me, can't you? It's Louella! Wake up, Adam!"

"The man's in a bad way. We'd better call an ambulance—"

"He said no doctors; seems like he don't like 'em much. Adam's a strange feller, like I told you. Lord knows what he's got squirreled away. He wants to give it all to me, don't you, Adam? You want to make a will, Adam—and Jerry's here now. He's a lawyer, he'll do all the papers just like you want. . . ."

Adam opened his eyes. He saw Louella's strained, strangely thin features, a foxy-faced man in sharp clothing standing behind her, frowning. The latter ran a gold-ringed hand through slicked-back, thinning hair.

"I don't know, Louella—the legal aspects—"

"Just write it down, Jerry," Louella cut him off. "Now, Adam—what was you saying? About the store, and all?"

Adam gave instructions for the transfer of the title to the property to Louella. The man called Jerry made notes. The typewriter clattered briefly. Louella thrust a paper before Adam, offered a pen.

"Just sign here, Adam. You can do it for Sister Louella, can't you?"

Adam appended his signature to his last will and testament and sank back, exhausted. Louella and Jerry were talking, but he caught only snatches of the conversation:

". . . they said he skipped out on his bill . . ."

". . . going to do? Can't have a man in your place, the neighbors . . ."

". . . can't just put him out in the street . . ."

". . . not your responsibility. Call the police, tell them . . ."

Adam forced his mind to alertness, forced his eyes open. Louella and the man Jerry were at the telephone; Jerry was dialing.

"Wait," Adam said. "That won't be necessary. I wish to go now. If you'll assist me to the elevator. . . ."

Jerry hesitated, then hung up the phone. "Sure, fellow," he said heartily. He approached, gingerly put a hand under Adam's arm and helped him to his feet, urged him toward the door.

"Adam—are you sure. . . ?" Louella said in a faltering voice, but Jerry snarled her into silence. He hustled Adam into the hall, along to the elevator, Louella following.

"Maybe we better ride down with him," Louella said anxiously. Adam was only dimly aware of the elevator's halting, the doors' whooshing open, of Jerry and Louella's half-carrying him across the foyer, maneuvering him through the doors into the cold wind and pale sunlight of a late winter afternoon.

"Where was you wanting to go, Adam?" Louella inquired. "Where you staying now?"

Adam gave her an address. He waited, while vast, vague images swirled and ballooned in his mind. He heard tires squeal, heard a car door open, heard Jerry repeat the address he had given.

"That's the city dump," a strange voice demurred.

"Never mind, here's five, take him there. . . ."

"Poor Adam," Louella's voice came, faint and faraway. "He looks so bad. Jerry, are you sure. . . ?" Then the car door slammed and Adam sank back as the cab churned away from the curb with a clash of gears. He watched the changing patterns of lights, half-dozing. . . .

Hard hands hustled him out of the car. The door slammed, the engine gunned away into darkness. Adam *felt* about him, sensed the direction in which he wished to go. He made his way over heaped refuse, among drifts of rubble, past black pools of oily fluid, through stenches, feeling crumbling matter and broken glass and rotted wood underfoot.

The hut was as he had seen it last. He pushed aside the canvas hanging, groped his way to the pallet, sank down on the damp wads of decayed bedding. A rat scuttled away. Adam shivered violently, curled himself into a fetal position—and waited. . . .

A sound recalled him to the here and now: the creak of a board, the scraping rustle of stiff canvas. Cold air blew in on him; a short, grotesque figure stood outlined against a black sky in which a single star glowed. The beam of a flashlight probed, came to rest on him.

"Adam?" a half-familiar voice said uncertainly. "Is that you?"

"Yes," Adam said.

"Thank God! I finally found you! I'm Arthur Poldak, and I have to talk to you!"

16

[1]

The stranger had lit a kerosene lantern he had found among the litter. The yellow glow showed Adam a short, massive man with a crooked back. He wore a thick, bristly beard, black and gray, and thick lenses over his eyes. He was dressed in thick, lumpy wool. His fingers were short and thick, his lips thick and red. He sat on an upended apple crate beside Adam's pallet, looking at him with an avid expression.

"When you first contacted me—that fantastic night—I didn't know what to think. A dream, maybe a hallucination, a hypnogogic experience. But I checked out the name of the woman—Mrs. Knefter—just on a hunch, a wild possibility. And she existed! I knew then the contact had been a real, objective experience. I tried to call, then went there—to the little town, Jasperton. But you were gone. The police were no help; in fact, they held me, asking questions. I had to have my attorneys wire them. Fantastic. But I kept on. I found leads, traced you here to the city. That was over two months ago. At last I met a Mr. Baturian. Nice fellow. I knew I was close. It was a private detective I hired who located you at the hospital—and before I got there, you were gone again. But I was lucky, people remembered a one-legged man, the cab driver—but anyway, I persevered, and here I am!"

"Please go away," Adam said.

"But why, Mr. Adam? Why did you try to delude me?
184

And why are you here—in this foul place? Why, man—you'll freeze here! And—"

"Please go away," Adam repeated.

"Do you realize how long I've been searching—the expense, the time, the difficulty?"

"Why?" Adam inquired.

"Because," Poldak said solemnly, "you are the most important advance in human evolution since the discovery of fire. Bigger than that! Since man first swung down from the trees!"

"I don't understand," Adam said.

"Consider," Poldak said urgently. "Man long ago completed his biological evolution. Certainly, there are minor matters; the appendix, the vertebral deficiencies, the useless toes and hair and so on; but as a functioning organism, man is now—and has been, for a hundred thousand or so years—on a plateau. Man of the Old Stone Age was the same animal he is today. It took him most of that time to explore his capacities—to learn to use what he's got. Now his progress is halted. Why? Because of the failure of communication, man-to-man."

"Inasmuch as I've failed utterly to establish contact with humanity," Adam said, "I don't understand your contention that in some way I represent an advance."

"Why, man, you're a telepath!"

"This does not appear to have given me any advantage."

"Because you didn't know what you had—how to use it! You're like the first caveman with the innate capacity to understand calculus—but no one ever taught him! But I'll teach you! The possibilities—"

"No," Adam said.

"No? But—how can you refuse? You've got other plans?"

"No."

"Then—"

"I intend to die," Adam said.

"You want to *die?*" Poldak yelped. "With all your advantages, with an ability that can make you anything you want to be? Are you out of your mind, man?"

"I have not found living to be a pleasant experience. To wish to continue would be insane."

"Look, we all feel that way sometimes, you can't let it get

you down, Adam. You've got to fight back, to keep trying, if at first you don't succeed and so on."

"The prospect does not attract me."

"Look, Mr. Adam—all right, I'll agree you're under no obligation to me just because for almost six months now I've devoted my entire energies and my small available funds to seeking you out. But surely you'll agree you have an obligation to science?"

"Not insofar as I know," Adam said.

"Mr. Adam!" Poldak exclaimed. "What a thing to say! You of all people! I admit I don't understand you—*can't* understand you. The way you've been living all these months, the strange things you've been doing—naturally, your behavior pattern is beyond me. But to make the statement you have no obligation to science! You!"

"How have I incurred any such obligation, Mr. Poldak?"

"It hadn't occurred to me," Poldak said wondering. "I assumed the first characteristic of a superior intelligence would be the recognition of its own unique quality—of its responsibilities!"

"You're mistaken in imagining me superior," Adam said. "I was born an idiot. I've only recently learned to speak."

"Are you making jokes, Mr. Adam?"

Adam recounted what he recalled of his early life.

"Blows on the head, you say?" Poldak said excitedly. "A beating—it could have done it, Adam. A brain injury that had the effect of breaking down the barrier that kept you from developing—"

"To me that proposition appears basically illogical," Adam said. "To improve a delicate mechanism by damaging it is a contradiction in terms."

"The correlation is obvious man!" Poldak snapped. "Your mind was awakened, so to speak, by the blow. I'll admit it sounds somewhat paradoxical, but how else can you explain your sudden development—not merely of normal intelligence, but of the fantastic learning abilities you have? Do you realize you've mastered the whole body of normal human knowledge and skills in a mere six months? Plus your telepathic capacity—" He broke off abruptly.

"But I've been pursuing only one alternative of a dual

choice," he said wonderingly. "What if the blows to your head, by depriving you of intellectual capacity, *reduced* you to your present condition? Reduced you to . . . a mere superman!"

"I'm frightening myself, Adam," Poldak said. "I'm all over gooseflesh. But I'm a scientist; I pursue a line of thought to its logical end. In all species, the period of maturation bears a direct correlation with the complexity of the adult organism. A superman would require a longer infancy than a normal individual. Not physically—that part would proceed as usual. But mentally . . . the embryonic superman . . . like a normal baby that's still a drooling infant when a dog of the same age is bearing its second litter . . . might still be soiling diapers when a mere man was taking a degree in nuclear physics . . ." Poldak shook his head, amazed at his own thoughts.

"Now, if a normal infant is deprived of all training, his brain fails to develop properly; he reaches adulthood as an imbecile. In your case . . ." Poldak warmed to his subject, "by being reduced, by injury, to the level of the near-normal, you proceeded to function at that level—to mature as an ordinary man—at an accelerated rate, of course!"

"In fact," Adam pointed out dispassionately, "I function so inadequately as to render me nonviable."

"Adam, you're effectively only six months of age! Of course you're naïve in certain departments—women, for instance. But on your own, you've already discovered some fantastic capabilities—"

Adam coughed explosively. Little bright lights swam in darkness all around him.

". . . got to let me get a doctor," Poldak was saying urgently. "Don't you understand you can't die now?"

"No," Adam said. "No doctors."

"I'd go get one—but you'd be gone when I got back. I can't make you live against your will. . . ." Poldak pulled at his lower lip.

"But what ails you isn't really physical, anyway. It's what they used to call the sin of accidie. Not caring. You don't want to live. Only *you* can cure that."

"How?"

"I don't know—but—" Poldak broke off, looking thoughtful. "But maybe *you* do, Adam. Maybe—with your talent you *could* look at your own brain—and see more than any psychiatrist could ever hope to!" He smacked a fist into his palm. "Do it, Adam! Look inside you, find whatever it is that's acting up and fix it!"

Adam considered this proposition.

"Very well, I'll try," he said, and closed his eyes.

[3]

Formless shapes of light and darkness moved aimlessly against a nebulous background. Images appeared, meaningless, random; they faded, metamorphosed, coalesced, dissolved, and new images swam into view. . . .

Corridors, broad, bright-lit, and branching from them, narrower, dimmer passages, which in turn led to dark and twisting ways leading deeper and deeper into the unexplored abysses of his mind. He followed them, pressing on as the walls closed in, constricting him; and then he could go no farther. A barrier blocked his way, though through it he could sense dimly the continuation of the endlessly branching proliferation of complexity. . . .

He withdrew, opened his eyes.

"No," he said. "The way was blocked."

"Try again," Poldak ordered curtly. Obediently, Adam turned his thoughts inward. He saw a great machine, wheels moving intricately within wheels, levers describing precise arcs, gears soundlessly meshing. He traced the sequence of forces, saw how the initial impetus was multiplied, rotated, converted, in a pattern which extended on and endlessly on. . . . And jammed. Somewhere beyond sight a bearing was frozen, a joint locked.

"Again," Poldak snapped. This time it seemed to Adam that a plant grew upward, stem thrusting, branches spreading, twigs intertwining, leaves deploying in an ordered sequence. He traced their growth and development, sensed the shape of the final flowering. . . .

But the leaves at the farthest tendril-tips were withered and brown; tender shoots were shriveled and blackened.

188

No buds formed to signal the consummation of the promise of the stunted life force.

Adam delved deeper, sensing the aborted pattern, searching for the inhibiting element that robbed the structure of its fulfillment. He probed along twisted paths, tracing them backward, searching out the roots from which all else sprang. On he pressed, caught up in the fascination of the quest; deeper and deeper, probing, tracing, searching. . . .

Then it lay before him: the tap root, fractured at its base, robbing the organism of the nutrients it needed, negating the integrity of the pattern.

He reached out with intangible hands, joined the broken parts—

Green life flooded into dying leaves. With a grinding and shuddering, the jammed machine started up. In the corridors, the barriers fell. In darkness, light grew and swelled into a blinding brilliance. In utter fascination, the entity that was Adam watched the unfolding of the grandeur that was himself.

Then from faraway, he heard the voice of the man calling to him, and reluctantly he returned from the place where he had been.

[4]

Poldak—a strange, small pattern, an amalgam of fragile beauty and ancient ugliness, of tentative power and pervasive weakness—stared at him from across a gulf wider than the space between worlds.

"My God, Adam—what . . . what happened? I saw it on your face—and then . . . and then you *changed!* Before my eyes, you *grew!* I saw the color come into you—I saw—for the love of heaven, Adam—I saw your leg regenerate! You turned into—what? A superman! A god!"

"I'm no god," Adam said. He sat up, an effortless motion of perfectly functioning muscles. "I don't know what I am—or why. . . ."

"You're no man," Poldak said with conviction. "No wonder you couldn't function as a man among men, Adam! It would be like a man trying to live as a monkey among monkeys. He'd be a misfit—an ugly duckling; he couldn't swing through the trees, or hang by his tail, or fight with his teeth—and his human abilities would never develop. He'd be a failed ape, not a superape. And of course the females rejected him; they'd realized he wasn't of their kind!"

Adam looked at the short, ugly man before him, seeing him simultaneously as a powerful and brilliant, though deformed man—and as a strangely warped transitional creature, caught between animal and . . . whatever name there might be for what came after man.

"I arose from the massed mental emanations of the human race," Adam said. "This much is clear to me now. I bear the same relation to the individual human as does the entity known as Arthur Poldak to a single cell of your body.

"I came into being, and existed for a time—a day, a million years—until the proper matrix for my incubation occurred. One day I found this mindless husk and occupied it for a time. Now I have no further need for it. . . ."

"Adam! My God, don't *do* that! You started—you started to *fade,* man! Like a light going out!"

"The maintenance of a material matrix is no longer essential," Adam said. "But though I've now emerged on a higher plateau of existence, I perceive that in essence nothing has changed. Consciousness can only exist as a pattern among patterns; and—therein lies the ultimate trap—a cage so vast that it can never be outstripped."

"An infinite cage, Adam? Perhaps—but think of it this way; a cage that's infinite in extent is no cage at all, eh?"

"A peculiarly human sophistry," Adam said. "I have never laughed—but now, almost—I grasp the meaning of a joke."

"Wait a minute," Poldak started—and grunted. He gasped, cried out. His body jerked, twisted—and grew straight.

"Good-bye, Poldak," Adam said and tuned his awareness to the new spectra of phenomena now open to him—the bewildering variety of sensory impressions, ultracolors, hypersounds, superscents—and a thousand other impacts for which he knew no words. For a long moment, he watched the swirl of overlapping continua about him; then, deducing the rhythm of one of the simpler patterns, he . . . *stepped up.* . . .

New worlds opened out, new universes unfolded. On their threshold, he stood, staring at the vastness of the undreamed-of, the unknown, and the unexplored cosmos that was to be his.

With a tiny portion of his mind, he glanced back, saw the man Poldak—tall, sturdy, straight-backed—and the man who had been Adam, lithe, powerful, keen-eyed.

"Adam—are you—did you—" Poldak said.

"I'm Adam," the other replied. *"He's* gone. Whoever and whatever he was . . . I wish him luck; better than he had here."

"Amen," said Poldak.

[5]

And then the being of pure intellect that had been born of humankind expanded outward at the square of the speed of light, to claim man's inheritance.